To Victoria!

MW00619773

Sharon M

Stephen H. Provost

ALL HALLOWS' NIGHTMARE'S EVE

Sharon Marie Provost

No part of this book may be reproduced, or stored in a retrieval system, or transmitted in any form or by any means, electronic, mechanical, photocopying, recording, or otherwise, without the express written permission of the publisher.

Cover images: Public domain
Cover design: Stephen H. Provost
Interior images: Images on title page and page 255 adapted from photos by Stephen H. Provost; all others in the public domain
Cover and interior design: Stephen H. Provost

The contents of this volume and all other works by Stephen H. Provost and Sharon Marie Provost are entirely the work of the authors, with the exception of direct quotations, attributed material used with permission, and items in the public domain. No artificial intelligence ("AI") programs were used to generate content in the creation of this work. No portion of this book, or any of the author's works, may be used to train or provide content for artificial intelligence (AI) programs.

©2024 Sharon Marie Provost and Stephen H. Provost
Dragon Crown Books
All rights reserved.
ISBN: 978-1-949971-50-7

Dedication

For all those brave enough to face their fears, confront their demons, and make peace with their past.

"This is my costume. I'm a homicidal maniac, they look just like everyone else."

— Wednesday Addams
The Addams Family

Contents

Acknowledgments

I have to express my sincere appreciation to my husband for agreeing to write a dark Halloween-themed short story collection with me. It was such a joy to collaborate with him on *Christmas Nightmare's Eve* last year, that we had to do it again. I can't express how much my mother's and his support have meant to me as I explore this new career.

I must also thank two dear friends of mine who won contests I held asking for story ideas to inspire me. Dr. Sara Hogle's story idea inspired the story "BFF." Her very last sentence describing her story idea was such a perfect quote that I used it as the last sentence in her story. I couldn't have come up with a better line myself.

Chrissy Boyles responded to a contest where I asked people if they wanted to be a victim in one of my stories and if they had a preference for how they died. Chrissy—the sassy, hilarious person that she is—immediately volunteered and suggested she die by her own clumsiness. Anyone who has ever met Chrissy knows if anyone could do that, it would be her. Thankfully, she seems to be bulletproof, so she has survived all her mishaps. I hope she will enjoy her story, "Tiny Terrors."

I hope that my fans and Stephen's will enjoy our exploration of the other side of the veil. Be sure to watch for our next collaboration early next year when we look at the *Shades of Love*.

Sharon Marie Provost,

June 14, 2024

First and foremost, I would like to thank my co-author, Sharon Marie Provost, for sharing this title with me. This is our second short-story collaboration, following *Christmas Nightmare's Eve*, and I can heartily recommend each of the yarns she's spun for your benefit here.

Sharon has a special affinity for human horror, and that's reflected in stories such as "BFF" and "Mischief Night," but she's also got some great spooky paranormal tale to offer, such as "The Manor." Her expertise in both forensic law enforcement and paranormal investigations shine through.

For my part, this volume contains more time travel and a philosophical debate with the Grim Reaper, and my first work of historical fiction, "Once Upon a Star." It's set in Chinese Camp, the subject of a nonfiction book I released this year as well as the setting for "Solinsky Alley," the lead story in Sharon's solo collection *Shadow's Gate*.

I would also like to thank our faithful readers, who I know appreciate that this is a book of horror. Scary things are about to happen as you turn these pages. They're designed to frighten you and stick on the inside of your skull after you turn out the light (hence the series name, *Nightmare's Eve*). It is not for the faint of heart, so I'll leave it at that. I will tell you that there's no graphic sex, but I won't spoil the surprise with any trigger warning. I'll simply remind you that this is a book of fiction. No actual animals, humans, extraterrestrials, or paranormal creatures were harmed in its writing.

And no, the cat doesn't really die. We love cats too much for that, and Freya—our honorary feline co-author—would never forgive us.

Stephen H Provost, June 14, 2024

Sharon Marie Provost

BFF

Tallulah ran headlong down the hallway, searching madly for someplace to hide. She knew he, or at least she thought it was he, couldn't be far behind her. She should never have agreed to go out with her friends tonight, not with all the threatening messages she'd been receiving the past five days. But they'd promised to stay right by her side and keep her safe.

Tallulah had just walked out to the front porch for one moment to call her mother and check in. When she returned, her friends had wandered off without her. They must have gone somewhere into the far reaches of the imposing structure because she couldn't even hear them talking or laughing anymore.

She started down the main hallway toward the dining hall, the location they had talked about exploring next. However, when she turned the corner and went through the double doors, they were nowhere to be found. She remembered she had heard the *ding* signaling she had received a text message while she was talking to her mom. *Maybe Kitty texted me to tell me where they were going.*

However, when she pulled her phone out of her back pocket, she found it was another message from that *same* number—the one that had threatened to gut her—the same one that had sent creepy selfies of a person in a gunny sack mask with her in the background in various settings. She didn't want to look at the message, especially not right now when she was all alone in an unfamiliar location. Yet she was afraid to not know if he were here right now.

Originally, she had thought maybe the messages were from Kitty playing a prank on her, until two days ago when Kitty had accidentally seen one of her messages and freaked out. It was clear she had nothing to do with it.

How does this asshole know that I am terrified of that mask from "The Strangers?" How do I not notice someone wearing that mask and taking a picture so close to me over and over?

She took a deep breath and clicked on the message. It read, "Hello, Lulu," and there was a picture of her, taken from a distance, standing on the porch and talking on the phone. Once again, it was a selfie showing that he must have been standing at the edge of the forest to the west of the building.

Fuck! He's here. Now what the hell do I do? Nobody ever calls me Lulu, except for my sister Aine, and she wouldn't scare me like this.

She began punching the keys to call Kitty when her phone dinged once more. On the screen, the little preview dropped down from above showing the text she had just received from him... again. Her mind spun as she tried to process the one word that appeared, "BOO!" as she turned in response to the small noise behind her. She saw him standing at the corner of the long hallway, only 150 feet from her. She screamed and ran toward the stairs leading up to the second floor. She turned her head as she started up and saw that he was pursuing her.

Tallulah focused on her breathing and her steps—her cross-country training coming back to mind. She turned to the left as she reached the top of the stairs and darted into the first open room, closing the door without a sound, hoping he had not seen her enter. The room had a large picture window, so she ducked underneath it, out of sight. She heard footsteps approach and then pause right above her. Quieting her breathing, she held deathly still as she waited for him to be satisfied that the room was empty.

When Tallulah heard the steps move away, she slid along the wall and made her way over to a freestanding coat closet in the corner. She slid inside and closed the doors. They did not fit snugly together where they met, so she was able to see most of the room through that sliver. Her heart skipped a beat when her phone emitted that notification beep. She ripped it from her pocket and muted it before it gave her location away any further.

To her horror, she heard the footsteps approaching rapidly. She heard the side entrance door to the left of the cabinet open. Holding her breath, she placed her hands on the lefthand door.

When she felt pressure on the door from a hand on the other side, she turned her shoulder and slammed into the door with her entire weight behind her, bouncing the door hard off her attacker's forehead. She heard a brief "oomph" before the man slumped to the ground in a heap. He was still breathing but appeared to be unconscious.

Tallulah darted out of the cabinet and fell to the ground as his hand reached out, grabbing her ankle and pulling her down. She pulled her other knee up and donkey-kicked him squarely in the face. She felt a sickening crunch of bone as his nose broke under her heel. She clambered to her feet and broke for the stairway to the third floor, hoping she would find her friends in the auditorium.

All thoughts of calming her breathing and taking well-spaced steps vanished from her mind. She was running for her very life. A broken nose wouldn't stop him for long. She had maybe a minute to find somewhere to hide. She mounted the last step, her chest heaving, and dove to the right, hoping to find the auditorium. She would either find help or a hiding place along the way.

As she rushed past the first doorway, she heard him behind her and felt his fingertips brush against her back as he tried to grab her.

Where the fuck did he come from? Is he fucking Usain Bolt... World's Fastest Man?

She leaned forward and strained her muscles, hoping they would carry her faster. She fought to ignore the searing pain of the lactic acid buildup in her screaming calf muscles. She realized too late that she had turned the wrong direction, away from the auditorium. Not knowing what she might find at the end of the hall, she burst through the door at the far end.

Her ear-piercing scream was cut short as her body impaled itself on a twisted piece of rebar sticking up from the ground. Her mind had only seconds to comprehend she had mistakenly run toward the side of the old building that had partially collapsed after an earthquake. The door was still in place, but it opened to a sheer 30-foot fall to the ruins below. As blood dripped from her mouth and her eyes flickered as she fought unconsciousness, she heard a shocked gasp. Then all was black as her heart slowed... and then stopped.

Two years later...

Cendrina's fingers were a blur as she lounged on her bed, texting back and forth with Kate about their Halloween night party plans and their college acceptance letters. Her mom used to call the two of them Frick and Frack because they were always by each other's sides. She had never seen such a pure, devoted friendship develop so quickly: They had only met a year ago when Cendrina's family moved to town. Cendrina's mother was very spiritual, in her own way, and had explained to them that they were platonic soulmates, destined to meet and befriend each other throughout time.

Cendrina and Kate had grown even closer over the past three months, since Cendrina's mother had passed away suddenly from an undiagnosed aneurysm. She felt alone much of the time because her father was lost in his own grief and busy working overtime now that they had become a one-income household. She frequently spent nights over at Kate's house. Cendrina sometimes worried that she had become a nuisance as a frequent third wheel hanging out with Kate and her boyfriend Colin. However, they assured her that they enjoyed her company.

Colin was the stereotypically egotistical, rich boy quarterback of the varsity football team. Cendrina hated the way he and the rest of their group treated the nerds and other outcasts at school. However, he had a heart of gold when it came to his relationship with Kate, his family and friends and even with Cendrina herself. She had discussed the issue with Kate, who felt much the same way, and they had vowed to lead by example and hopefully help Colin change his ways.

Their social group included the lead cheerleader, Corinne; varsity linebacker Carlton; varsity pitcher Holden; and Portia Kensington, the self-proclaimed leader of the pack. Portia came from money, and she made sure that everyone knew it. Her father owned many of the large office complexes throughout town, along with several large hotels; he was the CEO and founder of Kensington Enterprises, and a descendant of the town's founding father.

The group had welcomed Cendrina thanks to Kate, but she spent as much time as possible with just Kate. Kate came from a wealthy, pretentious family as well, but she was different from the others. She was loyal, kind, caring and giving; even volunteering her time on weekends at a local children's hospital.

Cendrina came from a working-class family that doted on her, but she didn't have the wardrobe and spending money available to her that most of the other kids at school did. She'd felt out of place and worried that she would be bullied when she first arrived in town. However, Kate had been assigned as her orientation ambassador at school and had welcomed her with open arms. A friendship had developed within the week, and they were each wearing one half of an expensive 24-carat gold heart-shaped Best Friends Forever necklace, which Kate had purchased, within one month of her arrival.

The two of them shared their deepest secrets, darkest fears and wildest dreams of their futures with each other—even things they had never shared with anyone else. Kate had grown up with the other members of their friend group since kindergarten, but it quickly became clear that none of them knew some of the private information she had shared with Cendrina. Cendrina appreciated that Kate was far more down-to-earth than the rest of them and enjoyed some of the same simple activities she did, like reading and baking.

Kate struggled with her father's grand expectations for her life. She came from a long line of lawyers, and it was expected that she would continue the family legacy. She had never even considered deviating from "the plan" until the past six months. Cendrina had expanded her horizons and made her realize that she had never wanted to be a lawyer; she'd just wanted to make her family proud. Kate liked to help people, especially children, so she was interested in becoming a child psychologist. Cendrina had been helping her figure out the best way and time to have that talk with her parents.

"I've been accepted to Yale and Vanderbilt, which my father is thrilled about because they both have excellent law schools," Kate texted. "I can choose either one because they both have child psychology programs as well. I don't know if I should tell my family before I go that I have changed my major or wait until I get through my first two years of core classes and tell them I changed my mind."

"I can see why you're uncertain about how to proceed. I think you should be honest and upfront though. Your family might think, rightfully, that you have hidden this from them and feel betrayed if you wait. I know it won't be easy. I know they'll be disappointed at first. But I've spent a lot of time with your family, and it's obvious that they love you very much and want you to be happy. Besides, it's not like you are saying you want to be a dog groomer. LOL"

"I suppose you're right. Maybe we can stay over at your house next weekend and figure out how I should bring it up."

"Definitely. Now on to the Halloween party on Saturday. Are we really going to go? Who exactly is throwing this party? I asked Corinne and Holden, but they didn't know. Portia turned up her nose at the 'quality of the invitations and the location,' but I think she's going to go because of the exclusive invitation list. I'm not sure what I think about this whole situation."

"I really don't know what to do. I thought maybe Colin was doing it on the sly, but he swears he has no idea. It must be someone pretty exclusive because I can't imagine anyone else having the guts to invite all of us."

"Well, why did they invite me? I am a nobody."

"You aren't a nobody. You are a part of the group. You are my best friend. Anybody with a brain knows they better invite you if they want me to attend."

"Why do you think they're holding the party at the old, abandoned boys' reform school?"

"Probably because of its isolated location. There are no homes within miles of the property, so there's no one to call the police if we get too loud. We'll be free to party as much as we like and have alcohol. To be honest, there used to be a lot of parties there... that is until two years ago."

"What changed?"

"Some kids were partying up there, and there was an accident. A girl ran out a door that opened out into nothing and fell to her death. Her family tried to sue the property owner for not having the place boarded up. It was a big scandal in town, and the family ended up moving away when they lost the case."

"That is terrible. Is it even safe for us to go there?"

"Yes, of course. The property is still in good shape, except for the west wing that collapsed. We'll stay on the bottom floor or the east wing if we go upstairs. And nobody will be dumb enough to be running around. If we don't like whoever is throwing the party, we can just leave and go to my house. Deal?"

"OK. Sounds good. So, are we still wearing costumes?"

"Of course! I am going as a vampire seductress. Do we need to go to the mall for you?"

"Yes, I suppose so then. Want to meet there in 30 minutes?"

"Yes! This is so exciting. We are going to pick out the perfect sexy costume for you. I have seen Holden looking at you lately. We'll let him see a little more of you on Saturday."

Cendrina texted her the eye-roll emoji and then grabbed her coat and purse before heading out to the car. It was a quick drive over to the mall, but parking was always a hassle. She finally found a spot near the food court and headed inside to find the Spirit Halloween store. It was not surprising for her to see Kate already inside with an armful of skimpy costumes.

"There you are! I came right over to pick out the best ones for you to try on. No arguments!" she said as she wagged her finger at Cendrina's skeptical look.

Cendrina laughed, knowing she was outmatched by Kate's enthusiasm, and grabbed the stack of costumes as she walked toward the dressing room. "I should have known better than to accept your help. I am not picking any costume with my butt or breasts hanging out. You can give up on that right now."

Kate giggled and held up her finger as she motioned to the words, "Cross my heart and hope to die. Stick a needle in my eye. I solemnly swear that I will respect your wishes."

Cendrina spent the next 20 minutes trying on the multitude of costumes that Kate whisked in and out of the dressing room after she refused the first three for being too sexy. They finally agreed on a form-fitting Old West saloon girl costume with a corset and a short skirt. It was sexy, but still modest enough that Cendrina felt comfortable wearing it.

They stopped at the food court to grab dinner before heading over to Kate's house to study. While they were sipping their smoothies, Holden and Carlton passed by and stopped to say hi.

"What are you two doing?" Carlton asked with a wink, as he grabbed Cendrina's shopping bag sitting next to her. He reached in and pulled out her costume.

"Hey, wait!" she pleaded.

"Nice, Cen! You are going to be smokin' hot," Holden said with a mischievous smile.

Cendrina looked down, the unmistakable glow of a blush spreading across her cheeks as she whispered, "Thanks."

"So, I take it that you two are going to the party on Saturday at the old Bartholomew's School for Boys?" Carlton asked.

Cendrina nodded as she asked, "Are you going too?"

"The whole gang is going," he replied.

"The weird part is... I haven't heard of anybody else going but our little group of friends. I tried asking around quietly because I didn't want to invite in the wrong crowd. Some are going to see that new retro horror movie *Frat Party Bloodbath.* The Loser Brigade is either staying home or going out trick-or-treating like the immature babies they still are. Most of the jocks are going to be out pulling pranks, including stealing Barton High's mascot," Holden said.

Carlton saw the concerned look on Cendrina's face and hurried to say, "I still think Colin or Portia must have planned this party. I can't imagine her going to a party like this in the middle of nowhere, unless she knows it is going to be up to her standards."

Cendrina looked up and smiled. "I'm sure you're right." Their conversation was interrupted by a loud disturbance just down the hall out of sight. A few seconds later, the cause became apparent as Colin appeared with some of the other football players. They had surrounded Alexander, the president of the science club, as he made his way down the hall with his model rocket in hand. He must have been headed to the hobby shop to get more supplies when he was accosted by the jocks. The boys had encircled him and were pushing him back and forth between them, randomly sticking their feet out to trip him.

Colin sneered as he spoke in a high-pitched whine, "Hey, Alexander! Nice toy you got there. Can I play with it?" Colin reached out and plucked the rocket from Alexander's hand, making sure to poke him in the chest with the nosecone as he did so. Alexander reached out for the rocket, pleading with his eyes to be left alone. "Oh, you want it back? Here you go!" Colin spat, tossing it into Alexander's waiting arms as Robert pushed him down on his face hard.

The rocket split in two and parts scattered across the mall floor. Alexander sat up, cradling the ruins in his arms, as his eyes filled with tears. "My... my dad helped me build that just before his last deployment. It is the last thing I have from him."

"I think you mean 'had'...," Colin said as his voice drifted off before all the boys broke into raucous laughter. Cendrina looked over at Kate with wide, horrified eyes. She'd thought that they were getting through to him. He hadn't been tormenting other students like usual lately... well, at least, not in front of the two of them he hadn't. Kate jumped up, her chair screeching across the tile floor as she glared over at Colin and his buddies.

Colin looked up and met Kate's angry eyes. He excused himself from his friends and started toward her, head hanging low. Kate brushed past him with a solid shoulder-check as she proceeded over to Alexander to help him pick up the pieces. Upon closer inspection, it was clear that the rocket was beyond repair. Alexander's tears were drying as anger replaced it.

"Don't bother! Like you really give a shit. You were Little Miss Homecoming Queen to that asshat! You just want to have your own fun at my expense." Alexander screamed, red-faced, as he threw down the wreckage of the rocket.

"No... I want... I'm sorry," Kate stuttered.

"Go to hell! All of you, go rot in hell. You will be sorry. You're going to pay for this."

Kate's anger boiled just below the surface, but all Cendrina could see was her devastation at how Alexander had yelled at her. She rushed over and put her arm around Kate and led her out of the mall. Colin tried to follow them out, but Carlton and Holden held him back when Cendrina told him no. Cendrina made sure Kate got in her car and then ran over to hers to follow her back to the house.

"We'll find a way to make it up to him," she told Kate as they walked up the flagstone walkway.

"How? You know I could buy him a new rocket, no problem, with just my lunch money. I can't make it be the one he built with his deceased father though. Colin pisses me off so much sometimes. How can he be such a kind, gentle boy with those he is close to but such a rotten asshole to everybody else? You know how much I love him. You know I want to spend the rest of my life with him. But how do I accept this kind of behavior? When does enough become too much?"

"I don't know, Kate. I can't decide that for you. All we can do is keep trying to make him see the error of his ways. Don't answer his calls tonight. Let him see the depth of your anger. Let him worry that he might lose you this time. The test isn't until next week. We can skip studying tonight. Let's just order some late-night pizza and watch movies."

The two girls rose late the next morning and had to hurry to get ready, so they were not tardy for school. Kate came out to find a dozen roses lying on the hood of her car. She threw them in the backseat, determined not to let him off that easy this time. When they arrived at school, Colin was waiting next to her parking space, with Alexander standing next to him. Alexander looked uncomfortable, but he didn't appear to be there against his will.

"Kate, I am really sorry for my behavior. I apologized to Alexander as well, and he accepted it. I collected all the parts from his rocket, and I took it to the hobby store. I will pay whatever it costs if they can repair it. Please forgive me."

"It's true. I did forgive him. I am sorry for yelling at you. I was just upset. Can I go now?"

"Yes, of course. There is no need for you to apologize. I completely understand your reaction, Alexander."

Alexander shuffled off to class as Cendrina waited for Kate. Kate hugged Colin as she said, "I appreciate you doing that. I forgive you, but I will not tolerate you continuing to treat people that way."

"I know. I know. I am really trying to change... I swear. "

The next two days of school passed quickly and before they knew it, Saturday had arrived. Carlton and Holden were going to pick up Corinne and bring her to the party. Portia was getting a ride from her father's chauffeur. Cendrina came over to

Kate's place to ride with them, since she had never been out to the old school. Colin had raided his father's liquor cabinet to make sure the party would be aptly supplied with beverages.

The music could be heard thumping down the road as they approached, as well as a generator that had been set up in the back to supply power. All the entrances to Bartholomew's had been chained up after the accident, but whoever was throwing the party had used bolt cutters to remove the lock and chain on the back door. The girls walked inside as Colin began unloading the liquor. They found Portia, the social queen that she was, already seated on the richly upholstered Queen Anne chair in the lobby, like she was sitting on a throne.

"So, who's our host?" Kate asked.

"I don't know. I haven't seen anybody else. When I arrived, it was just like this... lights on, music playing, door open, but no one in sight. I haven't looked around though yet. Maybe they're still setting up somewhere else."

"Woohoo, the gang's all here!" Corinne squealed as she rode in on Carlton's shoulders. Holden followed closely behind, helping Colin carry in the last of the booze and some chips. Corinne looked around, puzzled, "This party is a little quiet for my taste, even if the bass is pumping hard. Where is everyone else? We can't be the only people here. Whose party is this anyhow?"

Everyone's head turned toward Portia with an expectant look on their face. "Don't look at me. I told you guys I didn't arrange this party. I mean, seriously, does this look like the kind of location I would choose?"

"Why yes, Queen Bee, what were we thinking? You are much too sophisticated and hoity-toity to ever hold a party in a dirty, abandoned building," Carlton retorted with a deep bow.

"I think the word you are looking for is grandiloquent. You are not the only one who scored above 1300 on your SAT," Portia replied with a sneer. Corinne's brow furrowed as the rest of them laughed and clapped for Portia.

"Seriously though, I think we should see if anyone else is here. If not, let's get the fuck out of here. We could have more fun at my house or Colin's. This is boooorinnng!" Corinne whined.

The girls set off to explore the east wing, while the boys puffed out their chests, extolling their own bravery by investigating the "dangerous" west wing. To no one's surprise, Portia called the first floor. Cendrina and Kate opted for the third floor, while Corinne went up to the second. Even though the boys always teased the girls for going to the bathroom together as a group, it didn't stop them from exploring their wing of the structure as a group. It was easy to know where they were at any given moment just from the sound of their thundering footsteps and bellowing voices as they roughhoused their way down the halls.

As Portia approached the far west front corner of the building, she heard a resounding thump on the floor above. Portia rolled her eyes as she entered what appeared to be a small art gallery. *Goddamn! It sounds like there is a herd of elephants in here. If the rest of the party didn't know we were here before, they sure as hell do now. I thought the boys were loud, but now the girls are just as bad.*

She spent the next ten minutes looking through the old school's collection. She couldn't understand why such quality art would have been left behind when the school closed. She realized how long she had let herself be distracted, so she proceeded on to explore the last few rooms, entering what appeared to be the kitchen.

As she looked around the room for refreshments, she heard what sounded like the big oak door in the back shut with a resounding thud. She turned to go check out the noise and noticed the door to the dumbwaiter had what appeared to be a handwritten note taped to it. Portia walked over to the far corner to read it, hoping she might finally find an explanation.

It simply read, “Open me.”

Portia noticed a dark substance coming from underneath the door and dripping onto the black tile floor. She placed just the tips of her fingers on the gold handle, so as not to get the mysterious substance on her. The door slid up with a loud screech, exceeded only by the blood-curdling scream from Portia. Her pupils dilated as wide as saucers as she took in the sight before her.

Sitting on the dumbwaiter platform was a large metal platter in a pool of dark blood holding the head of Corinne, her long flowing, golden locks spread out before her. The word “Deception” had been written in black Sharpie on her forehead. Portia’s eyes darted around the room, assessing any danger nearby.

She ran to the drawers and began ripping them out one-by-one; the drawers thumping on the floor and the utensils and serving spoons clattering as they scattered across the tile. None of the drawers contained a knife or any other item suitable for self-defense. Portia climbed to her feet and began screaming for her friends as she ran back toward the lobby where they had all congregated earlier.

“Guys! Guys! We need to get out of here now. Colin! Carlton! Holden! Help me.”

She could just hear the boys as they moved around on the far side of the building. It sounded like they might be descending to the second floor. Portia looked around the room again to make sure no one had entered behind her, before letting loose with another ear-splitting scream. This scream had the desired effect. Soon, she heard rapid steps approaching from both directions.

"My God, Portia! What has gotten into you?" Kate snapped as the two girls appeared at the top of the stairs above her.

One look at her face, and both Kate and Cendrina rushed down the stairs to comfort her. "Are you okay?" Cendrina asked, worry in her eyes.

"I'm fine. But Corinne is dead! Someone cut off her head and put it in the dumbwaiter in the kitchen."

Colin sniggered, disdain dripping in his tone, "Fuck, Portia! You *did* plan this dumbass party. I should have known. None of us want to play one of your parents' stupid murder mystery games. What did you promise Corinne to get her to participate?"

"Fuck you, Colin! This is not a game. You can be such an asshole. If you don't believe me, go look for yourself."

They descended the stairs to join Portia in the lobby. "We all go together then. Don't want another 'victim' to fall prey to your blackmail or bribery," he replied with a glare.

"Not a fucking chance! I'm not going to look at her like that again. I'm getting out of here right now. I'll call the chauffeur from outside… unless you'll give me a ride, Kate?" Portia looked back at Kate with pleading eyes as she stormed toward the back entryway.

"Colin drove Cendrina and me. Colin?" Kate asked, raising her eyebrows.

"No way! Let her get a ride with Carlton and Holden. AND CORRINE! Let's not forget her little cohort. She will need a ride home, too."

Portia turned on her heel and stormed off to the back of the school. "Fuck you! I hope you die, Colin Masterson!"

The rest of the group proceeded toward the kitchen, only Cendrina looking back with regret. *She seemed so scared... for real. It all must be a game, because who would murder Corinne so horrifically? Fuck it! She is upset. I am going to see if she needs anything.* Cendrina turned away from the rest of the group and headed back toward the rear exit of the school.

"NO! Fuck!" Portia raged at the door as she slammed her body against it.

"What's wrong?" Cendrina asked.

"It's a little obvious, isn't it? I can't get the door open. Somebody locked us in here. I can't make a call either. There's no signal."

"Here. Let me try. You're so upset right now. Maybe I can get it."

"Have at it, Little Miss Perfect!"

Cendrina tried the handle repeatedly, but she couldn't get the door to open. It was unlocked, so the handle turned without any effort, but the door wouldn't open more than a crack. She bounced her shoulder hard against the door and was shocked to hear chains rattling against it. She pulled out her cell phone but was puzzled to find she didn't have a signal now either, even though she'd had one when they arrived.

"You're right. Somebody chained the door closed again. Is there a caretaker that checks the place periodically who might have come by and noticed the chain cut?"

"I'm sure that's it. High-quality help there... notices the chain gone but doesn't check the place out or call the police. That makes a lot of sense, genius!"

I'm happy to help anybody, but there is no reason to treat me so rudely. She's on her own. I'm going to find the rest of them and figure this out. Cendrina left the back entryway and turned the corner quickly, running into Kate, who was sobbing so hard she could not catch a breath.

"She's dead! She really is dead," Kate exclaimed in a breathless rush.

"Oh my God! What are we going to do? Portia and I just tried the door, and we are locked in here. I'm so... "

"Fuck that! No one is keeping us in here. Leave it to us," Colin interjected as he brushed past with the other boys in tow. The boys rushed the door, throwing themselves against it with a crash. The solid oak door rattled against the chains but didn't budge. Three more tries only succeeded in making the boys sore. Their next attempt was interrupted by the blaring BWWWAAAA-BWWWAAA of *The Purge* siren coming from the speakers set up in the lobby.

The entire group ran out to confront whoever had played the siren sound, only to find the room still empty. As they looked around, an electronic voice emanated from all around them.

"Greetings. I am so thankful that you were able to attend my very special Halloween party. I am hosting this party just for you. I know I am going to enjoy it... immensely. You, on the other hand, I am not so sure about that. You might ask why I invited all of you here. But let's not beat around the bush: WE ALL KNOW why you are here. There is no escape, as I am sure you have already found. In case you haven't noticed yet, there is no cell signal out here, so don't bother. I jammed it. Confess your sins and beg for my forgiveness—convince me that you have seen the error of your ways—show me that you have changed. Then maybe, just maybe, I will let you live."

"What is going on here?" Cendrina begged Kate.

"How should I know?" Kate asked in a high-pitched tone as she cast a downwards glance at each of her friends in turn. No one met her gaze head-on, except for Cendrina.

"You must know something. You seem like you are feeling awfully guilty to me," Cendrina said to her. "I sure as hell don't know what is happening. Maybe it's because your friends are all egotistical assholes who torture the rest of the kids at school. You don't do it, but it's like you condone it by staying friends with them. You didn't try to change Colin's ways until you met me, and only since we have worked on it together."

"What did you guys do?" Cendrina screamed, turning her accusations on the others as she dared them with her eyes to look down.

"We didn't do anything, you pathetic bitch!" Portia spat. "You were no one when you moved here. I am sure you have always been no one. But Kate felt sorry for you and brought you into our group. Against our wishes, I might add. You know you don't fit in. You never have... never will. If you are so innocent, then why are you locked in here with us? I seem to remember you getting an invitation, too."

"Probably guilt by association," Cendrina said, as tears ran down her cheeks. " I admit that I was desperate for a friend. I should have tried harder to make you treat people better or stopped hanging out with you. I should have done more to help your so-called Loser Brigade."

"Whatever! I don't have time for this shit. I'm getting out of here," Holden said as he ran off.

The group split up to begin checking all the doors and seeing whether the bars had been removed from any of the windows. Cendrina headed upstairs to separate from the rest of the group as she began checking for some means of escape. After 20 minutes of searching to no avail, she returned to the first floor to find Carlton, Kate and Portia waiting downstairs.

"Where are Colin and Holden?" Kate asked in a whisper.

"I don't know. I haven't seen them. I thought they were both down here on the ground floor," Cendrina replied.

"They were, but they went up to check the third floor about ten minutes ago, and Holden wanted to make sure you were okay."

"We need to go look for them," Carlton stated as he stood up.

A muffled grunt and creak far above them drew everyone's attention to the third-floor banister. Carlton jumped out of the way, just in the nick of time, as Holden's body hurtled to the floor. He landed on his chest, driving the long boning knife that was protruding from it through his spine. A large pool of blood began to spread around his body.

He'd hit a newel post on the way down, leaving a large laceration on the side of his head from the massive blunt-force trauma. Shards of bone and small chunks of brain matter were poking out of the wound. Kate's uncontrolled screams tore through Cendrina's shock as she looked at his injuries, then began pointing to the message that had been scrawled on his forehead.

Once again, only one word appeared, "Treachery."

Kate's scream ended as she jumped to her feet. "We have to find Colin... before it's too late." Carlton and Portia met her incredulous gaze.

"You have got to be joking," Portia scoffed.

"No, I'm not. We need to stick together. We have... "

"We can stick together right here. Right, Carlton?"

"Umm... yeah. I don't know if it's a good idea for us to go upstairs."

"Colin would look for you. He would try to help save you. We need to take care of each other and then stick together from now on. Are you with me or not?" Kate begged.

"I guess so," Carlton replied.

"This is so stupid. I refuse to go up there," Portia said. "I will sit right here with my back to the fireplace. Then I can see from every direction. I'll call out if I see or hear anything. But I don't trust her." She gestured toward Cendrina. "So take her with you."

"Fine. You are on your own. I don't have time to argue with you," Kate said, exasperation overtaking her desire to be polite.

Carlton led the way upstairs, feigning bravery, even as his tremulous voice betrayed his fears, "Where should we start?"

Cendrina had put aside her anger and questions for now. The situation had become a matter of life and death. Kate's friends may be despicable human beings at times, but they certainly didn't deserve to die. Survival was paramount now, and the rest could be sorted out later.

"The two of them said they were going up to the third floor, and that's where Holden fell from, so that seems as good a place as any to start," Kate replied.

The three friends made their way up the stairs, trying hard to stay quiet as they looked ahead for dangers. As they reached the third-floor landing, they could see where the struggle had occurred with Holden, but there was no sign that Colin had been there. The west wing's dangerous condition made further investigation of the third floor slow and, ultimately, unproductive.

They decided to proceed down to the second floor via the

east wing staircase.

About halfway down, they heard what sounded like a muffled cry for help on the second floor. "Shit! Don't tell me Portia came up here alone!" Carlton exclaimed. Concern for Portia's well-being overrode their caution, as Carlton rushed down the stairs and across the second floor to the main central staircase, with the girls not far behind.

A flicker of movement in a doorway off to the left drew his attention. He merely had seconds to dodge the onslaught, but that would have left the girls squarely in the attacker's range. Instead, he attempted to put his football skills to use, hurling himself at the attacker for a crushing tackle. But the brief glimpse he'd had of the figure from the corner of his eye had missed a crucial detail: the large fire axe in the assailant's hands.

"Uhhhh… " Carlton wheezed, as he sank to the floor. The head of the axe was buried deep into his chest cavity over his heart, pulsating ever more slowly as his heartbeat faded. Kate screamed and continued forward past the carnage toward the staircase. Cendrina's mouth gaped open as she fought for a breath, unable to tear her eyes away from the sight. As the assailant let go of the handle, she could see a word written in Sharpie on the handle, "Betrayal."

The killer's eyes met hers for a moment before turning away to pursue Kate. Cendrina finally broke through her panic-induced paralysis and retreated to the side staircase. She continued down to the first floor and found a cupboard tucked away under the stairs that was nearly impossible to see in the shadows. She hid there while she racked her brain for a way to save her friends.

Kate is in trouble. I don't know if Portia is still alive. We still haven't found any trace of Colin. There doesn't seem to be any way out of here. None of our cell phones work. Fuck! What do I do?

Cendrina activated her phone's flashlight mode and looked around in the cupboard. There were several bins filled with odds and ends one might expect to find in a junk drawer. As she dug down to the bottom of the last one, she felt the long shaft of a large flathead screwdriver. *Better than nothing, I guess.*

Cendrina climbed out of the cabinet, with the screwdriver clenched upside down in her hand, the blade of it tucked tightly against her forearm out of sight. She tiptoed down the hallway to where Portia was still waiting—hopefully—and where Kate should have just come down. As she peeked around the corner of the hall into the large lobby, she could see that Portia looked unconscious.

She got down onto her knees and crawled across the floor, trying to stay out of sight behind furniture as much as possible. She reached up to palpate Portia's neck, and her neck rolled to the side at the touch. She could see the word "Pig" scrawled in the same dark black handwriting on her forehead. The old school was frigid from the late-October temperatures, so Portia's body had already cooled considerably. As she looked closely at her body, Cendrina noticed the dark purplish ligature marks around her neck, so deep in the back where the garrote had been twisted tight that it had begun to cut into her skin.

Cendrina yelped in surprise when the booming electronic voice emanated once more from the speakers. "Okay contestants, we are down to two. I gave you time to suspend this game and survive. All you needed to do was confess your sins and apologize, but you couldn't even bother to do that. Tallulah was a sweet, innocent girl. You murdered her. Now you are going to pay!"

Cendrina's frustration had reached its boiling point. She

screamed out into the void, "I didn't kill her! I don't even know who Tallulah was. My friend Kate would never hurt anybody either. You have the wrong people. Please let us go."

Cendrina took a couple of deep breaths and fought to suppress her emotions. *At least I know that Kate is still alive... for now.* She climbed to her feet and began the slow process of searching the ground floor for any signs of Kate. To her dismay, she found footprints in the dust coating the west wing stairs. *Damn it, Kate! You told me the west wing was compromised. Why would you use these stairs?*

Cendrina began a tedious, laborious climb up the stairs, her body pressed against the wall where the structure was most stable. As she neared the room closest to the second-floor landing, she could hear hushed, tense voices. *That's Kate, but who is she talking to?* Cendrina considered entering the room but decided to stop and listen for a moment to assess the danger.

"She doesn't know anything," Kate assured the listener.

"Are you sure? Are you telling me the truth? I know you two had your private little talks... all those secrets you wouldn't even tell me... your boyfriend," said the voice in Colin's unmistakable growl.

Are you fucking kidding me? I thought Colin was dead or badly hurt. What the fuck are these two hiding? Is this all some sick game to them? I have half a mind to... Cendrina thought as she reached for the door handle. But then she paused. *Let's see what else they say.*

In her anger, all thoughts of the other, more pressing, danger had left her mind.

"Yes, we have our little secrets as you call them, but I would never betray you or our friends. We discussed our futures and my worries about life in general. Thoughts I didn't need to burden you with."

"Fine. I believe you. Could she have figured it out though? If we ever get out of here, how do we hide the truth? She will spill her guts to the cops about what that voice said: that we needed to confess. They won't let that go. The questions will be endless."

"I know. But she really is a true and loyal friend to me. She doesn't have anybody else... no other friends besides us, no siblings, and the few family members she has are estranged. They blame her father for not taking her mother to the emergency room sooner. She had been in pain for a couple of days. Even her own father is too busy with work and his own grief to support her. I think I can come up with an explanation that she will buy, and I can get her to shut up about what she knows."

"You really think you can do that?"

"We might have to see each other in secret for a while. Make her think I broke up with you to make you pay for your transgressions. Then we will work to convince her that you've changed."

"Okay. I trust you. But how do we get out of here? Who is holding us here and killing our friends? Do you think it is Aine? Whoever attacked me caught me by surprise. The person didn't seem all that strong but instead knocked me off balance. When I fell, I hit my head on the corner of an oak dresser, which knocked me out. When I woke up, I found these fucking pieces of rebar impaling me. It reminds me of the way... "

"Stop it! You need to calm down. Every time you get animated, you bleed more. But you're right, it does look a lot like how she died. Plus, there's..."

"Plus what? What else is there?"

"It's the word written on your forehead... 'Murderer.'"

"No fucking way!" Colin tried to sit up again but fell back against the dusty painter's drop cloths piled in the corner as the pain seared through his abdomen. Another large glut of dark blood poured from his wounds. He rubbed his head as a wave of lightheadedness washed over him.

"Colin, I am scared. You are losing a lot of blood. We need to get you of here... the sooner, the better."

Cendrina couldn't wait any longer. These people needed to be held accountable for their actions, but Colin dying would not be justice. She couldn't handle that on her conscience. She turned the handle and pushed into the room with a slam, as the door bounced off the wall. "What the fuck is going on here, Kate? You said you didn't know what that person was talking about earlier? You said you were all innocent. Who is Tallulah and how did she die? And who is Aine?"

"It is all a misunderstanding. Remember I told you about a girl accidentally dying at a party on Halloween two years ago? She was our friend. She liked to pull pranks on everyone, so Portia and Carlton decided to pull one on her. Turnabout is fair play and all. It was just supposed to scare her.

"Portia bought a burner phone from the convenience store and used it to send a scary message to her while she was here... you know the 'I'm watching you' kind of thing. Then Carlton wore a burlap sack mask, like from that movie *The Strangers, and* snuck up on her when she coming up to the third-floor auditorium where we were partying. How could any of us have known that she would panic and run away like that? We didn't know she had phobia about that character—that mask. She knew the west wing of the building was dangerous, just like we did. She opened that door at the end of the hall and ran right out, falling to her death on some rebar protruding from the foundation. It was a tragic accident."

Cendrina, hearing a slight scrape behind her, turned to see who was approaching. When her attention was diverted, Kate dove forward and pushed Cendrina to the right... onto the razor-sharp point of an icepick, before feinting to the left herself. The hand holding the icepick rapidly stabbed Cendrina half a dozen times in the abdomen before wrapping an arm around her neck and pulling her close. The screwdriver slipped from Cendrina's hand and bounced away. "Don't move, or I will kill you right here and now."

The person reached up and removed the Lady Justice mask covering her face.

"Aine! It is you! Why are you doing this? Your sister was our friend. You know her death was an accident," Kate cried out.

"Cendrina, that's your name, right?" Aine asked as she thumped Cendrina's shoulder.

"Yes."

Returning her gaze to Kate, Aine asked, "Accident? Just like you pushing your friend here into my path and onto the point of my icepick?"

"I stumbled. I was trying to push her out of the way."

"Sure. That sounds like one of your stories, Kitty. Just like the story you told the police about my sister's 'accident.' That she had gotten drunk at the party and just walked out the door by accident. In that story, there was no mention of this supposedly harmless little prank you just played like you told Cendrina here. But what about the truth? How about we skip story time and go right to the truth? What do you think, Cendrina?"

"I think you are right. Tell me, Kate. Or is it Kitty?"

Kate couldn't even lift her eyes to meet Cendrina's glare. "I don't know what she's talking about. I told you the truth."

Aine smirked as she laughed to herself. "Okay. If that's the way you want to play it. More fun for me then because I am going to make you pay... with pain... with blood... with soul-crushing torment as I take everyone away from you that matters. So, let's start at the beginning then: You never liked my sister. She was not your friend. It was all a big game with you and your friends to see which one of you could hurt and betray her the most.

"Portia may have been book smart, but she was lazy. She couldn't play the long game. She was just a pig who went for the easy target: making fun of the way Tallulah dressed and acted.

"Carlton went for the long game of making her think he truly liked her. He set her up to be humiliated at the upcoming Homecoming dance.

"Holden? Well let's face it, he was a pretty face and not much more. He was just the wingman backing up Carlton in his boyfriend farce.

"Now Corinne, she got in deeper, with you and your little boyfriend's devious plan. She was the eyes and ears to pass on information to you when you weren't around. She told you about Tallulah's reaction to the evil little prank you pulled to terrify and torment her.

"Now we get to the part involving the two of you," Aine said as she waved the icepick at each of them in turn.

"I was her friend. I swear! I didn't mean for her to get hurt. It wasn't even my idea. It was Carlton and Portia's prank."

"It is super easy to blame two of your dead friends. They aren't here to defend themselves. But I have the proof! I hacked into all of your social media accounts, email and cell phone records—every one of you. I know exactly what you did. Shall I continue now?"

"Yes, please," Cendrina replied in a whisper.

"Kate here got into the *super* long game... the kind meant to cause the most harm. She pretended she was Tallulah's very best friend. She convinced her to spill all her secrets—as she prattled on about her own supposed secrets as well. She told Kate her heart's desire, as well as her deepest fears. Tallulah made the mistake of letting Kate know how traumatized she had been by that movie. She told Kate about her irrational fears of the dark, being alone, staying in the woods and most of all... that mask.

"Portia, rich pig that she was, bought all of them burner cell phones, so they could torment her throughout the day when the others were busy. One of them was always nearby, so they could target her when she was alone and felt most vulnerable. They sent her disgusting messages, threatening her life with descriptions of the most depraved acts.

"Then lover boy here began showing up outside our house, in the woods she walked through to get home, in an empty parking lot next to the convenience store by our house... anywhere she was out alone, and he would stare at her while wearing that mask. Follow her. Wave at her. Brandish a knife at her. She was utterly terrified. She didn't want to go to that party that night, but they all insisted. They begged her to come 'have fun with them.' They promised to keep her safe."

"You guys are hateful. How could you do that to her, Kate? What did she ever do to you? I thought you were a good person. Were you setting me up, too?"

"Never! I would never do that to you. You are my best friend. I was going through a hard time back then. This was two years ago. I have told you about the issues in my family. We never... I never meant for her to come to any harm. We were just having fun. It truly was a terrible accident. We hid the real story because we didn't want to ruin our lives over a simple accident," Kate pleaded.

"Fun? You call what you did fun! Didn't you consider what you were doing to her emotionally? I, of course, assume you didn't intend to hurt her physically, but you were doing real, long-lasting emotional damage. You can't pretend you didn't know that. If it was truly an accident, then you had nothing to fear from telling the truth. You owed her that at least... Certainly her family deserved to know."

"I suppose you're right. I just wasn't thinking right back then."

"I hate to break up this tender fucking moment. Let's get back to the truth. Shall I finish?" Aine snarled.

Cendrina nodded, holding her hand tight against her oozing abdomen.

"When Tallulah went outside to call and check in with our mother, they all hid. Each of them had a matching costume and mask, so they could move throughout the building, tormenting her. It was lover boy over there who chased her up the stairs and across to the west wing, where she fell to her death in a state of utter panic. They were all at the end of the hall, standing outside the auditorium, watching her. She was so scared that she didn't even notice them. They all saw her running that direction, into danger, but not one of them tried to stop her—no one even called out to her. Then to rub salt into the wound, they called the police and blamed the whole accident on her drunkenness. Given their families' standing in town, no one mentioned the fact that all of them were minors intoxicated that night."

Cendrina rubbed at the tears running down her face. She realized that Aine's grip around her neck had loosened. She turned to give her a hug as she said, "I'm so sorry for all you've been through. They should be punished for their vile behavior. But killing them is not the answer. I will go to the police with you and back up your story with what I heard myself tonight."

In that brief moment, with the two of them distracted, Kate saw her opportunity to get free. She lunged forward, grabbed the screwdriver, and plunged it over and over into Aine's back just below her ribcage, annihilating her kidney. As Aine hemorrhaged, Cendrina dropped to the floor, weakened from her own blood loss. "Give me your coat now, Kate!"

Kate dropped the coat at her feet and ran over to check on Colin. He was pale and weak but still conscious. Cendrina wadded up the coat and pressed it hard onto the punctures in Aine's back that were oozing a river of blood. She searched through Aine's pockets until she found a set of keys. Against her better judgement, she tossed them to Kate. "She must have come in through the basement. There should be an entrance up from the basement somewhere down on the ground floor. Go outside and call the police. Tell them we need two ambulances!"

"What are we going to tell the police? If she lives, she will tell everybody what happened." Kate asked.

"Of course, she will. But it is time that the truth came out. Your daddies won't let you go down. This is not the time, Kate."

"You are right... she will," Colin mumbled.

Cendrina lurched forward, skewered by the screwdriver—the blade puncturing her lung before slicing into her heart. Kate swiveled her wrist, inflicting maximal damage before removing it. Her arms wrapped around Cendrina, holding her tight, as she whispered, "I'm sorry, Cendrina. I never wanted it to come to this. You were my very best friend. But I love Colin... we are meant to be. We are just about to begin the most exciting part of our lives. I just can't let you take that away from me."

Cendrina's eyes closed and, before long, the gurgling stopped as her struggle to breathe through the blood ceased. Judging by the pool of blood on the floor, Kate doubted that she had to worry about Aine, but she checked for a pulse just the same.

"Kate, I can't believe you did that. I love you, baby! Let's get out of here. I think I can walk if you will help me. So, what do we tell the police?"

"The truth... Aine blamed us for that horrible accident with her sister. That she trapped us here and killed all our friends. And that I saw her attack Cendrina, and I managed to kill her in defense of Cendrina."

"Perfect! I am sorry about Cendrina."

Kate winked at Colin as she helped him up, "She should have been more careful about who she trusted. Sometimes those you least suspect are the ones most thrilled to destroy you."

Stephen H. Provost

Don't Take the Girl

"I need to talk to my daddy." Carly narrowed her eyes, forcing tears aside through determination channeled as anger.

"Now, dear," the woman across the table said, her voice soothing but firm. "If you want my help, you have to set aside your emotion."

Carly balled up her fists, then forced herself to relax them. There was no one there to hit, anyway. The woman seated across from her, a middle-aged woman dressed in a flowing yellow dress that matched her long, straight hair, didn't seem like a medium to her. She seemed more like a refugee from some hippie commune, with her patchouli perfume and her half-moon silver necklace.'

Madam Liliana reminded Carly of her mother, which didn't help. The woman had left Daddy for another woman (her Pilates instructor), and then had tried to get custody of her.

Daddy had fought it, of course. He had been angry, the same way she was now. But he had always told her, "Let anger motivate you, but never let it control you. If your haters see it, they'll use it against you."

She'd already let this hippie medium with the long blond hair see it. First mistake. But was the woman a hater, or was she really trying to help her?

"Don't trust, but don't judge until you know," Daddy had told her. "Trust is earned, but if you're too quick to judge, you'll lose the trust of others."

Carly blinked several times quickly. It was involuntary: something she did without realizing it when she was trying to ground herself and force herself to focus on the present.

The past was simply too painful.

Carly had been close to her mother, once upon a time. She remembered Mom singing her to sleep when she was very young, and taking her to the park while Daddy was at work. She'd climbed on the monkey bars and slid down the bright red and yellow swirling slide. When her parents brought home Wolfie, their new Siberian Husky puppy, her mother took Carly out into the backyard and showed her how to play fetch with him. They'd gone through so many of Daddy's tennis balls that he finally gave up playing tennis with Willie Banks, his friend from work, and switched to racquetball instead.

But all that was before Max came along. Max was Carly's brother, six years younger than she was, and from the day he arrived, Mom had stopped being Mom to her. She was just her mother, a distant presence who spent all her time doting on her new baby boy—who acted like a spoiled brat almost from the moment the doctor pulled him out of the birth canal.

Max became her favorite right away, and she stopped singing Carly to sleep the night after he came home from the hospital. Those serenades were only for Max from that day forward, and Carly was all but ignored on those trips to the park: All the other mothers would gather around to gawk at Max, and her mother would go on and on to them about how much he looked like her and what a "cute little cuddle bun" he was. They all made faces at him and cooed like they were babies themselves, and they didn't notice Carly making faces of her own at them.

When she grew up, she decided then and there, she would *not* have a baby boy. She didn't know how it worked, but her six-year-old self was sure that she'd be able to *choose* to have a girl when the time came.

As Carly's relationship with her mother became more distant, she'd become even closer to her father. He must have sensed she was feeling left out, because he started doing more of the things with her that her mother used to do. Even when he was tired after getting home from work, he would make a point to go outside with her and throw the tennis ball for Wolfie. When her mother was busy with the baby, he'd sit her down on the couch and they'd play charades together, or he'd help her with her first-grade reading lessons.

Gradually, the family became less of a unit and more of two competing teams. On one side were Max and Carly's mother, who complained more and more that Daddy wasn't helping enough with the baby.

"I get up with him every time he fusses in the night, and you're just snoring away."

Daddy had tried to be patient. "I wonder if you're not spoiling him too much," he'd said, as diplomatically as he could.

"If we go running every time he starts fussing, doesn't that encourage him to do it more?"

"If *we* go? When have you ever changed his diapers?"

Carly hated when they argued like that. They'd never seemed angry at each other before Max had come along. It was all his fault—and Mom's for being so... so... so... selfish. Why couldn't she see that Daddy was spending time with her—something her mother never did anymore? Why was Max more important than she was? Yeah, he was a baby, but that didn't mean she had to forget about her daughter, did it? Daddy was just being a good father to *her*, but Mom never gave him any credit for *that*.

Besides, it had been Mom who'd gone on and on about wanting a second child. Daddy would have been fine just having her, but if Mom was the one who'd insisted, why was she being so unreasonable about changing a few stinky diapers?

Things only got worse when her mother had gone to take a shower one day and asked Carly to watch Max for a few minutes. She'd been nine years old at the time, and he was three, which meant he was "getting into everything," as Daddy put it. The minute her mother had left the room, he had gone over to Wolfie and started blowing on his nose. Wolfie shook his head briskly from side to side and sneezed, then let out a low growl and turned away. But this only made Max start laughing his annoying SpongeBob laugh and run around in front of Wolfie again. This time, he grabbed the dog's head on both sides to keep him from shaking it and blew into his nose hard.

Wolfie had not been amused. Instead of growling this time, he snapped at Max. His teeth had missed, but the boy had fallen backward onto the floor, banging his elbow and letting out a howl of pain and fury. Wolfie started barking, and the boy ran screaming from the room, yelling, "He bit me! Doggie bit me! Owwwwwwwaaaaaaaahhhhhhhhhhh!" He'd gone running straight for his mother and had pointed at an "owie" on his elbow. That wasn't where Wolfie had bitten him; Carly knew the he hadn't been bitten at all. The red mark on his elbow was from where he'd fallen backward, but her mother, naturally, believed him.

Carly came to her pet's defense, but it didn't matter.

"Mom, he was teasing Wolfie," Carly told her. "I saw it. Wolfie didn't bite him; he just fell over."

But her mother wouldn't listen. That night, she told Daddy that Wolfie would have to go, and if they couldn't find a home for him by the next day, she'd drive him to the pound herself. Carly had pleaded with him to believe her, and he'd heard him arguing with her mother.

"It's Carly's dog," he'd said. "She'll be heartbroken. You can't do that to her."

"She'll get over it," her mother had said. "Would you rather have your daughter be sad for a little while or your son be maimed for life? It's your choice, Thomas." Whenever she used his full name like that, Carly knew she'd made up her mind. Even if Daddy stood his ground, she'd just take Wolfie to the shelter the minute he left for work; there was nothing he could do about it.

He told Carly he was pretty sure Uncle Brewster would take Wolfie, which would be better than him going to the pound, but that hadn't stopped Carly from crying harder than she'd ever cried before. Daddy never forgave Mom for making her cry like that, and she was secretly happy that he didn't. Mostly, she was sad because she was losing Wolfie, but part of her—the part she wouldn't admit to—was hurt because her mother hadn't listened to her... and because she'd lost her mom, too. At least, that's what it felt like.

Out of self-protection, she'd turned that sadness into anger. And that anger had only increased when she found out her mother was leaving Daddy for another woman.

It was only a few months later that she'd lost Daddy, too. In the accident.

Now she just wanted to speak to him again, one more time, even if they were on different sides of the veil that separated life from death.

"I miss him so much... I can't... I just can't..."

"Your father is always with you, inside you," the medium said. She reached across the table and put her hand on Carly's. The girl tensed reflexively, then forced herself to relax. She was fiercely protective of her personal space, and when anyone touched her without warning—or permission—it made her want to run a thousand miles in the opposite direction. She squirmed in her seat but didn't pull away.

"Your anger is a barrier. Your grief is a barrier. He will sense that and think he's making you angry and sad. He will feel shame, and he won't appear."

Carly did pull her hand back then and used it to cover her eyes. "Of course I'm angry and sad," she said. "But how can he think I'm mad at *him*? He has to know how much I miss him."

But the woman was shaking her head. "It's not like that," she said, her voice full of sympathy. "Even when the veil is thin, as it is now at Samhain, those on the other side only have a vague sense of our world... until we make contact. Before that, they only sense raw emotion. It comes at them in waves, and it can be very confusing. Even frightening. He probably doesn't even know you're the one trying to contact him."

Carly stood up and started pacing. She wanted to run, but she felt like this was her only chance to make contact with her father, so she stopped herself before she got to the door, then turned to face the woman. "He knows me. How could he not know it's me?"

"Until you actually make contact—until we pull back the veil—he won't know where it's coming from. Put yourself in his position. If you just felt waves of anger, but you didn't know where they were coming from, wouldn't you be scared?"

Carly nodded reluctantly. "I guess."

She returned to the circular table, pulled back the padded folding chair across from the medium, and sat down. Trying to distract herself from her feelings, she looked around the room. Sheer purple curtains had been hung all around it, even though there were no windows. Five pillar candles burned on floor stands spaced at equal distances all around them, and a single book had been placed at the center of the table. It was bound in thick brown leather and looked impressive, but it didn't have any lettering on the front.

"Is that a book of spells?" Carly asked.

Madam Liliana just smiled. Nothing seemed to rattle her. Every expression seemed to radiate warmth and sympathy. Was this some trick to put her at ease? But if it was, then why? Madam Liliana hadn't charged her a penny, and she'd insisted that she did what she did for its own sake. She took joy in using her gift to help her clients find closure; of helping them across the veil; of reuniting the living and the dead.

"There is no magic to what I do," she said softly. "I am just a guide."

"Like those guys who climb Mount Everest?"

"Sherpas. Yes. The book contains no magic-at least not in the sense you probably think of it. It is a symbol of your own life. When you open it, you will be opening yourself to your father. Here," she said, pushing the book gently toward Carly, who just stared at it.

"Close your eyes and take slow, deep breaths," Liliana said softly. "Think of your father and all the good times you shared with him. Picture him right here with you, comforting you. You will be creating a mirror across the veil: As you focus your thoughts on how he used to comfort and reassure you, he will feel reassurance himself. Does that make sense?"

Carly nodded slightly. Her breathing had slowed, and she was picturing him there. She could almost feel the way he used to sit beside her on the couch, reading her *Green Eggs and Ham* and *Where the Wild Things Are* as she sat mesmerized by the pictures on the pages of those books. His voice was rich and full as he enunciated each of the syllables, never hurried, as though he were guiding her through the story.

Madam Liliana's voice felt similar. It reminded her of her father's: patient and always under control... but not forced control, like her own. It came naturally. Madam Liliana said she was a guide, too. Was it just a coincidence that she had a similar ability to put her at ease, or did she somehow sense that this was what her father had provided—and what she needed most to hear?

"Now," the medium was saying, "open your eyes slowly, and open the book."

Carly reached forward and took the book in her hands. Her fingers brushed across the cover, over the creases in the soft leather. The edges of the pages were uneven, like each of them had been bound individually. The book felt old... almost timeless... and somehow sacred.

She opened it, eager to see what she would find inside.

She was surprised to discover that the pages were blank.

"I don't understand," she said, looking up at the medium. "There's nothing there."

The medium smiled again. "As I told you, the book is a symbol—a conduit, if you will. By opening it, you have taken your first step toward the veil. Your father will sense this, but he will be hesitant. They always are. Now that your energy is more soothing, less erratic, his curiosity will be piqued. He will be open to discovering the source of it."

Carly smiled but kept her enthusiasm in check. She remembered when Daddy had brought Wolfie home to her. He had been wild and rambunctious, all over the place, but her father had taught her to remain calm and consistent. "He's a puppy. He wants to play!" her father had said. "Play with him, but let him know you're in control. Be firm if he gets too rough, and reward him when he calms down again."

Carly almost laughed: It felt like Liliana was asking her to train her father so he could hear her, the same way he'd taught her to train Wolfie.

Liliana brought her attention back to the book, holding its pages open in front of her. "It's time to let him know that you're the one trying to contact him," she said. "Write your name in the book."

She handed Carly a pen: one of those old-fashioned quills with a feather at one end and a point that curved on both sides toward the tip. Liliana had dipped it into an ink well, and it dripped a little onto the page.

Carly lowered it, pressed the tip gently against the thick parchment paper, and signed her name as neatly as she could. Handwriting had never been her strong suit, so it was legible, but hardly stylish.

"There," said Liliana.

Carly looked up at her again. "Now what."

"Now we wait. Patience is the key. If he senses you're anxious, he may believe you're trying to trick him and pull back."

"What are we waiting for exactly? Will he try to talk to me?"

The medium put an index finger to her lips. The message was clear: The ball was in her father's court now; anything she did now ran the risk of disrupting the channel she had opened to the other world. She would have to remain quiet and still, so she focused hard on doing so.

She only realized a moment later that she'd been holding her breath.

She exhaled slowly.

"It's OK," Liliana whispered. "Don't be nervous. Visualize yourself with him again, and relax into your memories. Focus on the times you shared. The door is open. It's up to him to step through."

Carly did as she was bidden, remembering the times she'd spent with her father. Two summers ago, they'd gone camping with her mother and Max. It had been one of the last trips they'd taken together as a family: They'd rented a campsite for the weekend beside a little lake south of the four-lane grade up to Shaver Lake.

On their first day there, they'd found an old tire hanging from a rope near a secluded lake, and Daddy had pushed her as far out over the lake as she could go. She remembered looking down at the water as she flew out over it; seeing the sunlight dance on the ripples, blurring into streaks on nature's wild canvas. The air rushed through her hair, blowing it backward, then forward across her face after she reached the apex of her journey and the tire swing reversed its course, racing again toward the shore.

Max had been there too, and he'd begged Daddy to let him ride on the swing, but her mother had said he was too young. So instead, he started pestering them to let him push Carly. Daddy hadn't been too sure about it, but in the end he had acquiesced... which had turned out to be a mistake. Max, seeking to show off how strong he was, had run up to the tire and pushed it too roughly, shoving it so hard that the rope began to twirl around madly like a spinning top—with Carly inside it. It had made her so dizzy that she'd fallen into the water without knowing whether she was going to land feet-first or head-first.

As it turned out, she did neither: Instead, she fell flat on her back, the unforgiving surface of the lake knocking almost all the air from her lungs as she gasped, in vain, for more.

She'd hit the surface and fallen quickly beneath it.

The next thing she'd known, she'd heard a splash and, a moment later, felt her father's arms underneath her, the water turbulent and full of bubbles as he kicked against it and pulled her to the surface.

Back on shore, she'd coughed and sputtered up water.

Max, of course, had run back the campsite to tell their mother what a klutz she'd been... and she'd believed him, the way she always did. She'd teased Carly about it later, chiding her for being reckless and going on the swing—even after Daddy had told her what had really happened. But he'd stuck up for her, the same way he'd stuck up for Wolfie. That was what mattered. And when Mom had wanted to ground her over it, he'd refused to let her. They'd gotten into a big fight that evening, raising their voices so much that someone from a neighboring campsite had yelled across at them to keep it down.

That had put a stop to it, and Carly hadn't been grounded after all. But their mother had still treated Max like a hero, as though he'd been the one who jumped into the lake and saved her. Their mother had stopped giving Daddy any credit for anything after Max was born. She treated him like a second-class citizen who couldn't do anything right...

...The memory of the camping trip faded from her mind and was replaced by a picture of him dressed up as Santa, climbing down from the roof and announcing that he'd been stuck up there all night.

It was Christmas morning, and Carly was twelve years old. The ground was covered with frost, but that was the closest they ever came to a white Christmas: It only snowed where they lived once every ten or twenty years.

Daddy wasn't fooling her with that Santa suit, but she figured it was more for Max's benefit than hers. Still, it was fun seeing him like that, and imagining him waiting up there on the roof for Mom to take them out into the front yard for his not-so-grand entrance.

"Your chimney's too small!" he said, stepping down off "Santa's" retractable ladder—which looked suspiciously like the one they kept in the garage. Carly tried not to laugh as she looked at him, with part of a pillow peeking out from underneath his red velvet coat and the cotton beard he was wearing starting to come loose from his face. He pressed it back down, but it wouldn't stick. Even Max had to know it was Daddy underneath that disguise.

"I guess none of the other children will be getting presents this Christmas," Santa Daddy said, doing his best to frown and look upset. But then his expression brightened as he said, "But at least the best little girl and boy in the world will!"

That Christmas, he presented Max with a new red bicycle and her with a fancy camera.

"You're the official Bartlett Family Photographer now," he announced. "From now on, you get to take pictures of every holiday and family gathering. I'll help you put them all together in a photo album so you can look back on all the fun times we had when you grow up and move out on your own."

"I'm never moving out," she declared. "I want to stay right here the rest of my life."

They'd worked on that photo album together over the next few years, and she remembered how proud she'd been when he told her how much she was improving.

"You've got a real eye for this," he'd said. "Maybe you'll be a nature photographer when you grow up. Or maybe work for a newspaper or do photo shoots for Vogue." He'd said that with a straight face: He really did think she was that talented.

Sadly, however, that praise had come just before everything went to hell. The divorce came three years later; then, six months after that, the unthinkable: the accident that had separated her from her father forever. Amid the chaos of that time, the album had somehow gotten lost. She had no idea where it was now, and she struggled to visualize the photos she had taken. How was it that such precious memories could fade so quickly behind a haze of time and tears?

Her thoughts were interrupted by a scratching sound coming from in front of her, and she opened her eyes to see, in amazement, the pen moving by itself across the parchment pages of the book. The writing was rough and fragmented, but she was still able to make it out.

"Carly, is that really you?"

She nearly jumped out of her seat, then saw Liliana motioning at her, palms downward, to stay calm. It was her way of saying, *You don't want to scare him away.*

"Yes, Daddy. It's me," she said aloud in almost a whisper. Then, speaking up a little more: "I'm here. Can you hear me?"

After a moment, the pen started moving again. "Yes, I'm here, Cupcake. Oh my God. I never thought it was possible."

Carly glanced at Liliana and whispered: "Why can't I hear his voice? Why is he just writing these things? I can hear him. Why can't he hear me?"

Liliana was shaking her head as if to say this wasn't the time for such questions. She could save them for later. It didn't matter anyway. All that mattered now was that she had her Daddy back—not all the way back, but as much as she could have hoped for. More, really. She hadn't dared to believe it was possible, but now there was no doubt of it: He was actually communicating with her from the other side.

"Oh, Daddy. What is it like where you are? Are you lonely there?"

There was a pause. Then the writing resumed, but more tentatively now. "I will always miss you, Cupcake," the words said. "I wish you were here with me."

"I wish *you* were here with *me*, Daddy. It's so lonely without you. I don't know how to keep going."

The writing resumed: "I am with you. I'm always with you. Just like you're always here with me."

It was the same thing Liliana had said.

She was staring so intently at the book in the center of the table that Carly was startled out of her seat by the sound of a door clicking open behind her. Light flooded the room from somewhere outside, and the candles that Liliana had kept lit were extinguished by a sudden gust of wind as Carly's mother strode through the door like a whirlwind in her own right.

"What's the meaning of this?" she demanded.

Carly stared at her, open-mouthed. "I was talking to Daddy," she said. "Really talking to him. But... how did you get here?"

Her mother looked around her, seeming suddenly disoriented. "I... I'm not quite sure."

Liliana seemed unfazed by any of this. She sat slightly more upright in her chair but didn't rise to confront Carly's mother. She just looked at her, the picture of calm and serenity, and spoke to her in relaxed but measured tones. "You just arrived, my dear, and I'm sure this is all very new to you. You're confused, and you don't understand any of what's going on, but I can help you."

Carly's mother looked at her, and the anger returned: "I don't need your help!" she spat. "And I understand perfectly well what's going on. You're interfering in my right to raise my daughter as I see fit."

She glanced over at the center of the center of the table, her attention caught by movement seen from the corner of her eye.

The pen was writing again.

"Roberta, I didn't know you were there. I'm so sorry. Please don't be angry with Carly. She didn't know..."

The woman's eyes widened in disbelief, and she pointed a finger at Liliana. "You're a witch."

"I'm just a guide, dear, but think whatever you will of me. Your eyes will be opened soon enough."

"Is that a threat?" Roberta demanded.

Liliana shook her head. "It has nothing to do with me. It will happen whether I am here or not. The journey is yours to take, not mine."

Carly's head was pounding. Her mother's arrival had jarred loose any sense of calm and patience she'd managed to muster. Images flooded her mind, tumbling and twisting into knots. They were memories, she realized: memories she'd somehow blocked out because they'd been just too painful. Her mother shouldn't be here with her. It should be impossible, just as Daddy couldn't cross the veil. Because...

The reality of it all pressed in on her, and she pushed back against it. It couldn't be.

The last memory of her time with him, the one she'd worked so hard to block out, now returned to her unbidden.

Daddy had visitation for the weekend, and he was taking her to see the Winchester Mystery House in San Jose, then up the coast to see the redwoods. The car radio playing country music, Daddy's favorite. After one song faded out, the deejay introduced the next selection, and more music started playing. Then Tim McGraw's voice came through the speaker, singing his number one hit, "Don't Take the Girl."

Daddy knew the song by heart. He mouthed the words as his head swayed slowly back and forth to the sound of the music and reached over and squeezed her shoulder. He took his eyes off the road for just a second.

Then he looked forward again.

In the blink of an eye, he pulled his hand away from her and sat bolt upright.

Both hands gripped the wheel and jerked it to the right.

Carly felt the car brake and swerve; she heard the screech of tires, and saw the big rig coming straight for them.

"Daddy!" she cried, and braced herself as they veered sharply away from the truck and off the road, careening through some low underbrush just off the shoulder... and directly into a giant redwood rising high above Highway 101. Carly heard the piercing sound of glass shattering, then it sliced through her skin a second later, shards of it slashing at her and lodging beneath her skin. As the car slammed to a halt, her head ricocheted off the headrest behind her, then forward into the dashboard.

She hadn't been wearing her seatbelt.

Somehow, the airbags didn't deploy.

She sat there, limp and motionless, frantic thoughts racing across the dark curtain of her now-closed eyes, before fading with her consciousness.

"Where's Daddy...? Is he all right...? It hurts so much... I can't see... I can't feel my legs. I can't..."

And that was where the memory ended.

Carly had never found any answers to those questions until today, when those words had appeared on the pages of that open book, a message from her father, answering her from across eternity. Now she knew he was okay... and so was she. She could see just fine, the pain was gone, and she had walked into this room—to Madam Liliana's—without so much as a limp.

"Mom," she said, suddenly calm again. "There's something I have to tell you."

Her mother was still staring down at her as she sat there at the table, but the anger was gone, replaced by dawning realization—one she was still fighting to suppress.

"Madam Liliana helped me contact Daddy because I needed to know he was okay without me. I remember him holding me in the hospital, and I couldn't say anything because I was... I wanted to tell him everything would be okay, but I couldn't. I could feel his sadness. He was afraid of losing me. And I was afraid of losing him, too. But I couldn't find my way back to him. I tried and tried and tried, but I just couldn't."

Her mother was just staring at the book.

"You can't contact the dead," she said. "It's just not possible."

Madam Liliana stood and took her head in her hands, looking directly into her eyes. "Yes, you can," she said, her voice soothing but unyielding. "And the dead can contact the living too. Your daughter has just done exactly that."

A look of panic appeared on the woman's face, and Carly knew the memories of her own death were flooding back into her mind—just the way Carly's memories had come back to her moments earlier. She didn't know her mom had died. Maybe it had just happened. And despite all the troubles they'd had between them, she felt compassion for the woman, a form of kinship that only trauma could have supplied.

"We're both dead, Mom. Daddy's still alive, and he's okay. I'm sure Max is okay, too. Maybe Liliana can help you talk to reach him the way she helped me talk to Daddy."

She took a tentative step toward the woman, who responded by stepping toward her. They embraced, awkwardly at first, then both began to cry. She had lost her father, but she knew now that he would be all right. So would her brother. Maybe now, after all this time, she and her Mom would be all right again too.

Sharon Marie Provost

The Manor

Madeline's eyes widened as she pulled up to park in front of The Manor, the affectionate name among those in the paranormal community for the large, decaying former mental institution. In its long and varied history, it had stood silent witness to the deaths of more than 200, with its own pauper's field across the way.

The land had been set aside for the site of the county courthouse when the town of Centralia was the seat of Frawley County. But then the county seat had been moved when the booming agricultural town of Victorville outgrew and eclipsed Centralia.

In the early 1900s, the courthouse and surrounding land had been converted into a poor farm to house the county's many indigents, chronically ill or disabled people and the so-called incurably insane, all of whom helped work the farm to help offset the costs the county incurred to support them.

The deaths and the mental anguish of all those sick and mentally ill people led to the enormous amount of paranormal activity being recorded there. Much of it consisted of residual hauntings: almost like recordings of the endless, repetitious activity of the poor ill and insane souls who lived here.

The Manor was still full of personal objects left by its last residents and employees, some of which were moved from one area to another time and again without explanation. Noises had been heard issuing from the padded room, , including unintelligible moans and whimpers. A number of paranormal investigators had recorded this activity, but nothing they tried changed it: It did not respond to stimuli of any kind. Exciting for novice investigators but pretty standard fare for someone as experienced as Madeline.

The activity that brought Madeline here to investigate? Now, that was an entirely different story. There had been reports of intelligent hauntings and a malevolent shadow haunting in the basement. That shadow figure did not appreciate uninvited guests entering his basement. He could be downright violent and terrifying to those who taunted him. Most investigators who ventured down there vowed never to return after only a few minutes in his presence. Madeline was determined to get evidence of his presence and not let him scare her away.

Upstairs on the second floor, there is one spirit, that while benign, still enjoyed interacting with—or in some cases scaring—those that endeavored to climb up to see him. This shadowy figure enjoyed darting past a person's view, appearing only from the corner of the eye. At times, he even "bumped" against visitors, causing a chill or the sensation of a draft across their skin. Madeline was eager to catch video of him and see what activity she could incite from him with playful interaction.

Several spirits inhabited the first floor. The first entity was known to seek out and scare those who enter his domain. The room he occupied was the site of a brutal rape and assault of one patient by another. The entity there was believed to be the perpetrator of that assault. He had never done anything to hurt an investigator, but he definitely worked to cause great discomfort and unease, invading one's personal space with glee.

The final spirit that was commonly encountered was a joyful, little girl who ran up and down the hall, pranking and peeking at investigators. Madeline had brought along some toys and other trigger objects in hopes of enticing her to appear.

Madeline finished looking at her notes and then made sure she had all her paranormal investigation tools together. Once she was locked in for the night, there would be no one to let her back inside if she should leave. She glanced around the property and realized that the caretaker had not arrived yet. She used the opportunity to take her camera across to the pauper's field to obtain some pictures. There, against the vibrant orange and red hues of sunset, she focused her camera on the bare-bones plots with only small, unmarked wooden crosses designating each gravesite.

Just as she was taking a panoramic shot of the graveyard with The Manor as the backdrop, she saw a white Volvo pull into the parking lot. Madeline quickly ran across the street, waving to the stoic woman behind the wheel.

"Hi there. I am Madeline. Are you Anne, the caretaker?"

"Yessiree, ma'am. That is why I am here. This is private property, after all."

"Oh, yes... that makes sense. Thank you very much for coming down to let me in. I have been looking forward to this investigation for some time now. I am hoping to write THE definitive paper on paranormal activity for the scientific community—or at least for the paranormal community. I have been researching this location and the activity experienced here for the past three years. I brought every tool I could think of that would help me in this endeavor, as well as every one I could use to dispel any doubts about potential natural or manmade causes.

"I have heard rumors that an investigator died here a few years ago. Any truth to that? No matter how deeply I searched newspaper archives and police blotters, I could not find any reports of such an occurrence. Goodness... I apologize. I should take a breath here and quit rambling, so you can say something edgewise or answer my questions."

"Thank ya kindly," the woman said. "Yes, I need your identification and payment please... cash or check, no credit cards. And I need you to sign this waiver of liability... we are not responsible for your injuries or death... blah blah blah..."

Madeline laughed nervously. "Of course. I should have thought of that. Death, huh?"

"We get a lot of people trying to sneak in here. Can't be too careful. Hafta to make sure you are the one who made this reservation. And for accountability and all, should you vandalize The Manor. The building has been deserted for over 20 years now. Of course, there has been some decay—the stairs aren't even as they once were, so you could fall. That is all I meant, naturally."

"I understand your cautiousness completely," Madeline said, nodding. "I appreciate that. I would hate to lose my spot. I have waited 14 months for this opening in your schedule. Nor do I want to be blacklisted for damaging the place, when I have only the most honorable of intentions. To me, paranormal investigations are another way to immortalize history. Too many of these old buildings have been torn down or destroyed by hoodlums, and deprived humanity of the history they contain."

"Mmm hmm," Anne mumbled as she finished jotting down Madeline's identification information on an old envelope she had fished from her car. "Well anyhow, you grab your bags there, and we will head inside."

Madeline made two trips from the car to the top of the steep staircase leading to the front door. The basement was only two-thirds of the way underground, with windows that rose mere inches above ground level on the outside. Madeline's eyes were drawn to the one on her right as she climbed the stairs the second time. She could have sworn she saw a shadowy figure staring out at her.

With her attention focused elsewhere, she missed the last step and fell in a heap at the door. A searing pain spread through her hand as she hit the porch. She righted herself quickly, picked her bags up and limped through the front door. As she looked down, she realized blood was dripping from a cut in her hand, from which a large splinter of wood protruded.

"Oh God, I am so sorry. I didn't mean to bleed on the floor. Let me go find something in my car to clean it up. And a Band-Aid."

"You go take care of yourself," Anne said. "As for the blood, it's not the first time this place has seen a little blood. Nor I suspect, the last... uh, I mean given the state of the building... somewhat hazardous and all."

Madeline forced a small smile and ran out to the car to get

her first aid kit, surveying the interior quickly to make sure she had grabbed all her equipment. She didn't really expect to need her phone, but she retrieved the charger just in case. Electricity was available in The Manor to power a space heater, and for visitor use in a small room right off the entry.

Madeline set the charger and first aid kit on the table, then took a seat to clean and bandage her hand. Unfortunately, she had left a trail of blood through the vestibule leading up to the table.

"You are pretty brave coming here tonight."

Madeline looked at Anne quizzically and asked, "You mean the veil?"

The woman continued, "Especially with your intention to interact with the spirits. Aren't you concerned that they might give you more than you bargained for? This is their night to cross the barrier. We don't normally book The Manor on this date. Your professional reputation precedes you, so the owner approved your request for Halloween night. Despite my protestations."

"No, I am not concerned," Madeline replied. "I am not sure that I believe this whole veil concept. Yes, I agree that there does seem to be more activity during this time. But I cannot say I have ever seen, nor heard—from anybody reputable at least—evidence of a spirit crossing the veil. I didn't choose today because of the potential for increased activity, although I must say it would be a welcome bonus. It was more a matter of the next date for availability being three months away. As I said, I have already waited 14 months for this chance."

"I hope for your sake you are right. Do you want a tour of the building? If so, I would like to get started now. The sun has nearly set, and I do not stay here past dark."

Madeline shook her head. "No, that is OK. I have researched this place thoroughly. I even have a copy of the old blueprints, so I know where everything is located. What is the restroom situation though?"

"Should you need to use the facilities, there's not one inside The Manor. You would have to put that log over there in the door to prop it open," Anne said, gesturing toward a large piece of wood. "Around the back, you'll find an unlocked, fully functional modular... although, I can't promise what—or who—you might find back there or when you return. As I told you, people creep around here often."

"Noted. I will take care of that before you drive away."

This was one of the largest locations Madeline had investigated, but it was still surprising to see how expansive 13,000 square feet was in person. The walk to the bathroom was longer than she had expected.

No way I am coming out here at night. Real humans are far scarier than any ghost, veil thin or not. This looks like the perfect setting for the Creeper to come harvest my eyes.

Madeline whistled "Jeepers Creepers" as she made her way back into the building, waving at Anne as she drove away. The next hour was spent setting up cameras, infrared and full-spectrum lights; motion detectors; laser grids in the areas frequented by shadow figures; a BooBuddy interactive ghost hunting bear; some toys and a ball; and EMF meters. She placed her voice recorder in her jacket pocket, along with extra batteries.

Thankfully, the immense steel door to the basement was propped open with another heavy log, allowing her easy access with her armful of equipment. She set up the first laser grid near the padded room in the basement, where the shadow man had often been sighted, and started a video recording. On the first floor, she placed the toys in the hallway at the far left end. The BooBuddy bear sat on a wheelchair nearby, ready to interact with the little girl ghost. The camera at the end of the hall captured both locations perfectly. In Room 104, where the attack occurred, she placed a motion detector, another camera, and an EMF meter. Now it was time to head up to the second floor, where she placed another laser grid near the stairway landing. The shadow figure commonly traveled between the stairs and the two rooms at the top.

As usual, she started with a tour of the entire second floor, introducing herself to any spirits and asking if anybody wanted to speak to her. She did not hear any answers on playback of the video, which was not uncommon at the start of an investigation.

Returning to the stairway, she placed herself in the middle of the shadow man's path and began speaking to him.

"Hello. My name is Madeline. Is there anyone here who would like to speak to me? Thank you for letting me join you here today."

She waited a few moments before turning her back to the stairwell and starting again, "Would you like to play tag or hide-and-seek? I hear you like to sneak past people and touch them." Her eyes flitted from side to side, as she slowly began to rotate her body. A dark shape appeared, just at the edge of her vision, and then was gone before she could react.

"Was that you?"

She reached her hand out, beckoning in the darkness for something... or someone to come to her. She covered her eyes with her hand and began to count down from thirty, "5... 4... 3... 2... 1... come out, come out wherever you are." She opened her eyes and whirled around, catching sight of a dark shape running past her on the right and into the room behind her.

She dashed into the neighboring room and hid behind the door. "Come and find me," she called out. She peered through the crack in the doorjamb, waiting to see if the dark shape would follow. The hairs on her arm rose as she felt a cold sensation sweep across it, and she turned to see the dark form beside her. It disappeared just as her eyes took in the sight of it.

She pressed STOP on her tape recorder and played it back to see if she had obtained an EVP. Seconds after she had invited the shadow to find her and heard the squeak of the hinges, there was a faint whisper, "Right here," followed by her gasp.

Madeline whooped with joy. She spent the next half an hour interacting with the spirit until he seemed to lose his patience. He had started appearing in different locations, almost as if he was avoiding her. She kept following him around, asking questions. On the last pass by the stairs, she'd heard a whisper right by her ear as a cold draft rushed by her. Then she stumbled as a force pushed her, barely catching herself on the railing.

Her pupils dilated, and she broke out in a cold sweat. She had never experienced such a strong touch before. She gathered up her equipment and hurried down the stairs, thanking him as she went.

When she reached the landing in the middle, she played back the recorder to see what the voice had said as it knocked into her.

"GO AWAY!"

The clarity and vehemence of the voice on the EVP made her jump. She looked back up to see the dark figure standing at the top, looking down at her. She pressed STOP as she dashed down to the first floor, heart pounding.

Madeline retreated to the lounge room to rest and gather her courage, anxious to see if she had managed to record the spirit's movements. Much of his activity had occurred in front of the laser grid where the camera had been focused, which made tracking him much easier. Her unease melted away into pure joy as she watched the video. She clearly caught over 15 minutes of footage displaying intelligent haunting behavior. There was no doubt he had reacted to her questions and actions. She had never seen video proof of this caliber before.

As she replayed the video a third time, she couldn't help but notice a nagging feeling of being watched. When she looked up from the screen, she realized why. The lounge had two doors, one of which she had used to enter from the vestibule. The other door, on a wall that stood perpendicular to the first, opened onto the hallway directly across from the heavy steel door that led into the basement. She could have sworn this door in the lounge had been closed since her arrival. The door was now open about an inch, as if someone was peeking in on her. Madeline got up and closed the door again hard. She heard the latch click into place, and tested it to be sure it would not open again—no matter how hard she pulled on it. She sighed as she returned to her seat and restarted the video.

A short while later, the feeling crept up on her again. Her eyes flashed up to see the door cracked once again. She snatched the handle, pulling it open fully, and leaned out, searching the hallway for a person. The hallway was empty, and all was silent.

Except for the BooBuddy bear at the far end.

His paws glowed, showing a strong change in EMF energy, and his voice rang out, "Brrr...! Did it just get colder in here?" indicating a change in temperature as well.

Of course, you dummy. The little girl is here. She likes to play pranks and interact with toys up and down this hall.

Madeline grabbed her voice recorder so she could obtain

any EVPs in other areas of the hall. The BooBuddy bear had stopped detecting activity, so it started spouting the preprogrammed questions and statements, such as, "What's your name? How old are you? Count with me, 1... 2... 3..."

A ball began rolling toward Madeline from the opposite end of the hallway. "Can you tell me a secret?" she heard the BooBuddy ask, as first one paw and then the other began to glow. This was followed by the statement "I like hugs," indicating a vibration or motion had been detected.

Madeline darted into the lounge to grab a REM pod and then proceeded over to the bear, turning him off.

She placed the REM pod nearby and began an EVP session.

"My name is Madeline, sweetie. Who are you? Do you like playing with my toys? I brought you a new one. Do you see the metal antenna there? If you get near it, it will make a noise like this." A buzzing shriek emanated from the pod as her hand neared it. The shrieking increased in pitch and volume as her hand grew nearer and then touched the antenna. Madeline pulled her hand away, asking, "Can you try that for me?"

A doll she had placed against the wall earlier began to rise into the air and then glide across the hall to the REM pod. As the doll came within six inches of it, the shrieking sound began, intensifying as the doll came to a rest, sitting up against the antenna. Madeline giggled and thanked the little girl for her efforts. She continued to play different games with her until her energy and engagement seemed to fade.

"Thank you, dear one, for playing with me. I hope you had as much fun as I did."

She remained seated on the floor and replayed her voice recorder. Two EVPs had been captured... and they both chilled her to the bone. When the BooBuddy bear asked the little girl ghost for a secret, she had responded, "They want to hurt you."

The second response had come after she thanked her: "I can't wait to play with you forever and ever."

Madeline jabbed the record button, "Who wants to hurt me?"

This time, there was no reply. The little girl had left the area… or was too scared to respond.

Madeline began to regret her decision. She had become disarmed, her courage disintegrating, after her interactions with the two playful ghosts. She still had the non-violent spirit that sought to make people uneasy, and more concerning, the malevolent spirit, who had been known to be violent, left to investigate. A little liquid courage might be what she needed most at this moment.

Madeline was not one to advocate imbibing alcohol during investigations, but she had never known one shot to be a problem. She dug her flask out of the bottom of her duffel bag and took a long swig. She rested for a few moments, warming up by the space heater before she moved on to Room 104.

Upon entering the room, she was startled by the blaring siren of the motion detector, having forgotten she had set it up in there. She sprinted over to the chair behind the sensor to get out of its path and sat down heavily. As she waited for her heart to stop pounding, she turned on the voice recorder. Darkness surrounded her, and straining to see increased her discomfort. She had set up infrared lights in the room that provided no visible light but lit up the room perfectly if you were looking through the right kind of camera. She pulled out her handheld IR camera and turned it on, staring at the small screen on the back.

To her relief, it revealed an empty patient room.

Room 104 had two hospital beds: one to her left and the

other to her right. There were two large armoires, one partially open, revealing a few dresses. She noticed that she had narrowly avoided tripping on a walker near the door.

After surveying the room, she pulled a bed tray over and set the camera down on it, allaying her nagging fears by ensuring she was able to see what was in front of her. Then she pulled out her voice recorder to start an EVP session. She began by identifying herself, asking if anybody was there, and posing a couple of other introductory questions.

On replay, she thought she heard a whispered, "Leave me alone."

She knew better than to push a spirit, but she was hoping to get a little more activity than that. She restarted the recorder and said, "I don't mean any harm. I am not trying to bother you. I would like to set the record straight... get your side of the story."

The cold draft that followed should have been her first clue to leave. Instead, she chose to pick up the handheld camera and look around again. A flash of movement on the screen was the last thing she saw. The UV lights shut off. The camera screen went black and then powered off, as the sirens from the motion sensor began to blare.

She felt her way over to the main video camera she had set up for the investigation. As she realized its battery had died, too, she felt the hair on the side of her face move and heard a menacing voice whisper "Run" against her ear. Madeline jumped back, falling onto the bed behind her. She felt the bed depress next to her as something climbed onto the bed beside her. She dove off onto the floor and lunged toward the door, rolling out into the hallway. The door to Room 104 slammed shut.

She heaved in great lungfuls of air, her heart nearly

pounding out of her chest. Her legs too weak to stand, she crawled back into the lounge. Scrounging around in the bag finally produced her flask, and she gulped down the last of the whiskey inside. She needed to retrieve her equipment from Room 104, but maybe that was better left until the morning when the caretaker returned.

Three down... one to go. But should I even risk it?

Exhaustion overcame her as her eyes drifted closed. Madeline awoke at 3 a.m. to find The Manor quiet and still. The electricity she had felt crackling in the air all night seemed to have dissipated.

Now or never, Madeline. Get your shit together. You are a professional, so act like one.

Madeline struggled to her feet, her head spinning a little from the whiskey. She checked her voice recorder and found the batteries drained as expected. Whatever—or whoever—she had encountered in Room 104 had needed, and taken, a great deal of power to manifest his response to her.

From all reports she had seen, the entity in the basement was far more powerful.

She grabbed her backpack and filled it with batteries of all sizes as well as the REM pod and a handheld EMF meter. Given the power of the spirits tonight, she thought it might be best not to provoke this final spirit too much, and instead let him interact with some of the equipment on his own. She already had groundbreaking footage from the other three spirits.

Madeline approached the door with trepidation. She could feel the power emanating from below. Her foot was nearly swept out from under her when the large log holding the door open slid across the floor to the opposite wall. She stared down at the floor, pondering how it could have moved independently and why the door had not slammed shut. She had tested the door earlier and had found it would not stay open without being held or propped open. Once again, as she stepped forward, her movement was halted by the door slamming shut with a resounding metal clang.

Madeline resolved not to be dissuaded by a few cheap fear tactics. She yanked the door open and pushed her way through and down the stairs. She gripped her flashlight tightly as she made her way through the dark rooms full of objects, piled nearly to the ceiling. She made her way to the far back corner, where the laser grid was set up. All the equipment still seemed to be functioning properly. Just in case, she replaced all the batteries with fresh ones from her backpack and then turned the devices back on.

Madeline paced around the room quietly as she started an EVP session, taking care not to provoke an angry response.

"My name is Madeline. I came here to visit you. I think you are misunderstood and have been judged unfairly. You can tell me your name and your story if you like. I don't want to bother you if you want to be left alone. I will set this recorder down in the corner, and you can speak into it, only if you like."

Out of the corner of her eye, she noticed a dark shape pass through the grid and into the padded room. She tiptoed up to the door and placed the REM pod a few feet to the left of the door.

"You can touch that if you like," she said.

Madeline backed away carefully to sit on a wheelchair in the opposite corner. She placed the handheld EMF meter on the floor in front of her to alert her if the spirit approached. The video camera she had placed in the room earlier, along with lights, used full-spectrum light. Luckily, she had brought a full-spectrum handheld camera with her, so she used it to peer into the padded room. She could see what appeared to be some records stored there but not much else.

She turned her head as she heard a rustling sound to her left. She saw the dark shape lurching toward her just before pain exploded in her head. Strong hands wrapped around her throat, squeezing the air out. Her own hands struggled for purchase on the attacker's, but only felt empty space.

Lights flashed in front of her eyes as her head began to throb with each slowing beat of her heart. As her vision began to fade, she felt her body lifted high in the air and then a sense of weightlessness as she flew through the air.

Anne arrived early the next morning to check on The Manor. Madeline's car was still parked out front, but she did have until 10 a.m. to clear out. Anne parked behind her and headed inside. She was surprised to find equipment still set up all over the first floor hallway and in Room 104.

She looked down into the open basement and called out for Madeline, but there was no response. She walked over to the stairs and headed up to the second floor, but it was empty, save for the equipment set up at the top of the stairs.

Anne felt nervous when she couldn't find Madeline, so she began a thorough search of all three floors. In the basement, she found more ghost hunting equipment but no sign of Madeline.

Anne locked up The Manor and decided to go check the modular, in case she had accidentally gotten locked out and spent the night in there. The door was unlocked, but it was empty. In fact, there was no sign she had been in there at all. Anne called the owner of the property and explained the mysterious circumstances. He told her he would arrive shortly and call the police to meet them there.

The police searched the entire property, inside and out, fanning out across acres of rolling fields, both behind and in front of The Manor.

But no sign of Madeline was found.

Investigators collected all her recording devices and reviewed the footage, both audio and video, but that only deepened the mystery of her disappearance. When Anne was questioned, she verified that Madeline had seemed both sober and mentally stable.

They had found the empty flask and wondered if she had wandered out and gotten lost in a drunken haze. It was the most logical explanation given her erratic behavior on tape. They viewed hours of footage of Madeline appearing to talk back to someone, chase or hide from someone, even play with toys with someone... but there was no one else on tape. Madeline appeared very animated at times, as though she had heard or seen something—even giving thanks for various activities—but they saw and heard nothing on any of the videos or on the voice recorder.

The police asked the public for help, hoping that someone would report seeing her, but all efforts to find her proved fruitless.

The case remains open but unsolved to this day.

"Madeeeeelinnnnne! Come play with me."

Madeline turned around in the entryway and found a young girl in a long white dress, wearing ribbons in her long, blond hair. She appeared to be straight out of the early 1900s.

The girl was bouncing a ball. She had a mischievous smile on her face as she said, "I told you I couldn't wait to play with you."

A long, piercing scream echoed through the cold, empty halls.

Anne dropped the mop she had been using to scrub the blood from the floors of the lounge and vestibule when she heard the scream right in front of her. She ran out the front door, dialing her boss to announce her immediate resignation.

Stephen H. Provost

Reaper's Reward

"There are four lights!"

Professor Erich Von Prince pulled himself up out of his recliner, where he'd been happily ensconced watching Jean-Luc Picard's famous line from "Chain of Command." It was a classic *Next Generation* episode, and he never got tired of rewatching it. It was testament to the human spirit of resistance in the face of lies and brainwashing. There *were* four lights, despite the efforts of Picard's alien torturer to make him confess—falsely—that there were only three.

What he didn't like about the episode was its underlying premise that, for all of humanity's potential heroism, being human also meant having the capacity for brutal cruelty. The torturer in the episode might have been from a different planet, but the actor under the makeup was entirely human, and the story contained, at its core, a lesson about how far humans would go in their quest for power.

Other humans had come to his door that evening in makeup, taking part in the annual ritual known as trick-or-treat. One had been dressed as a Gorn, a dinosaur-like alien from the original *Star Trek* series. There had been a Darth Vader impersonator, courtesy of *Star Wars*, too. At least some of the younger generation remembered classic science fiction, even if they'd never heard of Bradbury or Asimov, let alone cracked open one of their books.

Of course, there had been other costumes among the doorbell-ringing visitors that evening: a kid dressed like Deadpool, the requisite witch, and a pillowcase-wearing ghost. But with the evening winding down, he'd only answered the door half a dozen times. Halloween wasn't what it used to be. More kids were going to parties and watching *Friday the 13th* or doing "trunk or treat" in school parking lots.

Halloween just wasn't the same.

The last of the visitors had come by almost an hour ago, so the professor surmised it was safe to call it an evening and head to bed. In his younger years, he'd been quite the night owl, staying up past midnight to work on research projects or do some light reading. But these days, pushing 70, he often fell asleep in his recliner before finishing a chapter or two.

When it came to aging, another quote from *Star Trek* came to mind: "Resistance is futile."

"To hell with that," he muttered. He would "rage, rage against the dying of the light." Resistance was never futile. It was the hallmark of the human spirit in its noblest form.

He had just shut off the porch light and turned back toward his recliner when he heard a sharp rapping behind him. Sighing, he turned back toward the door, flipped the light switch back on, and released the deadbolt. Turning the knob, he pulled back the door and glanced down in front of him, expecting to see a straggling group of young trick-or-treaters. Instead, his eyes were greeted by the lower end of what appeared to be a long black trench coat and a pair of leather boots worn by feet that were much larger than he'd expected.

That's right. It's the older kids who are out this late.

But as he lifted his eyes, he found his gaze pulled even farther upward. The hulking form on his threshold loomed over him like the shadow of that large pine tree on the front lawn. It could have been seven feet tall, the top half of its face obscured by a dark hood and the bottom half nothing but a toothy grin.

No choice was given him regarding trick versus treat. Instead, a man's voice simply greeted him, sounding even but hollow: "Good evening, Professor von Prince."

The professor didn't know how the man knew his name, and he didn't care. The figure itself was menacing enough, but he was holding something behind his back, purposely hidden there, it seemed. There had been a rash of home-invasion robberies a few neighborhoods over in recent weeks; now, it seemed, one of the perpetrators had seen fit to expand his territory... and use Halloween as a pretext for doing so.

"No more candy here," the professor stammered, moving hastily to close the door.

But the stranger chose that moment to reveal what was in

his hidden hand—a long-handled scythe looked like it was meant for harvesting wheat—which he jammed between the frame and the door itself, holding it ajar.

"I will come in now," the figure said. It was not a request but a simple statement of factual intent.

"Well, you're not welcome here," the professor replied, summoning his most authoritative voice.

"Oh, I'm afraid you don't need to invite me, Professor," the man said evenly, sounding just as authoritative, though the utterance seemed more like an echo than an actual voice. "I'm not a vampire." He chuckled briefly.

The professor relaxed just a little. Whoever this was had a sense of humor. Perhaps it was one of his old colleagues trying to put one over on him. But before he could say anything else, the scythe vanished, and the door slammed shut from pent-up momentum.

"Well, that was... interesting," the professor muttered as he bolted the lock again, shut off the porch light, and turned back toward his recliner... where the figure from the front door had somehow taken up residence, sitting back comfortably, legs crossed, staring at him. The scythe he had held before now sat propped up next to him against the side of the chair.

"How...?" the professor began, baffled. "Wait a minute, that's *my* chair."

The professor, who had lived alone since his divorce two decades earlier, had become extremely possessive of his personal space—and nothing epitomized that space more than his recliner. It had become his sanctuary, embracing him as he sank into its generous cushions and giving his back a measure of relief from the degenerative disk disease that had produced more and more discomfort as life went on.

If anything, the grin on the otherwise obscured face of his visitor grew wider. "You won't be needing it anymore," he said simply.

The professor scoffed. "If you plan to steal it, you'll have a hell of a time getting it out of here."

But the figure simply shook his head. "Oh, I have no use for it," he said. "I didn't say *I* wanted it, just that *you* had no use for it. You will, after all, be dead by morning. You'll die in your sleep of cardiac arrest. I already know this, and it's why I've come: It's my job to ensure that your transition from this life goes smoothly and as planned."

The professor just stared at him for a moment, then burst out laughing. "So you want me to believe that you really *are* the Grim Reaper? Whoever put you up to this has a pretty dark sense of humor. But since I do as well, you've got kudos from me. Well done! But please, now that you've had your fun, I'm tired and I'd like to turn in for the night. So if you don't mind vacating my chair, I'll see you out."

The figure in the chair did not join in his laughter, and he did not move, either. "If you think your own death is funny, well, that's up to you. But I'm not leaving until my purpose here is accomplished."

The professor scowled, resigning himself to the presence of his unwanted guest. He could call the police, but he decided to hold that option in reserve. The man wasn't making any move to threaten him at the moment, and despite the presence of that rather dangerous-looking scythe, the intruder hadn't shown any inclination to pick it up or use it against him. He was still convinced he was the victim of some sort of elaborate prank.

"All right," he said. "I'll play along. But if you would at least do the courtesy of telling me your name. 'Mr. Reaper' seems a bit contrived, if you get my meaning."

"My given name is Valerian."

"Like the root?"

"Like the Roman emperor."

"So, since it's your given name, that must mean someone gave it to you. Do your parents know you go around terrorizing people like this?"

"I am afraid you are under the wrong impression. I have no parents. It is my 'given' name because I gave it to myself."

"I see. And you do this sort of thing just for kicks?"

"Actually, it's my job."

"Well, I hope you take home a decent paycheck for it. I assume you are self-employed, and that your 'job' consists of burglarizing people's homes. You have a strange way of going about it, though, knocking on the front door. I imagine that eats into your profit margin a bit."

"As I suggested earlier and will state plainly now: I am not interested in your worldly goods, or anyone else's. Not that it's any of your business, but I am not self-employed and I do not receive a paycheck. My job is its own reward."

"Sounds like slave labor to me."

Valerian said nothing.

"Look here," the professor said when it was clear nothing more was forthcoming. "You're an interesting fellow, but if we're going to sit here getting to know each other, it's only right that I offer you a drink. Do you mind?" Not waiting for an answer, he got up and strode to the liquor cabinet. "Pick your poison."

"I do not drink," Valerian said stiffly.

"Well, I do," the professor said. "And this whole evening has put me of a mind to have a gin and tonic—minus the tonic, I think, this time." He pulled down a bottle of Tanqueray, twisted off the cap, and emptied what little remained into a cut crystal drink glass. "Cheers," he said, taking a prolonged drink and pulling up a chair opposite Valerian.

"That's part of the reason I'm here," his guest said, a hint of chastisement in his voice. "You've been drinking too much of that, which has contributed to your heart condition. You could have put me off a few more years if you'd followed your doctor's advice and sworn off that stuff."

"Seems I'm doing your job for you then," the professor quipped. "Why not be on your way and, if I'm going to die, let me do so in peace without hovering over me." He shot a glance at the scythe. "Or do you plan to decapitate me with that thing? Or maybe scare me into that heart attack you're so sure I've got coming to me."

"It's symbolic," Valerian grumbled. "I don't cause your death, I merely oversee it."

The professor rolled his eyes. "And who exactly is your employer, the guy who sends you out on these assignments."

Valerian shifted in the recliner for the first time, uncrossing his legs. "God, of course."

"Which one? Hades? Kali? The Morrigan? Osiris? Or maybe it's Shiva. Or Thanatos. Or maybe the Judeo-Christian god, in which case I'd have to ask whether your boss represents the Judaic or the Christian mythos."

Valerian's face was invisible, but the professor was sure he could feel the man's eyes boring into him. By his silence alone, he could tell he'd struck a nerve.

"Seems you don't like working for this god of yours. He expects you to do a rather unpleasant job for free. I hope he at least gives you holidays off."

Valerian shook his head.

"Not even Christmas?"

"No."

"As I said, it sounds like slave labor." Erich von Prince downed the rest of his drink, then returned to the liquor cabinet to open a new bottle.

"I told you that's not good for you," Valerian said.

"Why does it matter?" the professor responded. "You already said I'm destined to die tonight. Might as well enjoy a 'final meal,' as it were. Sorry I don't have a steak and some potatoes to whip up for you, but I wasn't expecting company. I'm afraid this will just have to do." He reached forward with the bottle, offering again to his visitor.

"I told you I don't drink."

The professor shrugged. "Suit yourself. But you see, I'm not ready to die just yet. I'm in the middle of a research project into the chemical makeup of sugar that could lead to a cure for diabetes. Your god, whoever he is, wouldn't want to stand in the way of that now, would he?"

"That's not his problem—or mine."

"That's right, because you're a heartless sonofabitch, just like he is. No wonder you work for him. He's got you snowed into being the same kind of sociopath it sounds like he is. And this serial killer *doesn't even pay you.*" He saw Valerian raise his hand to object but wasn't about to give him the chance. "Because that's what he is: a serial killer," he continued. "He clearly gets his jollies out of not only killing people, but preventing them from doing research that could actually *save* other people's lives."

Valerian leaned forward. "You don't understand."

"Oh, but I think I do," the professor said, leaning forward himself. He was beginning to enjoy this. Nothing fired his engine more quickly than putting an opponent on the defensive. He might have earned his degree in biochemistry, but he'd been a champion debater before that, in high school. He always enjoyed a good give-and-take, especially since he almost always came out on top.

"Your employer is taking advantage of you," he said, shaking his fist for emphasis. "There's no two ways about it. Have you ever thought about going out on your own? Maybe doing some freelance work or becoming your own boss?"

Valerian shook his head. "He'd never allow that."

"You sound positively scared of the guy. What's he gonna do? Fire you?"

Valerian sank back into the recliner again. His body language appeared to reflect an attitude of resignation.

This guy doesn't want *to keep working for his boss, but he's been stuck under his thumb for so long he doesn't know how to get out of it.*

At that very moment, an idea occurred to Erich von Prince. "How about a wager?" he said. "If I can convince you that your boss has been taking advantage of you all this time, you let me live. If I can't? Hey, I've had a decent life. Go ahead and do your worst. And if you don't care about that cure for diabetes, you'll have to live with the guilt. The proverbial blood will be on your hands. What do you say?"

He stuck out his hand, and to his surprise, Valerian took it. "Deal," he said. "Easiest bet I've ever taken."

"That's the spirit!" the professor said. "Now, you said your job is to 'oversee' the transitions of people who die to wherever they go next—not that I believe they go anywhere, but for the sake of argument, let's say they do. That sounds extremely boring to me. Kind of like the Walmart employee who stands there at the door with a highlighter, mindlessly marking receipts as each customer exits the store."

Valerian seemed to consider this for a moment. "I never thought of it like that."

"Now maybe it's not exactly slave labor, but it sure as hell sounds like a hostile work environment to me."

"No need to bring hell into it."

"Don't get hung up on semantics. I know this is hard for you. You've worked for the guy for... how long...?"

"As long as I can remember."

"See? He's got you wrapped around his finger. You can't get past the cognitive dissonance of it."

Valerian nodded slowly. "Okay, what if I admit you have a point—I'm not admitting it, but say I do—what do you expect me to do about it? Report him to the labor board or OSHA? He doesn't exactly recognize their authority."

The professor let out a sarcastic huff. "You don't need to do anything so drastic. Go on strike. How many other people work in your department?"

"It's just me."

"Perfect! Make him sweat a little. Let him see what it's like to meet his goals without your help. Think of it. The world population would skyrocket in just a few years. The entire system would be fucked, and he'd be powerless to do anything except come crawling to you, begging you to come back—on your terms!"

The Reaper dipped his head slightly and shook it from side to side, clearly dejected. "It wouldn't matter," he said. "He does all the dirty work. I'm just the grunt who oversees it. That way, I take all the blame while he comes out looking like Mr. Nice Guy. You're right. It really does suck."

The professor put his elbows on his knees and touched the

tips of his fingers on both hands together in a kind of pyramid. He was thinking.

"All right," he said finally, "then just quit. Find another gig. Hell, become a hit man. With your experience and expertise, you could make a killing at that... no pun intended."

But Valerian's head dipped even lower and his shoulders slumped.

"He won't let me."

"If that's the case, then you really *are* his slave. You have to stand up for yourself. Resist."

"The last guy who tried that got thrown into the hell you mentioned earlier."

"I don't really believe in that nonsense, but it doesn't matter: You've got that!" He pointed dramatically at the scythe. Even in the darkened room, its blade managed to give off a gleaming reflection of the little light available. It had obviously been sharpened to a razor edge, like a guillotine; the professor imagined that, if he'd wanted to, Valerian could have taken off his head with a single swipe.

"What are you suggesting? I told you, it's just a symbol."

"It's a weapon."

"To use against... HIM?"

"Precisely."

"Maybe I forgot to tell you, but my boss is immortal."

"And you are literally death personified," the professor reminded him. "Immovable object" —he pointed skyward— "meet irresistible force." He pointed directly at the Reaper. "Something's got to give, and you never know until you try."

Valerian cocked his head to one side, appearing to ponder this. Then, finally, against all odds, he said simply, "You're right."

A self-satisfied grin spread across the professor's face, and he tilted his head back, draining the last of his glass. "Then it appears I have won our little wager."

Valerian nodded. "So you have."

"What will you do now then? Are you going to confront him?"

The Reaper nodded, appearing suddenly resolute. "I am. Thank you for the pep talk, Professor von Prince. I have to warn you though, you will have to die eventually. If not tonight, then someday soon. I can't do anything about that drinking of yours and its effects on your body. And you might want to cut out the steak and potatoes too. My report on you says you're diabetic, so if your heart condition doesn't kill you, your glucose levels will. If I were you, I'd really start pushing that research of yours. It won't do you any good personally if someone else completes it after you're dead."

"Hey, you only live once, right?"

Valerian chuckled. "Some of us just live a lot longer than others."

The professor ignored what appeared to be a somewhat sinister tone to Valerian's laugh and reminded himself that this was just some elaborate prank. He might not know who was behind it, but it had been incredibly convincing, and the exercise of arguing someone who pretended to be the Grim Reaper into the plausibility of trying to actually kill the Almighty had been energizing.

Especially, of course, since he had come out on the winning end as usual.

The only thing he still couldn't figure out was how the man had initially appeared at the door, then seemingly rematerialized inside his house. Maybe he had imagined it.

Whatever the case, he was somewhat relieved when Valerian picked up the sickle, nodded and turned toward the door. At least he was leaving the old-fashioned way.

"Thanks for the entertaining evening," the professor said as the Reaper opened the door and took his leave.

"The pleasure was all mine," he called over his shoulder. "Be seeing you."

Erich von Prince awoke from a deep sleep around midnight in a heavy sweat. His heart seemed like it was about to pound its way through his chest, and he felt a pain radiating out across his torso from somewhere just below his left shoulder. He clenched his teeth as it grew worse.

He managed to fight his way through the pain and reach over to turn on the light, then slammed his hand down on the smartphone lying on his nightstand, wrapping his fingers around it.

The pain was so bad he could barely breathe, but he somehow managed to press his thumbprint to the screen and press the phone icon. His fingers were poised to dial 911 when he heard a voice from behind him, on the other side of the bed. He'd been so consumed with the medical emergency he was facing that he hadn't noticed the other presence there in the room with him.

Wincing, he forced himself to open his eyes to the sight of Valerian looming over him, armed with that razor-sharp scythe of his.

"Oh, thank God," the professor rasped. "I need an ambulance. I guess you were right about the drinking and the steak and..." He couldn't manage to say any more; the pain had grown too severe. He returned his attention to the cellphone and had pressed 9 when the scythe descended and knocked it out of his hands. It went flying through the air across the room.

"What...?"

"I took your advice," Valerian said calmly, bringing his face down level with von Prince's. "I confronted my boss. Turns out he was... amenable to my demands."

"Then... you didn't... kill him?"

"No no no. I knew that would never work. Really a stupid idea on your part. The guy who tried to challenge him before, well, you know that bit about hell—like I told you, that's where he ended up. I had no desire to follow in his footsteps. But our little conversation got me to thinking. Yeah, he was exploiting me, but he was just trying to make sure everything ran efficiently. I get that. It's a big responsibility, making sure the world keeps turning and all."

A look of horror, mixed with dawning resignation, washed over the professor's face. "You're not going to help me, are you?"

"Help you? Now why should I do that? You see, you had it all wrong about my boss, calling him a sociopath. He's really kind of a pushover: God of love and all that rubbish. *I'm* the sociopath, professor. I don't give a fuck what happens to you. I never did. And thanks to you, I finally stood up to him."

Even as the Reaper spoke, the professor could feel the tightness and pain in his chest begin to subside. Realization dawned: Somehow, miraculously, the heart attack wasn't going to kill him.

Valerian must have seen the relief on his face, because he was shaking his head slowly back and forth. "Don't get too excited, my friend," he said, chuckling. "I persuaded the man upstairs to give you a reprieve. But only it's a brief reprieve he granted, and for my sake, not for yours."

The professor frowned. "What do you mean?"

"I mean that my boss has agreed to give me a little more... shall we say... latitude in how I *execute* my duties. Under my new terms of employment, I'm allowed to be more... *involved* in my work. I've always been something of a voyeur. It's... exhilarating to see people die. But that's nothing: You get an even bigger rush if you do the deed yourself, if you know what I mean."

The professor's eyes widened as he saw the Reaper raise his scythe high over his head, its blade glinting mischievously, reflecting the three lights Valerian had turned on when he entered the room.

The blade, alive and ravenous, hung there for just a moment, as though savoring what was to come. The blood gushing and spurting out of the carotid arteries, the tendons and spinal cord severed in a single swipe. The detached head of a man who had reveled in the power of the brain encased inside it rolling off the side of the bed and onto the shag-carpeted floor.

Professor Erich von Prince saw none of that, but the Reaper did.

Oh, yes, he did.

And he savored every grisly moment of it.

Sharon Marie Provost

Papillon

Maria missed her grandmother more than ever. She could hardly believe it had been two years since she passed, yet at the same time, it felt even longer. Ever since her mother had left the family six months ago to go live with her cracked-out dealer-turned-lover, she'd found herself alone with no one to talk to about her fears and insecurities. Her mother had never been as engaged and compassionate a listener as her grandmother had been, but she at least was an actual corporeal being in front of her—one who always had an opinion to press upon Maria.

Maria now found herself talking to her grandmother in her head or even out loud at times when she visited their favorite park. In her mind, she could hear her grandmother's voice giving her the same encouragement she always had, but it wasn't the same as hearing her voice out loud. She missed the way her grandmother always had advice that pushed her towards making the right choice... herself. Her grandmother never forced her own opinions on anybody, nor did she judge someone should they make a mistake.

Maria had tried talking to her father, but he was too busy with work and taking care of her two teenage sisters to spend much time talking. Besides, most evenings were spent drowning his runaway-wife sorrows in a bottle of tequila. He was a good, hard-working man, but he was a man of few words, even fewer when he was dealing with a broken heart.

Maria had just turned nineteen. She excelled in all her classes at college, but she still couldn't decide on a field of study. Her first boyfriend, whom she had met the first week of school, had just left her... for her roommate, no less.

Maria's mind was a swirling mass of confusion. Should she move back home? Should she just change dorms? Then there was the question of a major. Biology major for physician assistant school? English Lit major to become a writer? Or say, "fuck school" and go work at Walmart? At least, she would be earning money rather than going in debt paying for food, clothes and any other necessities. She knew it was stupid to even contemplate that option, given she had a scholarship paying for her tuition, books and housing, but she felt overwhelmed.

There was only one thing she knew for sure at that moment: She needed to talk to her grandmother. She could only think of one possible way to accomplish that, but she didn't know the first thing about how to actually go about it. She used to watch paranormal shows with her grandmother in the evenings. Maria didn't know if she actually believed in the paranormal or the occult. To be honest, she didn't believe in much of anything spiritual. However, she had been intrigued by the "evidence" she saw presented on those shows. She discounted the existence of demons or the devil, so what harm could there be in trying to contact her grandmother? Worst-case scenario: It wouldn't work. But her grandmother, having immigrated from the Old Country, did believe in the supernatural, so she owed it to her to give it a try.

All those shows purported that Ouija boards could be used to contact the dead. Supposedly, the veil between the living and the dead was thinnest during Samhain, especially on the night of All Hallows' Eve, better known as Halloween. With only two days left before Halloween, she didn't have much time to research how to use the Ouija board and obtain the needed materials.

True to her generation, her research started... where else, but the internet? The list of dos and don'ts was astonishing and varied from one site to the next. Some even bordered on the ridiculous side:

You must have at least one partner to ensure each other's safety. There was no one she trusted to not laugh at her or deliberately move the planchette to fool her.

You must cast protection spells before starting. To protect yourself from what exactly?

You must close out your session properly by thanking any spirits that spoke to you and letting them know they are not welcome to linger, before grounding yourself and clearing the room with sage smoke. If using a Ouija board was so dangerous, it made no sense that anyone would ever do so.

Maria decided to focus on the "dos" that were supposed to ensure her successful contact. She needed to obtain some candles to light around the room, and, of course, the Ouija board itself. Crystals were also believed to help attract spirits, especially quartz. She needed to eliminate distractions, so she would need to seek out some quiet, dark place and remember to turn off her phone. Being respectful wouldn't be difficult because there was no one she respected more than her grandmother. She spent the rest of the afternoon trying to decide where to hold the ritual, before heading to work at the school library that evening. She was hoping she might be able to do a little further research at the library while she restocked the shelves.

The next day, Maria caught a bus headed downtown to visit the local metaphysical shop. The jocks in high school had always laughed as the school bus rumbled by the shop and called it Occult 'R' Us when they saw someone walk inside. The scent of patchouli washed over her as she walked inside. Soft ambient music surrounded her, almost as if it emanated from the air around her. A tall, dark-haired man in the center of the store looked up at her, his intense eyes boring into her, as she stood there looking around in confusion. She jumped as a melodic voice from behind greeted her, "Blessed be! Welcome to Crimson Moonbeam. Are you here for supplies for a Samhain celebration?"

The voice came from a middle-aged woman with long, flowing dark brown hair. She was dressed in a purple crepe dress adorned with stars and moons that draped around her figure flatteringly. A silver pentagram on a long chain hung from her slender neck. For the life of her, Maria couldn't discern where the woman had appeared from. She didn't see any doors along the side wall, and the front of the store had been empty when she entered. Maria realized she had been staring at her when the woman's smile beamed at her again and her eyes crinkled at the sides quizzically.

"Umm... yes... or no... not exactly."

"I'm sorry. I don't quite understand. Let's start over. How may I help you?"

"You have probably already figured out I am not Pagan."

The woman laughed kindly and held out her hand to Maria. "Here, my dear. Let's go sit over here where we can talk privately. You seem to have a lot on your mind. My name is Amaranth. And you are?"

Maria awkwardly placed her fingers in Amaranth's hand and followed her over to the table surrounded by six willow chairs in the far corner in a curtained alcove. A variety of items had been laid out on the table, which was adorned with a large, red circular tablecloth and seemed ready for a Ouija board session. There were candles in silver holders, crystals, a variety of dried herbs, a bundle of sage, and an ornate hand-carved wooden spirit board.

Amaranth waved Maria over to a chair before calling out to two customers in the back of the store, "If you need any help or are ready to check out, just ring the bell on the counter." She turned toward the man who was still peering at Maria, as he drifted toward the nearby table of herbs. "I'll be right with you in just a few minutes, Alaric." He nodded as he began a close inspection of the phials and apothecary jars.

Amaranth drew the curtain closed and turned back to Maria with an understanding smile. She turned her chair to face Maria and sat down, grabbing both her hands and squeezing them softly as she said, "Now then..." Maria felt tears begin to trickle down her face. Embarrassed, she couldn't bear to look up into Amaranth's sympathetic gaze. "Now. Now. Nothing is ever so bad as we think it is in the moment. Talk to me. Let me help you, child," Amaranth cooed as she reached up to wipe away the tears.

Maria sniffled as she began her story. She told Amaranth about her relationship with her cherished grandmother and then about her passing. She explained her mother's departure and her father's depression. She even told her about her relationship troubles and school woes. Finally, she met her eyes as she got to the point of her visit. "I need my grandmother. I must speak to her. Only she can help me figure out what to do. Only she can make me feel better. I want to contact her with a spirit board," she whispered as her eyes slid over to the one on the table beside her.

"I see. There is a lot more involved with contacting the spirit world than just lighting some candles in a dark room and placing your hand on the planchette. You should not embark upon this endeavor so lightly.

"Yes, you could have a rewarding interaction with your grandmother. But it's just as likely that she might not choose to answer you. She may not even hear your call. Contact with the spirit world is far from cut and dried... It is not simply a matter of asking and waiting for an answer. Furthermore, there is a real danger of inviting some darker spirits to interact with you. One should not take speaking to the dead lightly, especially without proper guidance, and especially at this time of the year. The veil is very thin right now, my dear. You don't want to invite the wrong spirit to this side."

Maria could see where this was going. Amaranth just happened to have a spirit board area set up in her shop. She was just like the psychic down the street with a similar, red-draped table, but with a crystal ball on it instead. They could both provide a supposedly paranormal experience for naive, gullible saps... but, of course, for a price. Maria was smart enough to know how to play this game. She looked up at Amaranth and smiled nervously.

"Oh yes! I know this is not something to be taken lightly. My aunt's friend is Pagan. She is going to help me contact my grandmother when she is in town next week for a conference. I told her I would get the supplies needed, but I was too embarrassed to admit I didn't know what to get. Can you help me get the candles and crystals we should have on hand? I know she always travels with her protection crystals and herbs. But I think there are supposed to be ones that attract spiritual energy, like quartz crystals. And do you sell spirit boards like this one? It has been made with such lovely craftsmanship; I thought it might be nice to gift it to her when we are done."

Maria saw the skepticism flit across Amaranth's face as her brow furrowed, but she smiled and rose with only a small sigh escaping her lips. "Of course, my dear. I shall be very happy to help." Amaranth slid the curtain open with a flourish, nearly running into Alaric as she turned the corner toward the cabinet with the crystals.

"Excuse me," she blurted out as she darted around him.

She turned back to Maria with a concerned look on her face and gently started again. "But child, I am serious: Don't take this lightly. If she cannot help you, come back here. I would be happy to assist you in contacting your grandmother, or at least teach you the proper, safe way to do so. And most importantly, do not try this alone."

Maria smiled and nodded her head in agreement. "I understand. I appreciate your kindness very much." They moved around the store, collecting quartz, amethyst and labradorite crystals to enhance spiritual energy and psychic ability, as well as facilitate communication with the other side. Then Amaranth took her over to the candles and selected white to create a sacred space for the ritual, purple to enhance psychic powers, blue to enhance communication, and pink to represent her unconditional, undying love for her grandmother. Finally, she went into the back room to obtain one of the antique, Victorian hand-carved spirit boards. Maria soon realized this endeavor was turning out to be a lot more expensive than she had anticipated, but communication with her grandmother would be worth it.

Amaranth gave her one of her business cards, but not before she wrote down her personal cell number on the back, in case Maria should need to reach her unexpectedly. Maria thanked her and headed out, wondering if maybe she had misjudged the woman's intentions. Before she boarded the city bus home, she tucked the store's bag into a reusable shopping bag, so no one there or at home would see where she had been shopping. She had too much to prepare before her ritual to invite unwanted, difficult questions.

She had promised to make an early dinner before helping her sisters don their costumes, and then drop them off at a Halloween party at a friend's house at 5:30 p.m. Then she would need to rush home and prepare for the ritual, so she would be ready to start once darkness descended. She had given herself an hour to communicate with her grandmother before her friends would arrive to pick her up.

They were going to the Halloween Fair at Lamplighter's Park before going to the 11:30 p.m. tour of the ScreamFest *Everyone Dies Here* haunted house attraction. The flyer proclaimed "You will scream until your lungs bleed, and you drown in your own blood. Or until you breathe your last when The Stalker plunges his blade through your heart. No one leaves here... alive, that is." The small print warned against anyone attending if they had cardiac, seizure disorders or other serious health issues. Even with all the stress in her life, she couldn't wait to blow off a little steam with an adrenalin rush.

Her father was supposed to pick up her sisters at 10:30 p.m.

on his way home from work. Once again, he was claiming that he had to work overtime, but most likely he would be drinking at the local bar. Maria really didn't care, so long as she was free to spend the evening with her friends and return in the morning. With any luck, tomorrow she would feel renewed, after a fun evening with her friends, and getting all the answers she needed to get her life back on track.

The afternoon passed in a blur as she helped her sisters with their last-minute costume changes before preparing hamburgers and Rice-a-Roni for dinner. The more she tried to rush them, the slower they went, but suddenly they were ready and rushed her out the door, complaining all the way, "Maria, you are going to make us late. Everyone already thinks we're freaks because Dad gave us the earliest curfew of anyone there."

"Chill out for Pete's sake. It only takes five minutes to get to Andrea's house from here. You are 14 and 16. The two of you could have taken a more active role in getting your costumes ready yourself, instead of keeping me from making dinner for you. I am doing the best I can. I have plans myself, in case you have forgotten."

Cindy and Bethany pouted in the back seat, grumbling to each other about how Maria wasn't their mother.

"Hallelujah! It is a miracle. You finally realize you aren't my problem. Good riddance. Here we are... ten minutes before the party EVEN STARTS!"

The girls exited the van quickly, rolling their eyes, then continued up the walkway chattering happily.

Bethany stopped and turned back saying, "Thanks. Sorry, Maria."

Maria smiled and waved. "See you tomorrow. Have fun. Don't do anything I wouldn't do."

The girls laughed and ran inside. Maria knew better than to

expect too much from them. If they were up to their usual antics, they would do precisely *everything* that Maria wouldn't do. But at least they weren't her problem tonight. Maria made a quick stop at the store to pick up some items for breakfast and tomorrow's dinner, along with her grandmother's favorite flowers, stargazer lilies, and a slice of carrot cake, another favorite of hers. Perhaps these things would entice her grandmother to visit; at least she would be making an offering to her deceased ancestor, a common practice in many cultures and religions.

When she arrived home, she shook her head upon finding the front door unlocked... as usual. Cindy could never seem to remember to lock the door, no matter how many times she had been reminded. Luckily, this time it was actually convenient, since Maria had multiple bags wrapped around her hands. After putting away the groceries she had bought, she brought her purchases for the night's activity into her mom's old sewing room, where she had prepared the sewing table for the ritual.

The table was covered in an old lace tablecloth that her grandmother had knitted. She had placed one candle on each of its four corners, with the white and pink on the corners nearest to her. The crystals were arranged in a circle around the Ouija board, which sat in the middle of the table.

On the back of the table, Maria placed the slice of cake alongside the flowers, which she had arranged in a crystal vase: a gift from her grandfather to her grandmother on their first anniversary. She retrieved the framed photo of her grandmother from the dresser in her room—leaving her cell phone there in the process—and set it in front of the vase. She closed the blinds to block out the light from the neighbor's security light and closed the door to bar any extraneous light or noise from the house.

Finally, I think I have everything just right. Well, it is now or never. Please come to me, grandma.

Maria walked over to the small boombox and pressed "play" on the CD player. The soft, dulcet tones of Glenn Miller's *In the Mood* drifted through the air in the background. She flicked the wheel of the lighter, and a bright orange flame appeared; she leaned over to light the candles. A small sigh escaped her lips as she seated herself at the table and tried to ground the swirl of anxiety and emotions pulsing through her body. Her eyes closed and lips pursed, she fought to still the nervous wringing of her hands.

As *Sing, Sing, Sing* began, her lips relaxed and a smile began to emerge as her memory played images of her grandmother dancing with the broom through the house; swinging and swaying, feet bouncing and kicking around to the Lindy Hop, jitterbugging and doing the Charleston through her daily chores. Maria remembered flipping her hands up and down through the ripples of her grandmother's skirt as she laughed and twirled like a whirling dervish across the hardwood floors of the sitting room.

Blinking away the tears that slowly slid down her face, Maria took a deep breath and reached forward to place her hands on the planchette. "Let's do this!" she whispered to no one in particular. "I am reaching out with the utmost respect to my beloved grandmother, Mabel McDonald. If your spirit has moved on to a better place, I do not wish to bother you. But, Grandma, if you are still here somewhere... if you are watching over me... I need you now more than ever. I like to think I feel you beside me—my own personal guardian angel—but I need to speak to you, to get your advice."

Maria stopped speaking as she felt a slight movement of the air around her. Suddenly, she was awash in the enticing aroma of her grandmother's old-fashioned rose perfume. "Grandma! Please, Grandma, tell me that is you. I love you so much. I miss you so much every day," Maria sniffled as tears poured down her face. A creak in the hallway, followed by the slight scuffle of movement outside the door, startled Maria, and she nearly fell off her chair as she whipped around in her seat. The air around her became heavy and tense, no longer the soothing cocoon of love she had felt only moments ago.

She quickly reached towards the planchette again as she called out, "Grandma, what is wrong? Have I upset you? Did I disturb the peace you so rightfully deserve?" The planchette quivered, ever so slightly, under her fingers; it began to turn so the pointer was headed in the direction of the door. "What are you trying to say? Do you want me to stop? Should I leave you alone?"

The air became oppressive—heavy with the feeling of both love... and angst. Maria's confusion grew. She became desperate to settle down her grandmother's restless spirit.

What have I done? How do I fix this? Should I reach out to my grandfather or maybe my aunt, even though I barely knew her?

The door creaked as though someone were leaning against it on the other side. Maria's eyes darted toward the door and then back to the planchette. She could hear the little wooden legs clatter against the board as it trembled beneath her soft touch. "Oh no! Is there anyone out there? Can anybody hear me? Please speak to me. Come to me. You must help me." Maria squealed in surprise when the planchette raced across the board. A screech announced its arrival at Goodbye.

Maria's plaintive cry echoed across the room, "No. Please

don't go. Don't leave me." Her fingers were pressed to her mouth as she tried to stifle her sobs. The planchette began to move on its own as it drifted from G to O and stopped again. "You want to go?" It wiggled in place impatiently before sliding to No. She placed her hands on it again, and its path across the board resumed from L to E to A to V to E. "Leave? Do you want me to leave you alone? Please talk to me. Is it you, Grandma? Are you okay?"

The planchette clattered in place, almost angrily. She felt pressure in her fingers as it was ripped from beneath them. It began to move again from G to O and then the pointer turned to face her, before resuming its path from N to O to W. It began to trace circles around the board before once again spelling out "now" over and over. The tears raced down her face, her neck and chest soaked. Maria couldn't understand why her grandmother would be telling her to leave.

"I love you, Grandma... I always will. I am sorry if I upset you or disturbed your rest. I just..." her voice trailed off as she felt a presence wrap itself around her, enclosing her in the tightest rose-scented hug she had ever felt. As quickly as it appeared, the presence withdrew its embrace as the planchette slid across rapidly from R to U to... Suddenly, it felt as if all the air had been sucked out of the room into the deepest reaches of the vacuum of space. Her head swiveled to the door when it creaked once more as if the weight against it had been removed, and she heard the sound of quick movement. At the same time, the planchette flew off the board to the other side of the room, crashing against the wall.

Maria screamed in surprise and jumped up as the laughter of her friends and a resounding call of "Mariiiiiiaaaaaa" rolled through the house. She rushed to the door and leaned against it, breathlessly calling out, "I will be right there in just a couple of minutes. Get a drink from the fridge if you want." She didn't know how she was going to explain her red-eyed, emotional appearance. She blew out the candles and began to gather the materials for the ritual together and placed them in an empty cardboard box sitting in the room. It occurred to her that she had not closed out the session, nor had she thanked any spirits she had spoken to, rescinded the invitation to come to her, or even told them that they were not welcome to linger. But then again, she didn't really believe in any of that anyhow.

She stowed the box deep in the back of her closet before heading to the bathroom to clear her face. She called out to Lacey and Daphne downstairs, "I just got out of the shower. I need to run a comb through my hair, put on my costume, and I will be right down."

"No hurry. We are a little early anyhow," Daphne replied.

"Can you guess who is coming to ScreamFest later?" Lacey queried in a playful tone.

"No! You didn't! Please tell me you don't mean Tristan. You promised. You said you wouldn't tell him."

"I told you she would be mad," Daphne mumbled to Lacey.

"We didn't tell him you had a crush on him... at least, not exactly. We just implied that you would enjoy his company tonight if he joined us. Please don't be angry with us," Lacey implored.

"Besides, he seemed really excited when we told him you were looking forward to seeing him. He asked if you were still seeing Brandon and seemed quite pleased when we told him no," Daphne added.

Maria had just finished wetting and then styling her hair to make it look like she had just freshly showered. She left the bathroom and leaned over the banister to call down once more.

"We'll talk about this more when I come downstairs." She ran back into the bathroom to apply a little makeup, now that she knew she needed to look her best. Then she trotted over to her room and put on her costume, a sexy French maid dress... At least she would look cute tonight. She retrieved her cell phone, in case her sisters needed to reach her.

She bounced down the stairs, determined to hide her recent distress. She didn't want the girls to know what she had done and certainly didn't want Tristan to laugh at her. Maria realized she was actually pretty eager to see how it went with Tristan tonight, which made pushing aside thoughts of the ritual easier than she had imagined. The girls excitedly discussed their plan of attack for the rides and attractions at the fair. Each of them had a different attraction that most interested them, but they wanted to be sure they didn't miss even one activity.

"I am absolutely famished. I didn't really have any time to eat dinner in the rush to get my sisters ready for their party. First stop: the food concession area? Footlong corndogs, loaded fries and funnel cakes like usual?"

Daphne and Lacey nodded eagerly.

"I told Tristan to meet us at ScreamFest at 11. We have to get in line by 11:15 for the 11:30 tour," Daphne explained.

The girls walked out of the house, a cacophony of voices talking over one another as they discussed the day's events and plans for that night. Maria locked the house up and returned the spare key the girls had used under the planter in the back corner of the porch. They climbed into Lacey's VW Bug and sped off toward the fairgrounds.

The next three hours passed quickly as the girls rode every ride at least twice, played most of the midway games, and ate until they thought their stomachs might burst. Maria's head was pounding—not due to stress for the first time in weeks, but from the nonstop side-splitting laughter. They ran into a few friends from the college and had a friendly competition to see who could complete the corn maze fastest. Screams abounded when they proceeded to the haunted cornfield, as monsters and killers of every ilk appeared from the darkness and chased them with rumbling chainsaws and long, sharp kitchen knives.

Maria couldn't remember the last time she had been this happy. She had just started her second year at college, and she was still in the middle of all the core courses required by all students. She still had some time to declare a major.

Maybe all that happened tonight was a message from my Grandma... not one of anger, but a warning... she just wanted me to get out, leave the house and go have some fun like a young woman should. There is so little time that one can be young, happy and carefree. Grandma always used to say, "Youth is wasted on the young." She warned me not to be in too much of a hurry to grow up and experience the stresses and tribulations of adult life.

The alarm on Daphne's Apple Watch went off, reminding them that it was time to head over to the old, abandoned slaughterhouse that had closed in the 80s, where ScreamFest was being held. Parking fees were at a premium in the event lot, so they decided to walk the three blocks over and leave the car at the fairgrounds to pick up later. As they crossed the parking lot, they heard Tristan's voice calling out to them. Apparently, he'd had the same idea about parking, so he walked with them to the haunted house. He quickly fell in line, walking next to Maria, a wide smile on his face as he chatted with her. Lacey and Daphne soon fell back a little to be less obtrusive.

They turned the corner onto Slaughter Lane to find a large crowd of people gathered outside the venue. The ticket line wrapped around the front of the building and continued all the way to the back corner. Those who already had tickets, like

Maria and her friends, were able to join a slightly shorter line that was at least moving, if only at a snail's pace. Groups of people who'd already gone through the attraction were still still standing around in the front yard, chatting excitedly about their experience. Of course, there was the contingent of younger teenage boys running around in costume, sneaking up on young girls, grabbing them to make them scream and run away.

The four college students began an animated conversation with some underclassmen they had known at high school last year as they waited in line. Maria hadn't realized there were actually two paths through the haunted house; one was billed as utterly horrifying and geared toward the majority of the customers; the other required participants to be 18 years or older and sign a waiver because it was billed as an extreme horror experience guaranteed to cause heart palpitations.

As a group, they quickly agreed to go for the extreme experience—especially once they realized there was no line and only a few people were inside. Lacey and Daphne joined hands and ran off giggling, making it clear they were trying to give Maria and Tristan time alone. Maria shook her head, letting out a nervous laugh, as she looked over at Tristan to gauge his reaction. His smile widened, and he reached down to grab her hand as they began their slow walk through the attraction.

Maria nearly knocked Tristan over when she jumped, issuing a small yelp, after she heard Lacey's blood-curdling scream—a scream that was quickly cut off. Her concerned eyes darted to his, but seconds later, they heard another girl laughing merrily. Daphne had probably done something to terrify Lacey. Maria let out a relieved giggle, as she gripped Tristan's hand tighter. Tristan took the opportunity to pull her in closer for a long kiss.

There didn't seem to be anyone else behind them, so

Tristan suggested they stop and chat for a moment. Maria was concerned that the girls might leave her if they didn't catch up with them soon, but Tristan assured her that he would get her home if needed. Their talk was interrupted a few moments later by another scream deeper into the attraction, so Maria knew her friends were still around.

"We should probably start moving again. It is getting late, and I don't know when they close up for the night."

Tristan nodded, but he kept his hand wrapped around her waist. A short while later, she let out her own terrified scream when a machete-wielding intruder reached out and grabbed her from a hidden alcove off to her left. She pulled away and ran off in terror around the corner, with the attacker in pursuit.

As she rounded the next corner, she realized she had lost sight of Tristan. She stopped and looked around the large, dark room where she was standing, but she couldn't see him anywhere. She peeked around the corner back the way she had come; still, he was nowhere in sight.

She noticed an elaborate staged area with a body butchered and hanging from a meat hook in the back corner of the room. As she waited for Tristan to catch up, she wandered over to examine it in more detail, impressed with the realistic display of disemboweled organs dripping from the human carcass impaled on the hook. The loops of bowel had been pulled out and swung gently in the breeze coming from the vent in the ceiling. A variety of other body parts lay displayed around on the table and in basins around the stage. There was even another body draped across the butcher's table.

The mannequin in back looked so realistic: no plastic or waxy texture, to distract one from the carnage on display. She could even smell the tangy, iron smell one associates with fresh blood. The display as a whole was amazing, but they had really outdone themselves with the girl hanging in full view. The body, dressed in clothes similar to those worn by the teenage girls outside—extremely similar, in fact, to the matching miniskirts and crop tops Lacey and Daphne were wearing under their flapper girl costumes.

Maria started to become overwhelmed by the sight of it, so she called out to Tristan that she was going on to catch up with her friends. As she quickened her pace she continued through the display, she was caught off guard by another terror-inducing scream. It seemed like no matter how fast she walked, she couldn't catch up with her friends or the few other people in the haunted house. The serial killers and monsters set up throughout the house for jump scares didn't startle her because she flew by too fast for them to even react to her presence.

As she rounded the next corner, she slid across a puddle of blood and landed with a splat, ruining her French maid costume. "Fuck!" she screamed into the empty room. "What stupid asshole didn't realize this is a safety hazard?" As she climbed to her knees and stepped out onto a clean patch of concrete, her eyes came to rest on the scene before and to the right of her.

Out of the corner of her eye, she could see a body laid out on a table that had been dissected, or rather butchered, into different cuts of meat. But she couldn't take her eyes off the stage directly in front of the place she had fallen. This area had been set up to look like a medieval torture chamber, complete with an iron maiden, a rack, a breaking wheel and a table surrounded by a variety of sharp instruments of pain, covered in blood.

Here she found another hyper-realistic body that had been gibbeted: ravaged but held together in a body-shaped cage. So much blood was dripping down from the hanging, broken carcass, that some of it had run off the stage and pooled up at the entrance to the room. Lashes from a cat o' nine tails across the stomach and legs of the victim had left bloody, raised welts. The face and upper torso of the victim had caved in and bore deep penetrating wounds from a ball-and-chain flail that hung on the wall next to the cage. The tongue had been cut out and lay on the table next to a sharp carving knife.

Maria realized that her love of extreme horror movies had done nothing to prepare her for seeing such graphic displays of carnage in person. She could hear movement in nearby rooms, even though she still hadn't managed to catch up with her friends.

I bet those fuckers are trying to freak me out. They saw my bad reaction to the scream earlier and think it is funny to hide from me. I just don't understand why Tristan would do that to me, since he supposedly likes me. Fuck them! I am out of here.

Maria ran across the room and made her way through the last two rooms of the haunted house without incident—until she knocked down one of the attendants when she burst out the exit door.

"Are you okay, Miss?"

"NO! I am not! Sorry. I didn't mean to yell at you. I can't seem to find my friends. I was with two girls my age, one blond and the other a redhead. They are about my height and wearing 1920s flapper dresses. They were with a sandy-haired guy, about six feet tall in jeans and a Metallica T-shirt. Have you seen them?"

"I can't say for sure that I saw them, but I did see some girls that kind of match that description leaving with a tall guy about five minutes ago laughing. I can't say I paid attention to what they were wearing."

"Damn them! Fucking bitches! Thank you for your help."

Maria stomped around to the front of the slaughterhouse to see if her friends were standing around waiting for her to emerge. She was surprised to find how much of the crowd had dispersed while she had been inside. To her dismay, she didn't see anyone she knew, let alone her friends. Maria sighed as she pulled out her phone and dialed her father to see if he would come pick her up. She was not surprised when the phone rang through to voicemail.

He probably passed out on the couch once he brought the girls home.

Maria began dialing her sisters, but she was surprised when neither one of them answered either. Most likely, they were busy eating junk food and watching horror movies, not paying attention to their phones. After one last hopeful look around for a friendly face, Maria gave up and began the three-mile walk back to the house. She didn't want to spend the last of her hard-earned mad money on an Uber after her expensive purchases a couple of days ago. A damp chill had developed in the air over the past hour, so Maria quickened her step. She had left her jacket back in Lacey's car at the fairgrounds.

A little over an hour later, Maria reached home. She retrieved the spare key and entered the house, calling out to her sisters as she entered.

Fuck Dad if I wake him up. He should have answered my phone call.

Her call was met with utter silence. No droning of the TV. No rocking music bouncing off the walls. No buzzsaw snoring from her father on the couch. Not even the incessant chatter from two excited teenage girls staying up late on Halloween night. In fact, even their dog Charley had not barked when she entered or come to greet her. She bellowed across the house,

"HELLOOOOO! Where is everybody? If this is some kind of joke, I don't find it fucking funny. If you are up there hiding with Daphne and Lacey, I swear I will kill the lot of you."

She set her phone on the side table near the door before meandering into the kitchen to grab a Coke and a banana, determined to appear nonchalant and ruin her sisters' fun if they, too, were trying to scare her. As she crossed to the other side of the kitchen to enter the empty living room, she saw a black candle, much like the ones she had been burning earlier, lit on the center of the coffee table. Her eyes turned toward the stairs to see if her sisters were hiding at the top, but all she saw was a message scrawled on the mirror on the hall tree across the room. It appeared to have been written in dripping blood and simply said, "I am here."

"Really fucking funny, assholes! I knew Lacey and Daphne were pulling a trick on me. Now you guys have to join in, too? I guess you guys figured out I was trying to contact Grandma. Daphne, did you stand in the hallway outside my door earlier and overhear me? I am really not in the mood for this bullshit. It has been a long day."

Utter silence reigned in the house still.

"Come out, come out, wherever you are! Seriously, guys, this isn't funny! I am tired. I want to go to bed."

Maria stood at the bottom of the stairs, looking up expectantly... waiting for someone to jump out and try to scare her. But once again, she was met with the stillness of a graveyard. As she began to scream in frustration, she heard a low whine coming from upstairs. "Charley? Is that you? Here, boy!" She heard his nails click across the wood floor in the hallway... his feet clumping down each step, sounding more like an elephant than a Basset Hound. He rounded the banister on the landing and looked down at her, sadder that she had ever seen him. His tail wagged slowly in recognition as he took slow, wary steps down the rest of the stairs.

His fur was matted with blood, but he didn't appear to be injured. Maria ran up the stairs and ran her fingers all over his body, but she couldn't find a single injury. "You assholes are fucking sick! This is not funny in the slightest. I was terrified that he had a serious injury." Charley continued to stare at her and whine pitifully. He turned his head and stared up the stairs. When she didn't follow, he began to trek back up the stairs alone, baying as he went.

Maria's blood ran cold. She began to feel dizzy as she realized she had not taken a breath since he turned his head. She rose and began ascending the stairs in one graceful motion. Her voice turned shrill as she called out, "Cindy! Bethany! Are you two okay?" As she reached the top step, she could smell it... the undeniable stench of blood and death. She burst into their bedroom on a dead run and stopped cold—willing her eyes not to see what lay before her.

Bethany's lifeless eyes bore into her very soul from across the room. Her body was staged—what else could you call it?—so that she was sitting up in bed cross-legged with a bowl of popcorn in her lap. A wide smile had been carved into her face, literally, by the kitchen knife sitting on her bedside table. The sides of her mouth had been cut, widening her smile until she looked like a perverse version of the Joker. She was positioned facing the television, where *Night of the Living Dead* was playing with the volume turned off. The immense pool of blood surrounding her and the number of deep stab wounds in her chest and abdomen told Maria that her sister was beyond help.

Maria finally tore her eyes away to look for Cindy—a

decision she immediately came to regret. Cindy had also been put on display: on the floor propped up against her bed with the laptop across her thighs and her fingers glued to the keys. Her face, like her sister's, bore incisions to widen her smile into a sickening laugh. Her head tilted back to expose a neck that had been slit open to the point of nearly severing her head from her body. Cindy's body had been turned in such a way that it appeared as if she was trying to show Maria what was on her screen.

The cursor blinked next to three sentences that had been typed in a new Word document.

You called out for someone to come to you. I am here now. Thank you for the invitation.

Maria tried to blink away the tears that began streaming from her eyes.

This can't be. Is it all my fault? Did I bring a spirit here and set it free to kill my family? I thought all that "thinner veil" shit was just that... bullshit. I didn't think a spirit could hurt me or anyone else. What kind of spirit did I invite?

Maria started when the laptop clattered to the floor. Charley knocked it over while nosing Cindy, trying to get her to respond to him. Maria ran out of the room and down the hall to check her father's room. He had been brutally bludgeoned, but his body had just been left on the floor where it had fallen. A large laceration on his right temple revealed small chunks of bone and brain matter that had been pulverized by the intensity of the blows. The walls were sprayed with blood cast off from the hammer that had rained blows upon his head.

What the fuck do I do now? Is the spirit still roaming around? It is past midnight now. Does that mean he has been sucked back into the other side? If he hasn't, I don't know how to send him back. Wait... Amaranth!

Maria ran into her room and began rummaging through the box in her closet where she had stashed the items for the ritual.

Amaranth's business card with her cell phone number must be in there with everything else.

She yelped and jerked her hand back as her finger slid across the card, opening a painful paper cut. Maria dumped the box out and grabbed the card. She dashed down the stairs and started across the living room to grab her phone to call the police, but she was stopped dead in her tracks by an item she saw lying on the hall tree. It was the feather headpiece Daphne had been wearing as part of her costume tonight.

Oh God no! Please! Maybe Lacey had a matching one and forgot it here earlier. I have to find out. I need to stop this spirit here and now before it kills anyone else.

Maria ran out the door and jumped into the car. She raced down the street and turned toward the slaughterhouse. Still blocks away, the flashing red lights and sirens in the distance told her all she needed to know. Those amazingly realistic bodies in the scenes had been real. Maria pulled over to the curb and found the card in her pocket. Her shaking fingers punched in the numbers, as she trembled in the seat willing her to answer.

A sleepy voice answered the phone, "Hello."

"Amaranth! I need your help. I was so stupid. I screwed up everything."

"Slow down. Screwed up what? Who is this?"

"It is Maria. I was in your store the other day. You helped me with the Ouija board. I contacted my grandma alone earlier. Weird shit happened. My friends arrived. I just quit. Now they're all dead."

"Whoa, whoa, whoa! You are not making sense. Take some

deep breaths. Meet me at the store. I live in the apartment above. I will leave the back door unlocked, so you can just come in."

Maria hung up and sped toward downtown. It seemed as if all the police in town were at the slaughterhouse, so there seemed little chance she would get caught. She screeched to a stop behind the store and ran in the back door. Amaranth was standing near the table where they had talked before. Maria ran into her arms, burying her face in Amaranth's chest, as she sobbed until she had neither breath nor tears left. Amaranth led her to the table and gestured for her to sit.

"Now tell me what happened. Don't leave anything out, and start from the beginning."

Maria took a few deep breaths and began the long, terrifying story. She explained to her that, while she was not positive, she believed that her friends had been killed as well and placed on display for her. Amaranth had tears in her eyes as Maria recounted her story. She nodded at times and held Maria's hands tightly, asking questions as needed to get all the details. Maria couldn't raise her eyes to meet Amaranth's gaze as she finished the story. Large teardrops fell into her lap as she sobbed.

"Oh, Maria! I am so sorry. I tried to warn you. It is a very dangerous time when the veil drops to attempt contact with the other side. Those rules you read about exist for a reason. In preparation, you should do spells to protect yourself. It is very important to be very specific who you are attempting to contact and never just call for *someone* to come to you. If you are unsure who is reaching back out to you, do not continue contact. You must thank any spirits who interact with you and let them know that they are not welcome to linger on this side. Then you must close the circle and the session by saying goodbye."

"Who did I let in? Why is he doing this? How do we stop him?"

"I don't know who it is. There are dark energies on the other side, and I think it is likely that one of them heard you. It will not be easy to send this spirit away. He is at his most powerful state until midnight on the 1st, but that also means we still have time to get him back onto the right side of the veil. Are you ready to do this?"

"Yes, please help me."

Amaranth rose and began to gather the necessary ingredients. This time *all* the proper supplies were gathered... not only crystals and candles to facilitate communication but also ones to protect the participants. She brought in the necessary herbs to protect them as well. Amaranth spread a circle of salt around the table, enclosing the two of them in a protective barrier to keep the spirit at bay. She then burned sage, frankincense, myrrh and dragon's blood to cleanse the space before they began. Then she led both of them through a brief meditation to clear their mind, ground themselves and visualize setting up a wall of white light around themselves.

Amaranth began the session by thanking any spirits in the area. "We come to you with the utmost respect for all the spirits who may hear us tonight. We want to thank our ancestors for your support and protection of us. We ask that our dearly departed ancestors help us tonight in our mission to banish this dark spirit that has come to Maria.

"We appreciate any spirit that came to talk to Maria tonight, but it is time for you to go back to the other side. You have crossed over from the world of the dead to the world of the living, but you do not belong here. I know the veil is very thin right now. I know that Maria invited you to come to her, but she did not understand. It is time for you to cross back over.

"You are not welcome to stay here. This is not your world. You must cross back over to the other side. We once again thank anyone who came to Maria earlier or to us now, but it is time for your visit to end. It is time for us to say goodbye."

Amaranth ended the communication by sliding the planchette over to the word Goodbye on the board. With that, the heavy air that had descended upon the room lifted, and a cool breeze swept past them, fluttering the heavy curtains that hung around them. Amaranth was whispering a small prayer when her eyes lifted at the faint sound of movement in the shop. She paused for a moment and then shook her head when nothing more was heard, before she lit the sage once more and cleansed the board as well as the area around the table.

Maria started crying softly as she realized that her nightmare was over. She sniffled and looked up at Amaranth as she asked, "What now? I have no one. I killed my entire family and my best friends."

"NO! You did not kill them. It is not your fault. I should have tried harder to make sure you understood the very real dangers. I knew you were hiding something from me. That is why I gave you my card. I was hoping that you would reach out.

"What's next? I need to get you a few things so you can cleanse your house and yourself. Just to be safe, I need you to do this before you repeat the meditation we just performed, along with the grounding and protection spell every day for the next week. This experience has left you very fragile and open to the world. The veil will still be quite thin for a while yet, so I need you to protect yourself.

"For now, you need to go home and call the police about

what happened to your family. I am available night or day... call me if you need me. I will be right back."

Maria closed her eyes and cradled her head in her crossed arms on the table. She felt exhausted but didn't know if she would ever sleep well again. She heard Amaranth humming a soothing tune as she moved around the shop, gathering items. Her eyelids began to flutter as unbidden sleep descended upon her.

Maria awoke a few moments later to the sound of Amaranth speaking to someone, "Oh! What are you doing here?" She didn't catch a response, but she did hear Amaranth returning. She turned toward the curtain as she heard a strange gurgling sound just outside. Amaranth was pushing through the curtain—her eyes wide with pain—as she choked on the blood pouring from her neck and seeping between her lips. Her body... for a moment at least... was suspended in air by the knife protruding all the way through her neck from the back and held by a tall man with dark features, glowering at her.

At that moment, he twisted his wrist to the right, and the razor-sharp knife sliced through up to her jawline before her body slumped to the floor. Her lifeblood pumped out of her, the bloody tableau on the floor brighter than the crimson tablecloth. Maria's mouth hung agape as she stared at the man towering above Amaranth as she breathed her last.

"We sent you back to the other side. You can't be here. We rescinded my invitation."

"Ignorant girl! Don't you remember me?" he asked as an evil smile spread across his face.

To her surprise, she realized that he did look familiar, but she hadn't quite been able to place him... until the moment he smiled. She shook her head in denial.

"Shake your head all you want. It won't change anything.

The only thing you might have sent back to the other side was your grandma or some other benign spirit."

"But how? Why?"

"You were irresistible... from the first moment I saw you that day in the store. I overheard your conversation. You need a real man. And you needed those other complications—distractions really—removed from your life. I followed you home. You were so lost in your own world that you didn't even notice me boarding the bus behind you.

"I entered your home when you left with your sisters. I heard your Ouija board session. I answered your call. I came, and I helped you, just as you asked."

Maria pushed her chair back as he approached, shaking her head. "Get away from me. I don't want you. You ruined my life! You killed my family and my friends. You are a monster!"

His face devolved into an angry grimace. He lunged at her as Maria jumped up and darted to the side. "You little bitch! After all I did for you," he bellowed as he swung his leg out sweeping her legs out from under her. Maria's body landed with a resounding thud; the breath driven out of her lungs as much by the blow as by the Bowie knife that was driven through her back and into the floorboards below, pinning her.

Maria gasped for each breath as her hands flailed behind her, trying to pull out the knife. Alaric walked out of the curtained alcove and returned a moment later with a camera in his hands.

"You bitches are all the same. You all claim to want a *real man*, but when you are presented with one you are all so fucking ungrateful. I am tired of being treated like an object. I am a performance artist by trade, so now I document my greatest works of art. You are the object now. I shall call you *Papillon*...

my pinned butterfly."

Maria struggled to breathe as her lungs filled with blood. She looked up at him, malice in her eyes, as she spit, "Fuck you!" As her head sank to the ground and her breathing slowed, her fingers released the phone she had hidden in her fist. A smile crept across her face as she heard the sirens approaching fast.

Stephen H. Provost

Creepstore

Ted Olsson stared up at the flaking paint on the sign over his shop, Creepstore & More. Housed in an old building at the corner of Mattox and Front streets, it had once been an A&P market. But Olsson had transformed it into a costume shop, catering mostly to acting troupes and adults holding costume parties. Their business wasn't enough to keep him afloat, so he relied on the Halloween season every year for the bulk of his income, the same way other stores relied on the Christmas season to keep them in the black.

That's why he'd chosen the name Creepstore: Sure, Olsson

sold all kinds of costumes there, as well as makeup and props for amateur magicians, but he knew that attracting the Halloween crowd was the key to staying in business.

Unfortunately, he'd been pulling in fewer customers every autumn for the past few years, which is why he hadn't been able to afford to repaint that flaking red-and-gold sign over the entrance.

Creepstore's location, tucked away in an older, mostly residential neighborhood built in the 1920s, meant his lease was cheaper. But it also meant lower visibility. The Spirit Halloween Store, which had been renting space in the Northside Mall, had a huge—albeit temporary—sign draped over the old Gottschalks building and drew all the foot traffic for impulse buys. Since it was a pop-up store that operated only from the end of July until November, the corporate owners didn't have to pay a full year's rent. And they probably got an even bigger discount for setting up shop in the cavernous, otherwise vacant old department store.

When he'd started out, Olsson had used his own reputation to build the business. He'd spent more than two decades working in Hollywood as a makeup man, turning ordinary actors into Great Apes, Klingons, mutants, Swamp Things, and Werewolves. But the advent of CGI had reduced the Reel Rembrandt Studios' demand for his skills, so the studio had let him go and he decided to get out of the movie business. Instead, he'd opened Creepstore, promoting it as Carson City's "only professional costume supplier." People who wanted the best costumes sought him out, and he could charge a bit more for his products.

You got what you paid for, right?

The problem was, fewer people were willing to pay for it.

Spirit was selling more sophisticated costumes of its own and could afford to carry a wider variety, while also undercutting him on price with bargain costumes for little kids (and their frugal parents). He had to find a new angle, something that would put him back in the game, and he thought he had found it with a new high-end product he'd been developing with Frasier Hart-Jeffries, a high school friend who'd gone on to get a Ph.D. in biochemistry. They'd reconnected by chance on Facepage when Ted was still working for the studio, and what had begun as a friendly conversation eventually morphed into a business partnership.

"You're a makeup guy," Frasier had said one day over a martini and a Fireball at The Elbow Room. "What would you think of a product that applied your makeup for you?"

"I think it would put me out of business," Ted laughed. "They're already using more of that CGI shit, and they laid off my assistant a couple of months ago. I'm afraid I'll be next."

"Not if you owned the copyright to the product. You could just retire and market it without doing any real work. Besides, the actors would love it: They wouldn't have to spend hours sitting there in a chair while someone else slapped on layer after layer of gunk they could barely see or breathe out of."

"Hey now," Ted replied, sounding wounded. "There's an art to this thing I do for a living. Not just anyone can 'slap on gunk,' as you put it. That's why it takes so long: You have to work to get it just right."

"That's the beauty of this chemical compound. The way I envision it working, you'd just pour it onto a person's face through a template, let it dry, and *voila*! It would mold itself to the person's face. Besides, you're what, 57 now? You could retire early and live off the profits from this thing. Like the song says, it would be money for nothing."

"And chicks for free?" Ted quipped.

"Well, maybe not that. You're not exactly Adam Levine, now, are you?"

"I guess you can't have everything. So how would it work?

Frasier paused for a moment, then continued. His voice changed slightly, like he was a salesman going into his pitch: "I'd create the product, you could use your reputation to market it, and we'd share the rights to it—split the profits 50-50."

"OK," Ted said. "Sounds fine so far. But it doesn't sound like this product of yours is ready for prime time. The way you're talking, it seems like you haven't even tested it yet. How far along is it?"

Frasier's tone was breezy and unconcerned, bordering on dismissive. "Oh, it's still in development," he said. "I'll let you know when it's ready for market. You just have to hold on to that job of yours in the meantime."

Unfortunately, he hadn't. He'd been let go less than a year later, and he'd forgotten about his friend's proposal... until recently. The two hadn't been in touch with each other for several years when, out of the blue, his cellphone buzzed just as he was about to close up, it was Frasier on the other end.

His friend offered a quick hello and a perfunctory "how are you," but he seemed full of excitement—eager to get to the reason for his call.

Ted decided not to make him squirm through small talk: "What's up?"

"It's ready," Frasier said, almost breathless.

"What's ready?"

"The compound. It's finally ready to go."

It took Ted a minute; then he remembered: "That magic

mask shit?"

"Yeah. bet you thought I'd forgotten about it, hadn't you? Listen, I know you're not with the studio anymore, but I bet you could use my Living Polymer—that's what I'm calling it—to promote your store. You could..."

Ted finished his sentence for him: "Offer it as a service to my customers."

"Exactly!"

That's how it had started. Ted received the first shipment of Living Polymer in two sealed 55-gallon drums marked, ominously, as containing "volatile chemicals." It was a variation on the moldable plastic, polyethylene. But unlike that material, it was moldable at room temperature. That was important, because you didn't want to pour scalding-hot plastic onto some trick-or-treater's face.

It was poured through a small hole in the mold—and set precisely at human skin temperature, between 96 and 99 degrees. Within 2 minutes of contact, depending which mold was placed over it, you'd come out looking like Groot, Thanos, or Worf. Then you just peeled off the mold, and you were set. The only catch was you had to leave the thing on until you were done with it: after that costume party was over or trick-or-treating was finished. If you tried to take it off beforehand, you couldn't reuse it: As Frasier put it, "you'd have a mess, not a mask, on your hands."

Frasier had sent him general specifications for the mask molds, and Ted had created three dozen specific "characters" to start out with (there *was* significant work to this, after all), including not just fantasy characters but celebrities like Danny Trejo, Joaquin Phoenix, Lady Gaga, and, for old-school impersonators, Princess Di and Humphrey Bogart. He'd procured real human hair for the coup-de-gras, which would take a little more time to apply but probably less than an hour.

He wasn't supposed to touch the material itself before it had set, not because of any danger to himself, but because it needed to remain pure in order to work properly. If anyone other than the intended wearer touched it, it would become contaminated by sweat or other residue containing that person's DNA, and in order to work properly, contact with the Living Polymer had to be restricted to a single subject.

"Remember *The Fly*?" Frasier had asked him. "The DNA from Jeff Goldblum got mixed up with the DNA from a fly, and they got fused together."

Ted had been appalled. "Are you saying...?"

Frasier laughed. "Haha. Gotcha. No, that's not going to happen here... at least I don't think so." He laughed again, and Ted couldn't tell whether his tone was totally playful or slightly nervous. "But you do need to wear gloves at all times, and sterilize the molds before placing them over your clients' faces."

"You *have* tested this, right?"

"Of course. Of course. It's perfectly harmless. It just won't work right if more than one person touches it. The DNA activates the 'living' part of the polymer, and if it gets mixed signals, so to speak, it will just stay a big pile of goo and won't set. It would all come out in the wash, though."

Ted supposed that was why the barrel had been labeled as containing "volatile chemicals." It was also why Frasier had supplied him with what he called an overhead applicator with a spout that funneled the material downward onto the customer's face. In principle, it seemed like a cement mixer, but it looked more like one of those cone-shaped X-ray devices attached to an overhead arm—the kind a dentist pointed at your teeth.

He wasn't entirely sold on the idea, but Frasier had given him the stuff for free, and Ted had signed a contract guaranteeing himself half the profits, so he convinced himself to go ahead with it... but he also thought it prudent to get customers to sign a contract of their own—or, rather, a liability waiver. He'd signed one himself before he and his wife had tried one of those escape rooms, and before they'd toured the basement of the Mark Twain Museum in Virginia City. He wasn't about to lose his live savings, or Creepstore, to a lawsuit.

The line at Creepstore stretched almost around the block on Halloween, two hours before the shop was due to open. It was like it was 1980 again and the new *Star Wars* movie had opened on just one screen. Ted hadn't counted on the fact that, since the material couldn't be removed once it was applied, all his customers would want their masks applied on Halloween itself. The thought had occurred to him just a week before the big day, and he'd called Frasier, frantically asking him if he could deliver a couple of more overhead applicators to deal with the expected rush.

Ted knew it would be busy because he'd borrowed several thousands of dollars to promote it. If it went well, he reasoned, he'd recoup it all on Halloween and word of mouth about the new "Magic Masks" as he called them (it was much catchier than Living Polymer) would stimulate off-season sales on top of that.

He had held off on trying the process on anyone until Halloween itself with two exceptions: a 16-year-old boy had come in, begging him to make an exception in his case because Halloween was on a Sunday this year, and his school was having a Halloween-themed costume dance on Friday night.

He'd wanted to look like Deadpool, with a mask that adhered to his face. Fortunately, Deadpool and the Hulk were the two superhero face molds he'd created,. The kid hadn't been back, so Ted assumed he'd won himself a satisfied customer.

The other was a 7-year-old girl who wanted to dress up as a skeleton for her birthday party and was pleading with her mother to buy her a skull mask. Ted hadn't felt too comfortable with this, not knowing if there were any special steps he should take to ensure the safety of a child undergoing the procedure. Frasier hadn't mentioned any, though, and when the girl's mother had arrived dressed in a Saint Laurent short jacket, carrying an alligator Coach handbag, and wearing Jackie Ohh-style sunglasses. She could obviously afford the price of a Magic Mask for her daughter, and when he hesitated because of her age, she offered to pay double what he was charging.

That was all the incentive he had needed.

But now here he was, having his morning coffee at home before heading over to the store, when he was interrupted by a call on his cellphone. He didn't recognize the number, but a lot of people had been calling about when the store was going to open, so he picked it up.

What he hadn't expected to hear on the other end was a woman's frantic voice.

"Is this Mr. Olsson?"

"Yes. Who is this?"

"It's Trudy Cartego, Shannon's mother."

Ted frowned. "I'm sorry, and who is Shannon?"

"My daughter!" the woman was nearly screaming into the phone, acting like it should have been obvious. "You put that filthy mask on her the other day, and now we can't get it off!"

Ted's eyes widened. Of course he hadn't remembered the

woman. She'd paid in cash and had never mentioned her name—or her daughter's.

"Did you hear me?" she was screaming. "We CAN'T. GET. IT. OFF!"

So why didn't the woman take her daughter to the Emergency Room? That's what any sane person would do in this situation. But the woman sounded so panicked that she clearly wasn't thinking straight.

"The mask is bubbling, like oil or something! What IS that?"

Before he had time to answer (although he didn't *have* an answer anyway), she was shouting again. "There's something black seeping up from inside it!"

Why was she calling him? How did she *not* know to take the girl to the hospital? He was about to suggest that she do just that when he realized something: He'd forgotten to make her sign the waiver! When the 16-year-old kid came in, he'd gotten his father to sign it. But he'd forgotten to give it to the little girl's mother. Thinking back on it, he realized why: He had assumed most people would be paying with a credit or debit card, so he'd made a mental note to give them the waiver then. But this Trudy Cartego had prepaid in cash by dropping a wad of bills on the counter, so the waiver had never entered his mind.

If the kid ended up in the hospital, she could sue him for the medical bill... not to mention the pain and suffering, and the mental anguish the mother was obviously going through. Yeah, she had a lot of money. But if they got their panties in a wad, those kind of Karens were more likely to use their money to get revenge, than they were to pay their own bills—even though they could obviously afford it.

If she wasn't thinking about the hospital, he wasn't going to put that thought into her little rich-bitch head.

"Hold on," he said. "I know just what to do. Can you give me your address? I'll drive right over."

He did *not* know just what to do, but he needed time to come up with a plan. He'd heard nail polish could get someone unstuck from Super Glue, and fortunately, his wife had some in her makeup kit. It took him a few minutes to find it—the kit was behind some scarves and a wool cap on the top shelf of her closet—but once he had it, he stopped in the kitchen to grab some disposable plastic gloves, before dashing out the front door. Reflexively, he checked his pocket for his wallet and his waistband for the concealed-carry holster that held his Glock 43. Shutting off the radio, which he'd left on the last time he'd been in the car and was playing "Voodoo Chile" by Jimi Hendrix, he plugged in his cell phone and set his GPS for the address Karen, or Trudy, or whatever her name was, had given him. It looked like it was only about five minutes away, so he still had time to solve the glitch with her kid's mask and get back to the store in time for the big opening.

She's just being overly dramatic. Those hoity-toity rich bitches always are. They think a hangnail is the end of the world. But let them try to work for a living and dealing with debt collectors instead of relying on their sugar daddies... then they'll REALLY have something to cry about.

He pulled up into the driveway of a two-story luxury home with a standalone garage and hedges carved like animals out front. It creeped him out because he felt like they were looking at him, silently condemning him for whatever had happened to poor little Shannon. He half-expected the tiger to pounce on him or the elephant to charge. Of course, neither of those things happened. And the irrational fear of it didn't make him move any faster—time was of the essence, and he was already going as fast as his 57-year-old legs could carry him up to the doorway.

He rang the bell, which produced a resonant Westminster chime, and was greeted two seconds later by Trudy Cartego, looking every bit as frantic as she had sounded on the phone. Ted could scarcely tell she was the same person who visited the store a few days earlier: Instead of the designer outfit and perfectly styled locks, this woman looked like she hadn't even run a comb through her frizzy brown hair since she'd gotten out of bed. As for her attire, she wore an old sweatsuit—unmatched hot pink top and teal pants—which were smeared with a sticky black substance that looked like it had bubbled up out of the La Brea Tar Pits.

"Hurry!" she shouted, although he was just a couple of feet in front of her, and grabbed his wrist, yanking him along toward an expansive room with a cathedral ceiling that must have been what they used to call a family room—the preferred term these days, he seemed to remember, was "great room."

The little girl lay on a heavily cushioned leather couch.

She wasn't moving, and she was barely breathing. Ted thought at first that she might be dead, until he saw her chest rising and falling—slowly and barely perceptibly—in response to irregular, shallow breaths.

The mask can't have done this to her, he thought as he approached and knelt down next to her. *Maybe she got sick at her birthday party.*

But he could see the skull mask was still attached to her face, and as he bent in closer, he noticed the black tar oozing out from inside it, around the edges. Reaching into his jacket pocket, he pulled out the gloves and slipped them on, then put one on either side of the mask and pulled gently.

The scream that followed sounded like it came from a dozen 7-year-olds who'd stumbled onto a sewer full of rats. The black stuff seemed to start percolating, like week-old coffee, bubbling and sizzling out the edges of the mask.

"Please!" Trudy begged him. "Don't hurt her!"

He nodded projecting an air of confidence he didn't feel as he struggled to fight off a wave of nausea, bile rising up to the back of his throat. He swallowed it back, reached into his other pocket, and pulled out the nail polish remover.

"What are you going to do with *that*?" the mother asked him. She clearly didn't trust him. Hell, he didn't trust himself at this point.

"It's what everyone uses to remove Super Glue," he said, sounding mildly perturbed. He'd noticed the woman's long nails, coated with pink polish accented with what looked like little trees, at the store. She probably had enough polish remover lying around to dissolve the caulk in a bathroom full of tiles. "Do you have a cotton ball or swab?"

Or course she does, with all that makeup she was wearing...

She disappeared and returned a moment later with several cotton squares; he took one of them and applied it to the place where the mask seemed to have adhered to the girl's face... producing another scream and more bubbling black goo, mixed this time with blood. Ted hoped the mother hadn't seen it. He was going to get this thing off, and he didn't have a lot of time if he wanted to get to the shop in time to open.

He ignored the bubbling, the blood, and the girl's screaming and dabbed the nail polish all around her face.

"Are you sure...?" the mother began.

"Yes, I'm sure," he snapped as he took hold of the mask

with his gloved fingers, curving them to try to get purchase under its edges. This was difficult, because there *were* no edges that he could identify. The mask was so completely stuck—more like bonded—to the girl's face, that the only way to tell where it ended and her skin began was the line of black ooze that was seeping out from underneath.

"My God!" the woman screamed. "Her eyes!"

Ted glanced up and saw that the mask's eyeholes, where the girl's eyes should have been, were covered in black as well, and that it was swelling upward and overflowing onto the surface of the mask.

Horrified and panicked, Ted dug his gloved fingernails into the girl's skin along the black line on both sides of her face. The girl wasn't screaming now; she appeared to have passed out from the pain, so he had nothing to distract him. Abandoning caution, he took hold and pulled as hard as he could, separating the mask from her face with great effort as the black goo clung to it, stretching itself out in what seemed like a desperate attempt to preserve the bond.

But it was just goo. It couldn't be "desperate" because it wasn't alive... or was it? Frasier had called it "Living Polymer," a name Ted had assumed was meant to hype the product. But what if it really *was* alive? He remembered Frasier talking about a person's DNA activating the "living" element in the polymer. What if, in creating this mask, he had literally brought some evil organism to life?

What if it was trying to possess or consume this little girl, and it was straining against his efforts to destroy that bond before it finished whatever malign process it had begun?

Ted pulled, then he pulled even harder.

The line of black became a thin ribbon of blood, like a razor cut dripping down the side of her face, and the substance bubbled and fizzed, like a seltzer tablet dropped in water, before finally weakening and giving way.

Ted's backward momentum as he pulled it free nearly sent him rolling over onto his back. But he didn't have time to worry about that, as Shannon sat bolt upright on the couch and glared down at him from black eyes full of malice. Or were they eyeholes? It was hard to tell because that black substance was still dripping from them like obscene, tarry tears. Whatever these "eyes" were, they were not Shannon's. And the face wasn't the little girl's either… if one could even call it a face.

It was as though the skull mask had made an imprint on her, melting away the skin and much of what lay beneath it until all that remained was the skull itself, with strips of pink flesh hanging there, loose and bloody and dying, clinging to the bone. How the girl could have survived this horror was hard to know, but she was, somehow, still breathing. Ted could see the hole in her throat that was still intact, opening up into the skull where a new passage to her nose bone and jaw had been created by the Living Polymer.

The mother gasped and retched, spewing her guts onto the just-shampooed soft white carpet. Then she fainted, hitting her head on the wooden claw arm of a chair and falling forward, unconscious, into the vomit.

"Why did you do this to me?" a voice rasped.

It wasn't the girl's voice; it didn't even sound human. Ted wondered whether it was the girl or the black goo that was talking, or whether the two of them had somehow become fused into a single grotesque entity.

The girl's hand reached up and picked off a piece of the barely attached flesh from the skeleton face and stretched it out toward Ted.

"Hungry?"

It laughed. It wasn't the kind of laugh that comes in response to a joke or gag, but that slow, steady cackle of insanity—the product of a mind twisted and deformed into something beyond recognition, just as the grotesque face in front of him had been.

Before he could answer, she flung the bloody strip of raw meat that had had recently been attached to her cheekbone, hitting him in the forehead.

Ted reeled backward, losing his balance and falling hard into a glass case against the wall, which shattered, sending glass shards raining down all around him. A crystal decanter, half full of some kind of liquor, crashed to the ground just beside him, inches from his head. Blood from a gash on his head, caused by one of those glass shards, dripped down into his right eye. But what had his full attention was the monstrous entity that had jumped to its feet with impossible agility and was nearly on top of him.

Reaching down beside him, he freed the Glock from its holster and whipped it around in front of him just as the thing that had been little Shannon Cartego leapt at him. In the split second before her body came crashing down on him, he pulled the trigger, sending the bullet slamming into the center of her chest. The momentum carried her forward, but the part of her that he'd shot was still human, and she convulsed as she landed, writhing in pain on top of him as blood began flowing out of her.

That blood and the tarry ooze from what was left of her face sprayed out onto him, and he kicked her off violently.

She lay there, writhing on the floor.

And then something astonishing happened: The tarry

substance that had created a breathing tube for the hybrid monstrosity began oozing downward, purposeful, toward its chest.

Ted aimed his gun at the goo and fired, which seemed to halt its progress momentarily before it resumed.

In a panic, Ted whirled around, looking for a weapon—any weapon—he might use to stop the thing. His eyes fell on the shattered glass case and the heavy decanter that had just missed his head. If it had hit him, the thing would have certainly knocked him out, and if it had hit at the right angle, it might have killed him. Spinning around, he reached down and grabbed it, ran over to where the girl-thing was lying on the ground, and slammed it hard down into the naked skull.

There was a sickly sounding crunch as bone gave way under the weight and momentum of the blow.

Ted raised the decanter again and brought it down again, with even greater force.

And again.

And again.

And again.

Bone fragments flew across the room, and the thing's breathing stopped long before Ted did.

Finally, winded and sweating, he stood and fired another round into the thing's chest for good measure. Just to be sure.

Then he turned to the mother, still unconscious, and fired two more rounds directly into her chest before hurrying out of the house. He still had 45 minutes to get back to the shop before he was due to open, and he would be damned if he'd let a little thing like a crazy Karen and her monstrosity of a daughter stand in the way of the money he was about to make.

On the drive to the shop, Ted's breathing slowed and he had time to think. What if the same thing happened to those customers at the shop that had happened to Shannon?

She just had a bad reaction, he told himself. Her DNA wasn't compatible with the polymer, and it just *looked* like the goo was alive. Of course, it couldn't have been. He had imagined that part of it, just like he'd imagined those topiary hedge plants in the front yard were about to charge at him. He'd need to get his eyes checked; he ruled out seeing a shrink, because the shrink wouldn't believe him—and he was convinced he wasn't crazy.

Worst case scenario: A few of his customers might have some mild allergic reaction, but whatever might happen, he'd have made enough money to close the shop and get out of the country. With that Karen lying dead back at her McMansion, and his fingerprints all over the place (not to mention ballistics that could tie him to the scene), he'd have no choice in the matter. He'd have to get out of the country, quietly and quickly.

He'd leave his wife with the house: She'd been threatening to divorce him anyway. Then he'd hop a plane to Colombia—which didn't require a visa or have a U.S. extradition deal—and start over there.

All he had to do was get through today, pocket the money from his transactions at the Creepstore, lock the door and throw away the proverbial key.

T.J. Harrington peered out from behind the bushes across from the costume shop, staring out at the line of restless children standing with their parents and teens clustered into the predictable cliques.

Idiots. They have no idea what's about to happen to them.

T.J.'s Deadpool mask had started itching shortly after he'd had it put on. Attached was more like it. Or grafted on. He'd been told that, if he removed it before the Friday night Halloween dance, it would be useless: He wouldn't be able to put it back on again. So he'd tried to grin and bear it, and he'd even made it to the dance—where everyone said how awesome he looked—before the itching became unbearable.

When he tried to take it off, though, he found it was stuck on… tight. The mask itself felt like it was resisting his efforts, and the longer he wore it, the worse the itching got: like fleas or mites burrowing deeper into his skin. The itching was becoming a hot tingling—so hot that was making his entire face sweat. But the mask blocked the sweat from escaping, and he felt it start to ooze out at the edges.

When put a hand up to wipe it away, though, it didn't feel like sweat. If felt thicker, stickier, like melted candle wax. Raising his hand in front of his face, he saw it didn't *look* like sweat either. It was black like crude oil, and it smelled like… he'd never been exposed to the odor of human flesh burning, but if he had, he would have known that this was exactly what it smelled like.

He'd been so distracted by the itching, burning sensation that he hadn't noticed that some of kids who had been dancing had stopped, and were now staring at him. They weren't admiring his cool costume anymore. They were gawking and pointing, talking excitedly and giggling.

At him.

"Hey," one of the guys said finally, "what's that shit on you? Looks like you hit a gusher there!"

"Fuck, that's some weird shit."

"He's supposed to be Deadpool, but he's startin' ta look

more like Venom."

Then the giggling turned to howls of laughter, and T.J. ran off to one of the single-stall restrooms designed for disabled students, locking the door behind him. He hurried to the mirror and was horrified to see the sticky black substance seeping out from under his mask at the edges. It felt like whatever the mask had unleashed on him was burrowing deeper into his head, affecting his equilibrium and making him feel drugged. He tried to fight the sensation, but it was getting worse by the moment.

Fuck! It has to come off!

He couldn't find the corners of the mask to gain any purchase with his fingers. Desperate, he dug his nails into the skin itself and began to pull it back, wincing in pain as the mask began to give way—taking the attached skin with it. It was still fighting him, but it hadn't gotten deep enough inside him to complete the bonding. It had not yet achieved full symbiosis, but it was far enough along in the process to begin altering his neural pathways—to begin making them compatible with its own genetic structure. Though T.J. had no way of knowing exactly what was happening to him, he could feel the madness bubbling up inside as his own genetics activated the Living Polymer's latent DNA. The madness was taking control of him, but it was also furthering his own desperation to rid himself of the mask.

He howled and screamed as he clawed at himself, ripping and tearing, heedless of whether he was pulling away the mask or his own skin. Or both. Blood mixed with black ooze to cover his face with a thick, coppery stew. Someone was banging on the door. He didn't know whether they needed to use the bathroom or were responding to his shrieks of agony at the self-inflicted carnage. It didn't matter. All he cared about was removing the parasite that was clinging to him, refusing to let him go unless he literally clawed it to death.

T.J. had finally gotten free of the mask, tearing it to an ugly pulp, but he hadn't been able to dig out the black tendrils that had bored into his skull. He couldn't see them, but he could feel them there.

And the madness never left him.

Those people in the line around that store were about to be fed, like fatted calves, to the same monster that had scrambled his brain and left him looking like *this*. He pulled out a jagged piece of reflective glass, broken off from the mirror he'd shattered in that restroom before he fled, and held it up to his face. Seeing it fueled his rage. His determination. He would *not* let anyone else end up like this: a mangled mass of blood and pus and sinew and black tar residue. His eyes still stared out from above what was left of his nose, the cartilage having been ripped away in his frenzy to free himself. He saw everything now through a hazy black filter that made everything look like storm clouds at twilight.

He laughed a low, mad laugh at the irony of it: He looked far worse than Wade Wilson's disfigured face beneath the Deadpool mask in that movie. You could still tell it was the actor, Ryan Reynolds; he just looked like he had a killer case of acne. No one could have guessed the grotesque figure crouching behind the bushes had once been T.J. Harrington. And no one could have imagined the pain he was still in from his wounds and what that leech had left inside him.

This was worse than death—far worse. If he had to kill every single person in that line, their ghosts would thank him. They would realize what he'd saved them from, and he would be a hero, if only to the victims of the slaughter he was about to inflict.

Ted Olsson had driven up and parked behind the store twenty minutes before it was scheduled to open. He unlocked the back door, put on a clean pair of gloves, and pried open one of the 55-gallon drums full of Living Polymer. Transferring some of it to a bucket, he brought it over to one of the overhead applicators, which he had installed in a room he'd set up behind the main store space. Then he climbed a short stepladder and emptied the contents into the receptacle on top.

He repeated the process with the other applicator, which his sales clerk would operate. He hadn't bothered to train the guy; there was nothing to it: Just put on the mold, position the applicator, and press a button. The viscous material was fairly thick, so there was little danger that it would overflow—as long as you were paying attention. There hadn't been any problems with the teenager or the Karen's daughter... at least not until this morning's fiasco at the McMansion. The application process itself had gone flawlessly in both cases.

Ted estimated that, between the two applicators, he had enough Magic Mask material to create seven or eight masks. Then he would have to go back and refill the machines between customers.

Striding to the front of the store, he flicked on the lights and unlocked the front door.

The customers who'd been waiting impatiently outside began to push forward immediately, crowding one another and jostling for position. It was like Black Friday: No one respected anyone else's place in line; the point was to get to the front, and "who got there first" didn't enter into it.

"Please, please, stay back," Ted shouted through the glass. "I won't open this door until you all settle down."

But they either didn't hear him or didn't care. They just kept pushing forward, and no one noticed the grotesque figure stepping out from behind a high row of dense shrubbery on the opposite side of the street, leaves sticking to an oily black substance smeared on the front of his shirt as he brandished an AR-15.

He was halfway across the street when one of the teenagers in line, a 15-year-old boy wearing a Punisher T-shirt and a straight brimmed Yankees cap noticed him.

"What the fuck is that?" the wannabe Yankee said, transfixed by the hideous mask of grotesquery where a face should have been. But no one heard him amid the clamor to get into the store. The figure's face was so mutilated, the kid didn't even notice the gun at first, until finally, as though waking from a nightmare, he shouted, "The motherfucker's got a..."

Some of people in line heard him then, but by that time, it was too late. He didn't even have a chance to finish his sentence before the unspoken "gun" exploded in round after round directed into the heart of the crowd. Screams filled the air, and those farther from the front door broke and ran, their excitement forgotten in a haze of fear and panic. Those closer to the entrance weren't so fortunate. Blood splattered onto the glass from the store's display windows, which were shattering in the same instant, slicing into flesh as those nearest the door dove to the ground. But their instincts were no match for the speed of the bullets that were spraying everywhere, slicing through shirts, jeans, backpacks, skin, and muscle without distinction.

Bodies that had been pressed close together, jostling for

position in front of the door, fell on top of one another, dying or wounded. Some crawled away, grimacing toward the gunman for fear that he might notice them and target them again. But he seemed oblivious to their plight or even their presence. The crazed eyes that stared forward from two tar-black sockets in that hideous visage stared past or maybe through them, toward the interior of the store, where plate glass lay strewn among rubber clown faces and Predator helmets, and Richard Nixon faces covering featureless polystyrene foam heads, some of them knocked on their sides and others blasted to small white fragments.

Somehow, Ted Olsson, who had been waiting to open the door for his eager customers, had escaped serious injury. A bullet had grazed his shoulder, but he was more in shock than anything at the tableau of horror that was unfolding before him. When his eyes finally focused on the figure with the gun—and realized it was headed directly for him—he turned to make a run for the rear door, expecting to feel the agonizing sting of bullets tearing through the flesh of his back at any moment.

But the attacker had stopped firing, and Ted's mad dash was halted by the shards of glass strewn across the floor. Slipping on them, he lost his balance and scrambled to right himself, looking like nothing so much as a novice on ice skates flailing as he tried desperately not to fall. His desperation, however, couldn't save him from falling head-first onto the glass, which sliced into the palms of his hands as he reached out to brace himself.

Before he could get back on his feet, he felt two hands grab him by the ankles and begin pulling him. He managed to kick himself loose, and rolled over to start up at the figure looming over him.

He did not recognize T.J. Harrington—or what was left of

him trapped behind that distorted, festering remnant of a face. No one could have. And the creature that was only part T.J. was not inclined to introduce itself. It was more interested in salving the searing pain it was feeling inside that misshapen head by inflicting well-deserved pain on the man who had done this to him.

That pain started with slamming the butt of his AR-15 into the forehead of Ted Olsson, rendering him immediately unconscious and primed for what the monster had planned for him.

The creature dragged the now-limp body of the makeup artist-turned-murderer to the back of the store and deposited him in the middle of the room.

Ted Olsson was still unconscious when the monster kicked over the mostly full
55-gallon drum of Living Polymer. This action caused it to spill out onto the floor and flow inexorably, like the slimy gray counterpart of molten lava, toward the prone and motionless figure on the floor. Even as it reached him, beginning to cover the fingers on his left hand and climb slowly up his arm, the second drum was unsealed and pushed over, its contents more than doubling the liquid's volume and hastening its journey.

As the substance made contact with the skin of its target, it was released from its dormant state, gaining purpose in its newly awakened form and instinctively focusing on its objective. Like a living shroud, it crept across the surface of the Creepstore owner's body until it had enveloped every square inch of it, even crawling underneath and cradling his legs and back as it lifted them from the floor.

T.J. Harrington had his revenge, but he barely noticed.

Now that the last fragment of his human identity had fulfilled its sole remaining purpose, it surrendered to that portion of the parasite still buried deep inside his brain. With the human element at last subdued, that parasite began to expand again, reaching out with syrupy tendrils that supplanted brain cells and fused neural synapses.

The creature stared down at its kindred, now covering Ted Olsson—bubbling up as it swirled across the surface of him, languor giving way to a frenzy that seemed almost ravenous. A sudden sound distracted the creature as it stood there, and it turned toward the source of it, absently brushing off the leaves that clung to its shirt. They drifted down and landed on Olsson's foot.

The sound was coming from the front of the shop, so the creature moved toward the source of it, grasping at elusive recognition.

What was it?

Full comprehension came gradually to the parasite as it conquered and transformed T.J. Harrington's brain. It had absorbed enough of T.J.'s knowledge into its own incipient awareness to walk over to the phone, pick it up and press the little green icon to accept the call.

"Hello, Ted?"

The voice on the other end belonged to a human male, but its cadence was somehow familiar.

"No," the creature replied.

"Oh, good. It's you... It is you, isn't it?"

"Yes."

"Password?"

The creature racked its brain, struggling to arouse it fully, then intoned something that would have sounded like gibberish to any human listener. But the owner of the voice on the other end was not human.

It understood.

More words came to the creature now, as it began to remember its mission. "It... was... not... without challenge," it said slowly.

"But would you say it's a success? You have completely overcome the host organism?"

"Yes... But..."

"Did something go wrong?"

"Juveniles... are not... ideal hosts...," the creature said, becoming gradually more articulate. "Their genetic material is... unstable because they are not yet... mature. The juvenile subject... once assimilated... does not adequately... resemble... the outward human form. But I am confident that a stable host will provide no such obstacle... to our objective of seamlessly assimilating the entire population."

"Then I've succeeded in perfecting the transfer process—and in the nick of time, too. It's only a matter of days before I'll need to abandon this temporary host. We can begin mobilizing for mass transfer immediately. Inform the commander that he's clear to begin deploying our forces to reservoirs and other water-supply stations on a global scale. I estimate the time from deployment to complete conquest at approximately six Earth months, with exponential spread likely once our agents are in place to expedite further transfers."

"Yes, sir," the creature replied.

The voice on the other end laughed. "You haven't quite remembered everything yet," it said. "I'm not your superior officer. We're equal in rank."

"How should I address you?" the creature asked.

"For now, just call me Frasier."

In the back of Creepstore & More, the swirling, bubbling mass that was in the process of possessing and transforming Ted Olsson's body paused. Still more instinct than conscious thought, it shifted its focus, moving toward the dying leaves that stuck to the human's foot and covering it as well, fusing its own DNA with the leaves' genetic material as it continued to bond with the human's genes.

Knitting the two of them together.

As Olsson's body absorbed the alien substance, he began to look more human again. The viscous gray "Living Polymer" turned black—the sign that it was awakening—but the black tar seeped inside him, leaving the surface untouched...

Except for one thing...

The leaves and branches that had begun to sprout from the surface of his skin.

Sharon Marie Provost

Mischief Night

Tommy Brewster leaned against the brick school wall. He was waiting for his friend Wilder Robins, star pitcher for the high school baseball team, to get out of detention. Tommy had narrowly missed receiving detention, or even suspension, himself, but the teacher had looked up mere seconds after he punched Neal. However, she *had* caught Wilder spitting on him. A crowd of students had encircled the boys, but all of them were smart enough not to rat him out. None of them wanted to be his next victim—pulling himself off the ground with a shiner to show for his trouble.

What a day to get detention, man! It is Mischief Night... good ol' Halloween eve. How often do you get two nights in a row where pranks and vandalism are not only expected but largely tolerated? We have a lot to do to prepare.

Tommy's reverie was interrupted by the appearance of Principal Williams. "Why, may I ask, are you loitering on campus after school has ended for the day, Mr. Brewster? I am not aware of any sanctioned extracurricular activities or club meetings today."

"I am just waiting for Wilder to get out of detention, sir. We are stopping at the arcade on the way home from school."

"Get going then. I will inform Mr. Robins that he can meet you at the arcade."

Tommy scowled and began walking away. When he was off school property, he lifted his arm high into the air and flipped off the principal. "Asshole!" he yelled. He knew he would pay for that little infraction next week when he returned to school, but he didn't care as long as nothing else interfered with their plans for the next two nights.

Tommy waited for Wilder on the bus bench across the street. Fifteen minutes later, he finally saw him exit the school. When Wilder noticed him, he began laughing and shaking his head. "You are crazy, man. You really don't give a fuck, do you? Principal Williams was livid."

The two boys bumped their right shoulders together in greeting and then walked down the street to Tommy's parked car. They headed into town first and stopped at the Piggly Wiggly.

They had come up with quite a shopping list:

- 4 dozen eggs.
- 2 family packs of toilet paper.
- 2 cans of spray paint.

- 4 boxes of saran wrap.
- Brown paper lunch bags.
- 4 cans of shaving cream.
- A tube of fake blood.
- A baseball bat.
- 3 containers of table salt.
- A bag of sugar.
- 2 onions.
- Caramel apple wrap.
- A package of raw chicken livers.
- A box with two prepared candy apples.
- 4 cans of Silly String.
- A can of tuna.
- 4 envelopes of cherry Kool-Aid.

As they loaded all the supplies into the trunk, Wilder noticed a feral cat trap and a stuffed animal. "Hey, what is your sister's Petsies cat doing in here?" he asked.

"Oh, that! Just wait and see. I have a special surprise planned for old Mrs. Clarke tonight," Tommy replied with an evil grin.

Tommy opened the box of candy apples, and they each took one to eat on the drive. He placed the empty box back in his grocery bag, then they headed out of town on State Route 3 to stop at Major Spaulding's Fireworks Emporium. They spent nearly an hour comparing all the firecrackers to find the loudest, most powerful one available. They finally settled on 15 Wolverine M100 firecrackers, two canisters of Keystone Kannonballs, 10 Giant Smoke Grenades and five Two-Minute Smoke Screens. The greaser at the checkout counter was too meth'ed out to care, so he didn't even card them.

"We don't have to worry about that asshole remembering us if the cops ask," Wilder sneered.

"Fuck, that dude barely remembers English. It's not just his teeth that have rotted out of his head," Tommy laughed.

Tommy dropped Wilder off at his house. "I'll pick you up tonight about 7. Sound good?"

Wilder nodded and trotted up to the door. Tommy unrolled the passenger window and leaned over to call out, "Don't forget to fill a bucket with dog poop." Wilder lifted his hand to acknowledge him as he went inside. Tommy returned home and brought the bag with the onions, caramel apple wrap, the empty box, and Kool-Aid in with him. He stopped in the kitchen to grab a paring knife and two wood Shish Kabob skewers before heading up to his room.

"Dinner is at 5. That is in one hour, young man. Don't be ruining your appetite," his mom called out as he left the room.

Tommy didn't bother to acknowledge her admonishment. As he passed by his older sister Tina's room, he saw her digging through her closet, looking for an outfit for her date that evening. Tina was the kind of typical buxom blond bimbo all the jocks love.

"When is Braaaaaad picking you up?" he asked, drawing out his name in the way that drove her nuts.

"In an hour. Don't you even think about tying up that bathroom, asswipe. I am about to take a shower," she chided.

"I'll just be a minute," he replied as he dashed in, locking the door behind him.

Tina began banging on the door, as she screamed, "Tommy Alan Brewster, you shithead. I told you not to take the bathroom!" Her screaming and pounding covered the sound of him stepping into the tub to quickly unscrew the shower head and pour the cherry Kool-Aid packets into it. He wadded up the empty packets and shoved them back into his bag, flushed the toilet and exited—to his sister's surprise—in under two minutes.

Serves that bitch right. I am sure she will love her new hair color for her date tonight.

He proceeded into his bedroom, locking the door behind him, before turning on his electric guitar and drum-laden heavy metal music, cranking it to ear-splitting levels. He sat at his desk to prepare the "special snack" for the twins, Jason and Jaden, his 10-year-old younger brothers. The six-year age gap between his brothers and him did not lend itself to a close relationship. They were always frustrating him with their immaturity.

He used the paring knife to cut off the ends of the onions. He even prided himself on the way he shaped the ends of the onions to create the gentle slope characteristic of an apple. Then he shoved the Kabob sticks into the onions before carefully applying the caramel wraps. When he was done, he had two perfect special caramel "apples" for his brothers, which he placed in the empty box.

If only there was a way I could videotape their reaction when they each take a big bite.

The "apples" had taken a little longer to prepare than he had planned. He needed to hurry up and get out of there before the shit hit the fan with his sister. It wouldn't do for him to get grounded tonight... not that it would stop him from going out. He grabbed his keys, a dark black hoodie, his mask and the candy apples. He knocked on his brothers' door before entering and gave them the treat.

"Thanks, Tommy!" they exclaimed in unison.

"No problem, little dudes. Don't eat those before dinner and ruin your appetite. Mom will kill me."

Tommy ran down the stairs and called out to his mom: "Wilder invited me to dinner and to watch horror movies at his house all night, so I'm going over there. I'll see you in the morning."

She stammered, trying to blurt out a reason to stop him, but the door had already slammed shut. As he opened his car door and started to slip in, he heard his sister's bloodcurdling scream, followed by a banshee-like scream of "Tommy!" He closed the door and turned the key in one swift motion, his tires squealing briefly as he took off. Tommy drove over to the Shake Shack to get some dinner while he waited until 7 to pick up Wilder. His allowance savings had taken a big hit with his purchases at the Piggly Wiggly, but it was worth it. He ran into Sarah, his on-again, off-again girlfriend, and they made out in the back of the parking lot until she had to meet her friends at the movie theater. He dropped her off at the theater before making one quick stop on his way to Wilder's house.

Parking down the block from the Clarke home, he got into the trunk and removed the feral cat trap and the can of tuna. Then he opened the tuna and placed it in the back of the trap. As he was walking toward the house, Mr. Clarke came out. He ducked behind the neighbor's hedge and hid until the man had left.

On the way down to his car, he heard Mr. Clarke call out to his wife: "I'll be home around 9, darling, as soon as the Elks meeting ends."

As soon as Mr. Clarke turned off the block, Tommy continued to the Clarke property and set the trap in the hedges, choosing the corner of the yard where Mrs. Clarke's cat liked to hang out. He looked around to make sure he hadn't been seen and then jogged back to the car to go pick up his friend.

Wilder was standing at the edge of his open garage waiting for him, a bucket sitting at his feet. He grabbed the bucket and sprinted down to the car, where Tommy popped the trunk so he could stow the bucket.

"Your mom thinks you are staying at my mouse, right?" Tommy asked him as he jumped in the car.

"Sure does. And your mom thinks you are staying here. Genius plan, bro. As long as we don't get caught tonight, we are going to have an epic night."

"Mischief Night 2024!" they both howled, their heads hanging out the window as they blazed down the highway into town.

"I thought we could hit a few houses on the other side of town first. Then, we can go to the Clarkes' house before Mr. Clarke gets home from the Elks meeting at 9," Tommy told Wilder, who nodded eagerly.

The two boys spent the next hour targeting the homes of some of their classmates. They stopped at Neal's house first with the express intention of vandalizing it. When they had targeted him earlier at school, he had been boasting about how his parents had rented out one of the theaters in town to throw him a huge All Hallows' Eve birthday party. Fortunately for them, that meant many homes would be unattended until around midnight.

Wilder grabbed the containers of salt and began to spell out "Dickhead" in large letters across the entire front lawn. By the time Neal and his parents saw it the next morning, those letters would be burned into the lawn.

Tommy grabbed rolls of toilet paper and began intricately TP'ing the house, with streamers running from one tree to the next. It almost appeared as if the yard had been decorated for the party to occur there, instead of at the theater. It would be a nightmare trying to remove all that after the sprinklers came on at midnight.

The two boys used two entire cartons of eggs to cover the front of the house.

"So much for that new paint job they had done this summer. Right, bro?" Wilder asked Tommy.

Tommy doubled over with laughter as he grabbed a can of bright pink spray paint, decorating the garage door with a crude drawing of a penis.

For the *coup de grâce*, the boys drew little smiley faces in shaving cream all over the brand-new Mustang Neal had received for his birthday. They gave the designs some time to dry before wrapping the entire car from front to back in multiple tight layers of saran wrap. It would take forever to unwrap the car before they found the permanent smiley faces that would have eaten into the paint by then.

As they drove over to the Clarkes' home, they stopped at other homes along the way to engage in less elaborate acts of vandalism. They ding-dong-ditched several homes, leaving flaming surprises for them on the porch. They couldn't stop laughing every time someone stomped on the lit bags to put out the flames and came up with a foot covered in shit. They even took turns driving, so each of them could use the baseball bat to knock mailboxes off their poles. They used the Silly String to cover the thorny bushes the Rogers family had planted to create an impenetrable privacy barrier on their front lawn. The salt and spray paint were used repeatedly to create more rude images or words to deface more homes.

They targeted cars at random along the route with eggs and shaving cream to ruin the paint jobs. When they spotted older cars without locking gas caps, they stopped to pour sugar into their tanks.

In the span of an hour and a half, they left many thousands of dollars of damage in their wake.

As they pulled up at the Clarke home on the corner, Tommy noticed that almost the entire street was black. Porch lights illuminated a few homes at the far end, but they didn't cast light far enough down the street to expose the boys.

They parked at the neighbor's house and walked over. Tommy crept into the yard to check the trap and returned smiling with a full cage. Mrs. Clarke's cat had taken the bait. He placed the trap with the cat in the trunk, so it wouldn't be seen.

"So what's this big plan of yours?" Wilder asked. "And what's your beef with Mrs. Clarke anyhow? She seems like such a nice old lady."

"That old bitch ratted me out to my mom last year. I was walking by here and stopped to pet her cat. I was scratching her back near her tail when she turned and raked me with her claws. Apparently, she doesn't like to be scratched there. How could I know that, and what cat doesn't anyway? Anyhow, I was bleeding from those deep claw marks, and it ruined my brand-new Green Day concert T-shirt. I was angry, so I kicked the cat. My foot barely grazed her side, and she took off running. Mrs. Clarke was just coming out the door and saw me. I guess, Petunia didn't return for two days. Mrs. Clarke called my mom and threatened to turn me in for animal cruelty."

"That's crazy, dude. Maybe she should learn to control her crazy cat."

"That's what I said. Instead, I was told I shouldn't touch somebody else's pet without permission. That's stupid when the animal is roaming around free unattended. It wasn't even in her yard at the time."

"That's fucked up. So, what are we doing to this old bitch then? Ummm... we aren't hurting the cat though, are we? I mean—it is evil and all—but I'm not down with hurting animals."

"The cat will be fine in the trunk for a few minutes. Once we're done, we can set her free again. But... we are going to make Mrs. Clarke think we killed her precious Petunia. Plus, a little vandalism is always fun."

"Awesome! I will go work on that while you stage the scene for Petunia."

Wilder began spray-painting "Old bitch" on the side of her house while Tommy returned to the trunk to prepare the prop. Tina had been heartbroken last year when the cat she'd had her whole life died. Their mother had bought her one of those Petsies: hyper-realistic stuffed animals made to look like your pet. Petunia looked very similar, so this would work perfectly.

He used his pocketknife to slash the side of the stuffed animal and pushed the stuffing deep inside. Then he opened the container of chicken livers and jammed some inside— leaving enough poking out that it looked like you could see the "cat's" internal organs—and covered the whole area with fake blood.

He carried the toy up and placed it on the porch, where Mrs. Clarke would see it as soon as she opened the screen and squeezed a pool of fake blood onto the concrete in front of the wound. Then he went around to the side of the house to see how Wilder was doing.

Wilder was a genius. Everyone in town knew about Mr.

Clarke's obsession with keeping a lush, vibrant green lawn, free of any weeds. Wilder had salted large spots throughout the lawn so it would soon sport many dead yellow patches. His prize-winning rose bushes were covered in silly string and toilet paper. Mr. Clarke would lose his mind when he saw what had been done.

Wilder went to the car to grab the supplies that Tommy requested and then went to the hedgerow to hide, while Tommy ran up to ding-dong-ditch the house, thereby summoning Mrs. Clarke.

Tommy joined him, and they waited in breathless anticipation.

Mrs. Clarke opened the door and looked around confused. She opened the screen to peer onto the porch, and that's when she saw the cat. "Pe... Petunia, my dear. Are you okay?" She walked out onto the step and began to shake.

Tommy flicked the lighter and lit the fuses when Mrs. Clarke grabbed the porch railing to steady herself as she began to try to crouch, tears dripping from her face. "Oh, Petunia, who hurt you, my baby?" she wailed. Her attention was so focused on the "dead" stuffed cat that she never noticed the two lit Keystone Kannonballs rolling her way. They exploded with an ear-piercing cluster of bangs that sounded like machine gun fire.

Mrs. Clarke screamed and lost her hold on the railing, falling to her knees with a sickening crunch. She yelped in pain and then wailed when her hand settled in the pool of blood stopping her forward momentum, her face only inches away from the carnage. She pushed herself up and then gasped, grabbing her chest. The two boys' cackles could be heard down the street.

Tommy heard a car approaching down the block and looked down at his watch. "Shit!" he exclaimed. "That is probably Mr. Clarke returning home. We need to get out of here."

The two boys ran through the hedge and over to the car parked next door. They jumped in and peeled out, stopping a couple of streets away for a moment to retrieve the cat from the trunk and release it.

Mr. Clarke turned the corner and saw two boys running from his house.

That's the Brewster boy and his friend. What were those two troublemakers doing here?

He made a quick turn into his driveway, but the boys' car was already pulling away, tires screeching. He ran around the hedgerow and opened the front gate, catching sight of his wife lying still on the porch.

"Beatrice!" he screamed as he ran towards her.

She was pale and clammy when he touched her, and her breathing was shallow.

Mr. Clarke ran inside to the kitchen phone mounted on the wall by the back door and called 911. He stretched the cord until it nearly pulled the phone off the wall as he returned to his wife's side. The dispatcher told him to cover her with a blanket while they waited for the ambulance to arrive. He held her hand and talked to her, expressing his undying love and how much he needed her.

The paramedics arrived 5 minutes later and began to work on Mrs. Clarke, one checking her vitals as the other locked the gurney in place. She was placed on the gurney and wheeled down to the ambulance. Mr. Clarke was informed he would not be allowed in the ambulance, so he ran to lock up the house and returned to his car.

When he arrived at the hospital, he was told that a doctor would be out to talk to him when his wife was stabilized. He sat in the waiting room, wringing his hands, as he pondered what the boys had been doing at his house and how that related to his wife's current state.

About an hour later, a solemn doctor approached him. "Mr. Clarke?"

"Yes, that's me. Wally, if you don't mind?"

"Yes, of course. Wally, your wife is in critical condition. She had a massive heart attack. She is very weak at the moment, and we are fighting to maintain her vitals. She is on a ventilator. The next few hours are critical."

"My Beatrice is a very strong woman. I have no doubt she will be fine. Can I see her?"

"Yes, sir. I think you should be with her. I want to warn you that she is hooked up to a lot of equipment by a lot of wires and tubes."

"I don't care. Nothing could change the beauty of my Beatrice. I need to hold her hand and let her know I am here."

"Yes, sir."

"Wally."

"Yes, Wally. If you will just follow me back."

The doctor brought Wally back to the room Mrs. Clarke had just been assigned in the intensive care unit. He asked the nurse to bring in one of the reclining chairs so that Wally could stay the night with his wife. While he waited, he carefully perched on the edge of the bed, as he contemplated which hand to hold: one had an I.V. placed, while the other had the pulse oximeter clamped on her index finger. He settled for sliding his hand under her left hand and wrapping his fingers around hers, caressing her ring finger.

The nurse brought in the recliner and offered him some

coffee, which he accepted graciously.

"Sweet Bea, I'm so sorry I left you tonight. I should've skipped that stupid Elks meeting. Most of the members didn't even come. They were all either at that party or stayed home with their families. What happened, baby? Did those boys do something to hurt you? I swear I'll make them pay if they did anything to you!"

Wally caressed her forehead as he watched her serene face for any sign of waking. He spent the next hour whispering sweet nothings and talking to her about the trip they had planned in the spring. As the hour grew late, he laid his head on the bed to rest for a spell, so he would be coherent when she awoke later.

At 5:23 a.m., Wally awoke to the sounds of multiple alarms blaring around him. The doctor and several nurses bounded into the room. A nursing assistant grabbed his arm, trying to lead him away. "What is happening? Is my wife going to be okay?" he asked her as he tried to pull away, back toward her bedside.

"Sir, you must follow me," the nursing assistant said. "They need you out of the way while they work on her. You can wait in this room just down the hall. Someone will be in as soon as they can to update you."

She led him to a chair in the intensive care waiting room.

Wally leaned forward, his head in his hands, sobbing as he waited for news. He didn't even believe in God, but he wondered if he should try to pray—not that he knew what that entailed.

Twenty minutes later, the doctor entered the room looking grim.

He sat down next to Wally and placed his hand on his arm.

"Wally, I am very sorry to tell you that your wife, Beatrice, has passed away. We did everything we could to bring her back. Her heart was just too damaged and her body too weak to fight anymore. Is there somebody I can call for you?"

"No, there is no one. I need to go home."

"Sir... I mean Wally. Why don't you take some time? This has all been a great shock to you. There is no hurry for you to leave."

"I need to get home now. She would want me to take care of Petunia. That's her cat. Thank you, doctor, for all you did," he said, as he held his hand out to shake the doctor's. Then he turned and began the slow walk down to the car. The young nursing assistant came rushing up to him in the lobby, a bag in her hand.

"Your wife's... belongings," she stammered as her eyes brimmed with tears.

"Thank you, dear," he replied, grabbing the bag before proceeding out the door and to the car.

He drove home in a daze. Anger coursed through his body as he wondered what those boys had done, but he felt numb at the same time. He couldn't imagine life without the love of his life by his side. As he pulled into the driveway, he vowed to set things right... whatever that might mean.

He entered through the front gate again and immediately noticed the bloody spot, on the porch next to what looked like Petunia, that he had been oblivious to last night. As he got closer, he realized it was only a stuffed animal.

Those motherfuckers! They made Bea think her precious cat had been brutally slain.

As he reached the porch, he noticed an odor... like some chemical or burning wires. He looked around the porch and noticed a small, scorched area on the lawn. He walked over and found two large, expended firecrackers.

They must have set those off just as she bent down to check on Petunia and scared the Bejesus out of her. Those sadistic assholes! No concern for others. I am going to make them pay. They are going to learn what it is to be scared.

"Hey there, Mr. Clarke. I see you were the target of some vandalism last night," a voice said from behind Wally.

He turned to see his next-door neighbor, Clyde, standing on the sidewalk and pointing toward the side of his house. He walked over and was startled to see the offensive words spray-painted on the side of his house. His blood boiled at the thought of anyone calling his sweet bride an old bitch. And the roses that he'd planted for Bea were covered with that awful Silly String and toilet paper. He didn't know how he could ever remove all that without damaging the plants that had brought her such pleasure over the years.

"I noticed a car parked out in front of my house last night, but I don't know who it was or if it was even related," Clyde said.

Wally only grunted.

Clyde continued, a nervous tone in his voice, "I saw an ambulance outside last night. Was that at your house? Are you and Bea okay?"

Wally turned to Clyde, tears sliding down his face as he whispered, "She's gone."

"Oh, man, Mr. Clarke. I am so sorry," Clyde said in a mournful tone. "If there is anything I can do for you, please let me know. She was such a dear lady. She will be sorely missed around here."

Wally nodded and turned away.

"Don't worry about those rose bushes. I know how much they meant to Bea. My son and I will come over later this morning and remove that mess. I will let you go, Mr. Clarke."

Wally was too lost in thought to respond. The only words going through his mind were revenge... retribution... vengeance... retaliation... blood for blood... eye for an eye... pain... death.

Tommy and Wilder laughed like hyenas as they drove out of the neighborhood. The cat had taken off like a bat out of hell.

"Who knows if that cat will ever come back!" Wilder crowed.

"Good riddance!" Tommy replied.

"It's getting late, but I think it is time for some more hardcore pranks," Wilder suggested.

"You read my mind."

Tommy pulled up next door to Tate Thibeault's house. Tate had come home from Vietnam with PTSD. All the kids at school knew that and loved to make loud noises to startle the school janitor whenever possible.

Tate lived in a ramshackle house on the edge of town, which wasn't fenced in like the homes in the nicer neighborhoods. The boys surrounded the house with the Wolverine M100s and threw out several Giant Smoke Grenades in the front to provide cover. Then they ran around, lighting the long fuses before taking shelter behind the copse of birch on the corner of his lot. When the firecrackers started going off seconds later, it sounded like they were in a war zone under heavy machine gun fire.

Tate's door was thrown open and bounced off the wall. The boys had picked a vantage point to the side, where they could see him crouching around the corner, an AR-15 in his hands. Tate was trying to see through the thick smoke. Tommy lit two more fuses and jumped up, tossing the smoke grenade at Tate's feet before rolling one of the Keystone Kannonballs up to the front steps. The boys heard Tate's panicked scream as he saw the grenade at his feet—all sense of reason lost upon seeing the shape of it, while he ignored the smoke issuing forth from it.

The boys used the distraction to run back to the car. Their raucous laughter was covered by the rat-a-tat-tat of the firecracker going off as Tate began screaming in terror, lost in a panic as visions of the battlefield filled his thoughts.

"Fuck, man! That was intense. You up for one more?" Wilder asked, shaking with excitement.

"Hell yes!"

Wilder directed him to the home of his deadbeat father. They pulled up around the corner and walked over.

"Just as I expected: The asshole gets so drunk by 4 p.m. that he passes out, forgetting to lock up the house or close the garage."

"What's the plan, Wildman?"

"Fill up one of those sacks with dog poop for me and meet me in the garage."

Wilder grabbed three of the Two-Minute Smoke Screens and ran over to the garage. When Tommy arrived a short time later, he saw that two had been set up near the entrance and one in the middle, toward the back of the garage. Wilder was Googling something on his phone.

"Now what?" Tommy asked.

"You light that bag of poop and the smoke screen next to it. I'll get the two at the front. Then run toward the corner when I give the signal."

"What signal?"

Tommy learned the answer seconds later when the sound of a fire alarm started blaring from Wilder's phone. Wilder stood there long enough for a light to come on before running to the bushes on the corner, right behind Tommy. They peeked over the top and saw Wilder's father stumble out the front door barefoot; then he saw the smoke billowing out of the garage and ran toward it.

Mr. Robins peered into the garage and must have seen the glow from the flaming bag because he began shouting, "Fire!" over and over, but none of his neighbors responded. He ran into the garage, and a moment later, the boys heard him shriek in pain. When he came limping out a few seconds later, they realized he must have tried to stomp out of the fire, forgetting he was shoeless, He looked down at his foot and, realizing it was covered in shit, he began to scream obscenities, "Fucking little cowards! You don't even have the guts to stick around and watch your little prank. I will find out who you are and make you little shits pay! Motherfuckers!"

Mr. Robins limped over to the faucet to turn it on, then out walked out onto the lawn where the hose was lying to wash the dog shit off his foot—which was bright red but didn't appear too badly burned. The boys stifled their laughter as they walked in a crouch until they were out of sight around the corner. They jumped into Tommy's car and decided to sleep at the rest stop out on State Route 3 for the rest of the night.

"I think Mischief Night 2024 was a resounding success, don't you, Wilder?"

"Hell yeah! Tomorrow the streets will be busy with all the little brats out getting candy. I think we will have to stick to the tamer pranks to be on the safe side."

"True. We still have plenty of toilet paper, eggs and shaving cream. We can use the last of the firecrackers and smoke bombs to scare kids who are out on their own. Tonight was epic though!"

The two boys fell asleep quickly, exhausted from the night's activities.

Wally threw away the used firecrackers and stuffed cat before spraying down his front porch. Around 10 a.m., he saw Petunia approaching the house cautiously. He went into the kitchen and opened a can of cat food. He then sat on the corner of the porch and offered it to her. Eventually, she wandered over and began to eat.

Once she was finished, she jumped in his lap purring, and he sat there petting her, while he contemplated his revenge plan. Wally knew he was in good shape for his age at 79, but he was going to be taking on two strapping young boys of 16.

Who will help me no questions asked? Who can I trust to not turn me in?

Suddenly, he knew just the friend who would fit the bill. He picked up Petunia and carried her into the house to keep her safe, then he retrieved his keys from the counter and locked up the house before heading out to the car.

This was a conversation that needed to be held in person.

Ten minutes later, Wally pulled up in front of Tate Thibeault's house. Tate was the younger brother of Wally's childhood best friend, Billy. Both Thibeault boys had fought in the Vietnam War, but only Tate had come home.

Tate had never been the same: Between the PTSD and his drinking and drug use, he had become a hard man. He spent most of his time locked in his home alone... that is, what time wasn't spent in lockup instead. Tate was not one to be overly concerned with the legality of his actions at any given moment. That, along with his loyalty to Wally, made him the perfect candidate for this mission.

Wally walked up to Tate's door and knocked with the same secret knock the three boys had used in childhood. He noticed what appeared to be a white plastic grenade lying on the porch. He heard some shuffling inside, but Tate did not open the door. Instead, he heard a strained voice: "I have a loaded gun. Get out of here now! No trespassers."

Wally felt deflated. *Another fucking nervous breakdown now of all fucking times!*

"Tate, it's me, Wally. Are you okay?"

"Wally? Is that really you?"

"I am going to come in now. Is that okay?" Wally asked as he slowly turned the knob. He stood back and gave the door a push to let Tate see it was him standing at the door.

"Oh, thank God!" Tate cried as he rushed Wally, nearly knocking him over with the force of his bear hug.

"What happened, Tate?"

"It was terrible. I was attacked last night! There was so much smoke and gunfire. They even threw a grenade at me, but it didn't go off."

Wally reached down and picked up the grenade slowly. "Is this what you're talking about?"

"Oh my God! Don't touch it!"

"Calm down, Tate! This is just a firework... a smoke bomb. Give me a minute to look around here." Wally walked around the property and found numerous expended firecrackers and smoke bombs.

Those little bastards were here last night, too, torturing an American hero!

He returned to the door with what he had collected and asked Tate if he could come in to talk.

Tate stepped back and waved him over to the dirty, threadbare couch.

Wally laid the pile of charred fireworks on the coffee table. "This is what I came to talk to you about. There were two young boys out last night playing pranks and torturing people, all over town apparently. They were at my house when dear Bea was there alone. They made her think that they had killed her cat, Petunia. Then they set off firecrackers, just like this, when she was checking on her." Wally's eyes began to fill with tears as he sniffled. "They killed her, Tate! She had a heart attack, and they couldn't save her. Those rat bastards need to pay! Look at what they did to you and my sweet Beatrice."

Tate began to sob uncontrollably. "Not Beatrice! Tell me they didn't kill her. She takes care of me. She is the only one in this town, besides you, that gives a damn about me. When I have an episode, she brings me food and cleans the house. It can't be true. Please tell me that."

"I can't. She is gone. My sweet girl is gone. I came to ask you something. I need your help."

"Anything, Wally. You know that."

"Really it's for Bea."

"I will do anything you ask."

"Let's get them... tonight. I have no doubt those troublemakers will be back out for Halloween. Last night was just a warmup—what do they call it?—Mischief Night or some such shit. You were a hero once. Let's be heroes for Bea. They need to pay for what they did, and we cannot let them hurt anyone else."

"I'm up for anything. What do you have in mind?"

The two men spent the next hour formulating their plan. Tate promised to gather the supplies they would need to handle the boys. He told Wally to come by at 6 p.m., and they would take Tate's van out that night. Wally ran into town to pick up some dinner for the two of them later, as well as a few essentials for the evening's coming attraction. As he drove through town, he could see the boys' path of destruction, from battered mailboxes to other homes covered in toilet paper or Silly String; some cars covered in shaving cream, others fully encased in a saran wrap tomb. The vandalism was the talk of the town.

As Wally exited the store, he was surprised to see Tommy standing in the parking lot talking on his cell phone. He was careful not to make eye contact as he slowly walked by. Even though he could only hear one side of the conversation, it was clear that Tommy planned to meet up with his friend at the park by his house at 7 p.m. The park was in the poor section of town, so it had fallen into disrepair years ago. It rarely had any visitors, and the only people who ever went there were up to no good.

It would be the perfect location to grab the boys.

Tommy and Wilder had awoken earlier that day as the first rays of sunlight streamed into the car. Tommy looked at his muted cell phone and saw he had missed multiple calls from his mother overnight. He listened to the voicemails and was relieved to find that she was just chastising him for his pranks on his brothers and sister. Wilder had no calls from his parents, so the boys felt confident that they had not been caught in their lie or for causing any trouble in town overnight.

Tommy called his mother back, and Wilder fought to hold

back laughter as he could hear Tommy's mother yelling from across the car. She told Tommy he had to come home immediately, and that he was grounded for the weekend. Tommy pleaded with her to delay his punishment until after Halloween because he and Wilder had tickets for the horror movie marathon at the theater.

After much pleading and many false promises, he managed to gain permission to be out until 12:30. However, he had to go home for the rest of the afternoon and do chores as punishment.

Tommy drove Wilder home and dropped him off.

Tommy spent the rest of the day cleaning the entire house after he gave his brothers and sister a formal apology. His mother did send him to the store to pick up some milk around midafternoon, and he stopped in the parking lot to call Wilder, updating him on his plans.

"Everything's set," he said. "Meet me at Jubilee Park at 7."

At 6:50 p.m., he was allowed to leave to meet Wilder. His mother reminded him of his strict 12:30 a.m. curfew, warning him he would be grounded until next year if he wasn't home on time.

When he got to the park, Wilder was nowhere to be seen. The only other vehicle around was an old beat-up white van in the back corner of the lot.

Tommy waited five minutes for Wilder before calling him, but there was no answer. A minute later, he received a text from him, "Sorry. I found some really cool shit when I cut through the back of the park on my way over. You gotta see it! I'm in the woods behind the Dumpster in back."

Tommy was annoyed and in a hurry, so he drove over to the back of the lot and parked a couple of spots down from the van. He didn't see anyone around, including Wilder. He started walking toward the Dumpster calling out to Wilder.

As he skirted around the side of the van, the door slid open with a whoosh. He saw a flash of movement out of the corner of his eye before he felt an arm wrap around his neck, choking him.

Then everything went black.

Tommy heard whispered voices as his eyelids fluttered. His head pounded in time to his heartbeat. At first, everything was blurry but slowly the scene before him swam into focus. As he blinked, his tears washed away the blood that had been obscuring his vision.

"Well, well, well, you finally decided to join us!" a voice off to side called out.

Tommy tried to turn his head toward the sound, but his head had been taped to the high-backed wood chair in which he was sitting. He tried to move his arms and legs but found them strapped to the arms and legs of the chair as well. He could see that he was in an old wood building, but he didn't know where. He heard a moan to his right and strained to use his peripheral vision to see what was happening.

"Wilder, is that you?" he asked.

He heard a mumbled, "Yes."

"And now we have two. Let's get this party started, boys, shall we?" came the voice again. It sounded familiar, but his head hurt too much to identify it.

Then Tate Thibeault came into view as he walked past Tommy and over to his side.

Tommy heard a loud scraping sound as Tate dragged Wilder's chair across the floor, placing it in front of him so the two boys were facing each other. Tommy knew the voice had come from a second person, that as yet had not come into view.

"Thank you, Tate. I think we are ready to begin then." Wally Clarke walked up to stand between the two boys. "Welcome," he said. "I think you both know why you're here."

The two boys tried to shake their heads no, but they couldn't move.

"Use your words, boys," Mr. Clarke told them.

"No, sir," Wilder said, as Tommy retorted, "I don't have a fucking clue! You better let us go now, or you will fucking regret the day you met me."

"Oh, I do already, Tommy. I wish you had never been born. By the time we are done tonight, you will wish that, too."

Tommy scoffed, "Oooh... I'm so scared!"

"You should be. Since you want to play dumb, I will tell you why you are here. I saw you! Last night, I saw you two running away from my house... from my beloved wife. She had a heart attack because of you, and you just left her lying there. She died last night."

Tommy tried to keep a cool look on his face, while Wilder crumbled. "I'm so sorry, Mr. Clarke. We never meant to hurt her..."

"Shut the fuck up!" Tommy bellowed.

Wilder continued, unfazed: "We were just playing a prank to pay her back for what she did to Tommy. We didn't hurt the cat... not really. We let her go a few blocks away. We never thought Mrs. Clarke would get hurt."

Tate came forward and screamed in their faces. "She's not hurt. She's dead!"

Mr. Clarke remained eerily calm throughout this entire exchange. "Turnabout is fair play they say. So, now we are going to see how much the two of you enjoy your little pranks. You see, Tate here got into your trunk, Tommy, and collected your little bag of tricks. What shall we try first? Any requests?"

Tate came forward with a container of salt. "Let's see how that salt burns you." He opened a bottle of water in his other hand and poured a large amount of salt inside before shaking it vigorously. Then, he passed the bottle to Wally. As Wally poured half of the bottle into Wilder's eyes, Tate poured salt into Tommy's mouth and held it closed. Wilder screamed in pain and fought to free his arms to wipe his eyes. His eyes turned bright red, and tears streamed from them.

Tommy coughed and sputtered, trying to spit out the mouthful of salt. Tate reached up and pinched his nostrils shut until Tommy was forced to swallow. Tate let go of his face and backed up just in time, before Tommy projectile vomited across himself and Tate. As he continued to retch long after emptying the contents of his stomach, Wally and Tate switched places to trade punishments.

Tommy screamed until he was hoarse when the salt solution was poured into his eyes. Wilder pleaded for mercy as Tate approached him with the container of salt. "You showed no mercy to that angel Bea, " Tate growled as he filled Wilder's mouth. Wilder's crimson eyes bulged as he vomited into his mouth. Tate refused to let go until Wilder began to choke, grainy bile running from his nose.

When Tate released his jaw, Wilder spewed vomit onto Tommy's face, as he choked and gasped for air.

"So, boys, did you enjoy that little prank as much as we did?" Wally asked as he appeared between them again. "I think you will enjoy this one a lot, Wilder. I mean after all, the two of you sure seemed to last night... I saw at least 10 homes with destroyed mailboxes on my way into town this morning."

"What about Tommy?" Wilder whined. "He knocked mailboxes off, too."

"Don't you worry about him. I have something special for him... another favorite of yours. Tate was the recipient of some of that fun last night."

Wally walked away and returned with the baseball bat in hand. He waved the bat back and forth... setting his aim for Wilder's right shoulder, then swinging it back past his shoulder as he prepared to deliver the blow with maximum force.

"Please, not my right shoulder!" Wilder pleaded. "That's my pitching arm."

Wally brought the bat forward like he was swinging for the fences and laughed as it connected hard with Wilder's shoulder, shattering the point of his clavicle and fracturing his humerus. Wilder shrieked, then passed out from the pain.

Wally looked back, shrugging his shoulders at Tommy. "No sense holding back," he said. "His pitching days would have been over anyway after we got through with him."

Even strapped to the chair, the shoulder hung limply at his side.

Tate approached from the other side, one hand behind his back and a wide smile on his face. His other hand was looped through a large roll of duct tape. "I guess it is your turn then." He pulled out one of the Keystone Kannonballs and held it up for Tommy to see.

Tate turned to Wally. "I am going to cut his arms free. I will keep him under control if you can place the firecracker for me."

"My pleasure, Tate."

Tate pulled his combat knife from the sheath at his side to cut the tape that held both wrists. Tommy began to struggle. Tate punched him on the side of his head. "I wouldn't recommend you continue that."

Tommy remained still as Tate guided his hands together so

Wally could place the Kannonball between his cupped hands. Wally placed two large pieces of duct tape across his hands to hold it in place.

Tate picked up the roll of tape that Wally had set down. "Oh, that just won't do. You see, I worked with explosives back in my military days. An explosive device detonated in an enclosed space will have a much more devastating impact than if that same device was detonated in the open. We need to bury that motherfucker in tape, leaving only the fuse exposed."

Tate began to wrap Tommy's entire hands and the firecracker in tape. When he was done, he asked, "Are you as excited as I am about this? I know how much you enjoyed tormenting me last night. Well here goes."

Tate lit the fuse, and both men disappeared from view.

Tommy heard the sound of a door closing behind them. He screamed for help, hoping they would have mercy on him, as he began to hyperventilate. As the fuse neared its end, he closed his eyes. Even muffled by the tape, the rat-a-tat-tat sound of the firecracker was still deafening. That first explosion blew the tape wide open, chunks of flesh and bone pelting the still unconscious Wilder. As more explosions followed, Wilder's face and body was spattered with blood.

Tommy screamed incoherently until he lost his voice as he looked down at the bloody stumps that were once his hands. Blood poured from them and ran down his legs in rivers of dark red. Wally and Tate re-entered the room when the blasts stopped, with bandaging supplies in their hands.

Tate looked at Tommy, a serene look on his face that he hadn't had in years. "I used to help the medics back in the day," he said. "We will get that bleeding stopped here in just a moment."

Tate and Wally worked together to apply tourniquets until

they could wrap the stumps of Tommy's forearms with pressure bandages. "We can't have you bleeding out now. We aren't done... yet."

After he applied the bandages, Tate turned to Wilder and held smelling salts under his nose.

Wilder awoke with a start and began to whimper.

Wally pulled up a chair to sit beside the two boys. "Well boys, we are just about done. I hope you enjoyed yourselves last night half as much as we have tonight. We just have one more prank left for both of you. I must admit I am getting a wee bit tired. I had a long night at the hospital and, frankly, all of this has been quite taxing. I think we should get on with it."

Tommy broke down, the cool facade he had worked so hard to maintain now utterly shattered. "Please, let us go. We learned our lesson. We will repay everyone whose property we damaged. We are both freaks now with permanent injuries. Isn't that enough?"

"And just how do you repay Mr. Clarke for the loss of his wife?" Tate asked with a sneer.

Wally stood up and replied, "With blood... with your lives!"

Tate pulled the boys' chairs farther apart so he and Wally would have room to work, as Wally dropped a stack of saran wrap boxes in front of Wilder's chair. The two men started at his feet and painstakingly wrapped his entire body in multiple layers of saran wrap, leaving only his head exposed. The layers were so tight that he strained to breathe, unable to expand his chest to capacity.

Tate tucked the roll between his neck and shoulder and moved over to help Wally with Tommy.

When both boys were fully secured, Wally retrieved two cans of gasoline and set them down beside their captives. The two men taped Tommy's forearms to the chair, then applied extra straps around his legs, chest and abdomen to be sure he could not free himself. Wally poured a pool of gasoline under his chair first; then the two men each used a can to dowse his entire body until he was dripping wet.

Wally stood between the two boys to make his final pronouncement as Tate began to wrap Wilder's face and head in saran wrap. "Wilder, at the store today I heard about your trouble at school yesterday with Neal. I also heard that his home and car were targeted last night. I'm sure you enjoyed your little act of revenge. I hope you will enjoy your little prank just as much in the hereafter. And as for you, Tommy, I heard about the flaming bags of shit you left at people's doors. You could have started a fire and killed someone. One person even got burned. Well, you can burn in hell, you little shit!"

With his final word, Wally struck a match and threw it into the pool of gasoline, as Tate wrapped the final layers around Wilder's nose and mouth. The two men stood there watching Wilder struggle to breathe and flail in his saran wrap cocoon until his body stilled. Tommy twitched and wailed until Wally could no longer stand it. He opened the gas can and splashed the last dregs of gasoline into his face, watching the fire race into his open maw when he inhaled the flammable fumes.

Silencing him forever.

Tate and Wally collected any items where they might have left their fingerprints and walked out the door. They waited in the van until fire had completely engulfed the building.

"I've built up quite an appetite," Tate declared. "What do you say we go to Bea's favorite restaurant and have a banana split in her honor?".

"I can't think of a better way to celebrate her life," Wally sniffled.

Note: Mischief Night, the night before Halloween, is a traditional time for youths to engage in pranks, vandalism, and mayhem. Also known as Devil's Night and Cabbage Night (for the practice of throwing rotting cabbage around), it is most common in the Northeast, but is also practiced elsewhere in the U.S. as well as in Canada and the U.K.

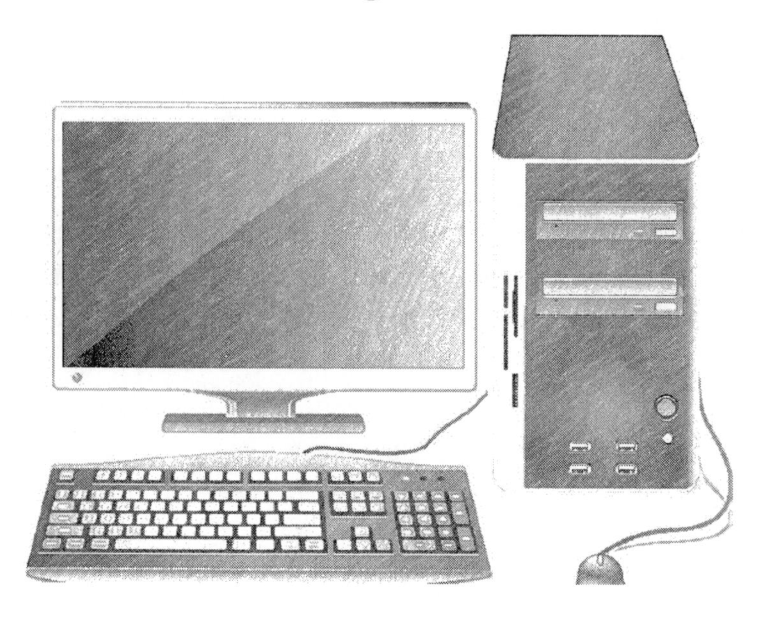

Stephen H. Provost

Three Simple Rules

Adopted children aren't all the same. Far from it. They come from a variety of backgrounds and, if they're older, bring with them memories—some traumatic—from their formative years. Some have been shuttled from foster home to foster home by temporary parents, some of whom have good intentions, while others are just in it to make a buck.

It's rare for older children to be adopted, especially once they hit their teens, and even more so if they're siblings who don't want to be split up. Dylan and April were just such a pair. Their parents had been brutally murdered when he was 10 and she was 8, and they'd been through a series of foster placements for the next five years until they finally hit the jackpot: adopted parents who actually wanted them.

Dr. Jonathan and Mrs. Benicia Thibault were the perfect couple: They'd been married for 15 years and had a stable home supported by a sizeable income. There was no doubt they weren't in it for the stipend the state offered foster parents. On the contrary, they had no interest in fostering children; they wanted kids of their own. After trying for years to have the first of two kids they always wanted—a boy and a girl—they'd been unable to conceive, so when they were shown Dylan's and April's profiles, they saw it as the perfect opportunity to create the family they'd always wanted.

Unfortunately, however, nothing is ever truly perfect in this world. And sometimes, especially when it comes to adoption, it's anything but.

Dylan and April didn't love their new parents. Forming attachments had never ended well for them. So, after so many foster-home false starts, they just stopped trying. Still, they knew a stroke of good fortune when they saw one: The Thibaults lived in a very large home out on the bluffs, with a colonnaded front porch and a pool in the backyard—some might have even called it a mansion. The property was massive and secluded, with the help of a dense forest and a 12-foot-high electric fence that ringed the ten-acre property.

The Thibaults did not take visitors.

But they did provide for the siblings' every need and desire. April didn't have to wear Dylan's hand-me-downs, and Dylan didn't have to wear clothes left behind in the closet by other foster children who'd come before them. Everything was new. The Thibaults let them pick out their own clothes, and nothing was off limits unless it violated the school dress code.

They each had their own smartphone and their own

desktop PC. April was even allowed to wear makeup. Dylan stashed porn under his bed and watched it online, but if they knew about it, they didn't care.

The school they attended was, of course, a private academy, with separate classes for boys and girls. This was very new to the siblings, but they had learned to adjust quickly and easily to new environments because they'd been forced to, and like little chameleons, they had no trouble easing into their new school surroundings as well.

If the siblings didn't actually love their new parents, it wasn't the tragedy it might seem. The Thibaults had spent the past decade and a half building a very particular sort of life together, and after being disappointed so often in their attempts to have children of their own, they'd resigned themselves to a more matter-of-fact, businesslike style. They weren't ones to show affection—not even to each other—and gave the siblings plenty of freedom. They could hang out with whoever they wanted, play video games, go to the movies, or even smoke dope. (The Thibaults were known to smoke a bowl themselves, so they couldn't very well place that restriction on the siblings.) All in all, they could pretty much "do their own thing"... as long as they followed three simple rules.

First, they had to attend school every day—no exceptions. If they said they were sick, Dr. Thibault's sister, Serena, would take them to the doctor and look after them until school let out. The siblings thought this was strange, since the Thibaults both worked from home, but they didn't complain because Serena always bought them pizza, streamed whatever videos they wanted, and allowed them to play on her computer.

Second, they were not to give out their home address, their parents' phone numbers or emails, or any other personal information.

Third, they were not under any circumstances to venture into their parents' home office or use their computer. This shouldn't have been too hard, either, since their parents were almost always home and kept the room locked. Since it was impossible to get into that room anyway, it didn't make sense that they would spend too much time thinking about it. The grown-ups let them do whatever they wanted anyway, so why should they care?

Except they did...

"What do you think they do for work?" April asked. "They never leave the house or anything."

She lay on the couch in her room, her feet kicked up on one of its arms. She did that so much that the upholstery had begun to wear thin. Not that she cared. Their parents would buy her a new one if she got up the energy to complain.

"Yeah, and look at this place," Dylan said, lying on the floor. "They gotta make their loot somehow. I figure they're day traders or some shit."

"You think that's why they don't want us going on their computer?"

"Could be." Dylan shrugged and tossed a tennis ball into the air, then caught it and repeated the motion. "Or maybe she just inherited it and that's why he married her. Maybe they're so rich they don't have to work. Maybe they spend all day playing Halo or League of Legends on there and don't want us messin' up their game."

April laughed. "That would be cool."

"Yeah."

There was a knock at the door. The Thibaults never entered either of their rooms without knocking. The doors even locked from the inside. They said it was a matter of respect for a person's privacy, and they couldn't very well ask the siblings to stay out of their office if they didn't extend them the same courtesy. "Weak people lead by barking orders," Dr. Thibault had told them once. "Strong people lead by example."

And get themselves screwed, Dylan had thought at the time. Still, the Thibaults didn't appear to have ever gotten screwed, no matter what they did. They were what some of the bleeding hearts (Dr. Thibault's name for them) called "privileged." Dr. Thibault hated that word. It made him cringe, and every time he heard it on the cable TV news, he flipped the channel. "You're only as fuckin' privileged as you make yourself," he'd said.

"Hey, you both in there?"

It was the mother. They felt weird calling her "Mom," so she just let them use Benicia.

"Yeah," said April. "What do you want?"

"To come in, if you don't mind."

April huffed, then jumped up off the sofa and unbolted the door. Benicia Thibault entered, her long brown hair shimmering with the combination of "product" and the sunlight that drifted in from the far window.

"We're going out of town," she announced, coming straight to the point as usual.

This was a surprise. The siblings had been living with the Thibaults for almost a year, and the couple had never left town, even overnight.

"We'll be going away on business, and the two of you have earned our trust. We believe you're both old enough to stay here by yourselves while we're away. Aunt Serena will look in on you every day to be sure you're OK, and she's just a phone call away if you need her."

Dylan got to his feet and cocked his head. "Why can't we just call you?"

"We'll be out of cell range," she said without missing a beat. "And we won't be able to get back here quickly in any case. Serena can help you with anything you need. The freezer in the garage is stocked with frozen dinners, and I'll leave my credit card on the kitchen sink if you want go out and get pizza. Just don't order in. And remember: The credit card has a $1,500 limit; there's nothing on it now, so please try not to go over."

April's eyes widened.

"And one more thing," Benicia said, her tone suddenly changing from breezy to serious on the verge of menacing. "The three rules are still in FULL EFFECT," she said slowly and deliberately, emphasizing the last two words. "I know Halloween is coming up, but there will be NO parties in this household. If someone you know is throwing a party, have at it: Serena will drive you wherever you need to go and pick you up after. But no one is to know any of our personal information, including and especially our address. Is that clear?"

They both nodded.

"When will you be back?" April asked.

"That's open-ended," Benicia said, her carefree, almost bored tone returning. "We'll be gone at least through Halloween, and probably longer than that. It just depends on how long it takes to wrap up our business."

"And where are you…?" but the full sentence wasn't out of April's mouth before Benicia had spun on her heels and exited the room, shutting the door behind her.

"Who cares where they're going?" Dylan said, laughing with glee. "They'll be GONE, and we'll have the entire place to ourselves. We can do anything we want."

"As long as we don't break the three rules," April reminded him.

Dylan grinned. "Yeah," he said. "As long as we don't do that."

The first few days the Thibaults were gone didn't pass much differently than the days that had gone before them. The siblings went to school, hung out with their friends, smoked dope, and in doing so built up an appetite for pizza, which they ate at Me-N-Ed's in the Tower District. Then they went home and crashed.

"I don't see why we can't just order in," Dylan said.

"Because we can't give the address to anyone, dumbass," April chided him.

"But it's boring here all by ourselves. There's nothing to do."

"We could watch a movie."

"That's boring."

"Maybe play video games."

"That's boring too."

April rolled her eyes. "Everything's boring to you."

"Some things aren't boring. Like doing what you're not supposed to do."

"But they let us do everything we want here," April reminded him.

"Not *everything*. Don't you ever wonder what's on that computer in there?" Dylan nodded toward the home office.

"That's one of the three rules," April whispered, as though someone might overhear them. There was no one else in the house, which was deathly quiet. Not only had the Thibaults installed a massive home security system with motion sensors and hidden cameras around the property, but they'd also had the house insulated so no outside noises could get in. "What if they've got cameras inside, too?" she said, sounding worried. "What if they can hear our conversation?"

"Will you relax?" Dylan said, raising his voice to make a point. "She said we had earned their trust, right? Besides, they're not worried about anything in here; they're just all paranoid about what's out *there*."

"But," April began, still speaking in hushed tones.

"Will you stop whispering already?" Dylan said, exasperated.

She acquiesced and started speaking almost normally again, but still not quite as loud as usual. "We can't get in there anyway," she said. "It's locked, remember?"

"Which means there's a key."

"Which I'm suuuuure they have with them."

"Probably, but... Alexa, release interior lock number 3."

A panicked look appeared on April's face, and she started whispering again. "Are you crazy? Doesn't Alexa keep a record of everything?"

Dylan shrugged. "Beats me. But if so, I'll betcha we can erase it from that computer in there."

No sooner were the words out of his mouth than they heard a click on the office door. "Too late now, anyway," he said, smiling mischievously. "C'mon!"

He opened the door and stepped inside, but what greeted them there was entirely unremarkable. A wide-screen monitor hung mounted on the wall across a spare desk with a metal top and a small drawer underneath.

"Now what?" said April. "The computer's off, and we don't know the password."

But there was a gleam in Dylan's eye. "There's a light on the power button," he said, pointing. "It's already on. It's just in sleep mode."

April stared at him. "It couldn't be that easy."

"Only one way to find out."

Dylan hit the space bar, and the screen flickered on. There, in front of them, was a website—one they'd never seen before called Doxx and Swat. The word "DISCLAIMER" was written in red, all-capital letters at the top of the site, followed by a few sentences that were part warning, part description.

"Doxx and Swat is a secure site hosted by a private overlay network, accessible only to authorized members through our proprietary software. The purpose of this site is to expose and hold accountable the conflicted judges, crooked politicians, dirty cops, and corporate raiders who have turned our society into a cesspool of corruption. For a simple fee, we will find these traitors, unmask them and bring them to justice. If you have a name, we will supply and publish your target's address, email, and phone number for the world to see. If you only have an address, we will spread the word across the planet via our network. We do not discriminate or pass judgment on the identity of your target. Your fee entitles you to our full services, rendered with complete discretion and anonymity: Your identity is completely confidential. We do not need your name or credit card. Once you have decided on a target, you simply need to contact us ON THIS SERVER ONLY, and we will reply with instructions on how to deposit your payment into our secure account."

"What *is* this?" April whispered.

"I think it's what they call the dark web. What do you think? Should we try it? We could give it the address of that girl who's always picking on you, Sherri Luzinski."

"Are you crazy? It sounds illegal. Besides, we don't have any money." April paused for a moment, then breathed, "What do you think they'd do to her?"

Dylan shrugged. "Who knows? Probably TP her house or crank her with one of those heavy-breathing calls."

"But we could do that ourselves."

"Yeah," said Dylan, "and get caught. They'd trace it right back to us using our phone number. If I'm right, and this is the dark web, they can't trace it. Plus we'd be having someone else do it, so who cares what happens? We wouldn't be responsible. We're just putting it out there."

April frowned. "I don't know..."

"C'mon. What can it hurt to look? If it costs money, we can't do anything about it anyway, right?"

"I guess."

April's eyes shifted to the right of the screen, where a sidebar listed a number of different addresses. "What's that?"

"It looks like a list of names and addresses that other users have submitted. Look! A new one just appeared at the bottom of the list, so someone must have just made a payment."

"I don't know any of these people."

"How would you? Like the site says, it's probably mostly judges and politicians and stuff. Who cares about them anyway? C'mon, April. Let's have some fun. Let's find the address for Sherri Luzinski and put it in to see what happens. They'll probably just ask for payment, and then we can X out of it."

April hesitated, then finally nodded, and Dylan moved the cursor over to a prompt that read "SUBMIT TARGET." When he clicked on it, a new page popped up with spaces to enter a person's name, address, email, and phone number.

"I don't have any of that," April said.

"Don't be stupid. The site said all they needed was a name." His fingers moved to the keyboard, and he typed in Sherri Luzinski, then hit enter. The screen disappeared and was replaced with a message that read, "TARGET ACCEPTED."

"Wait," said April. "I thought we had to pay?"

Dylan frowned and shook his head. "Me too. Maybe the system is just slow or something. Let's wait a minute or two."

But nothing happened.

Then, finally, the message disappeared, and the computer returned to the website homepage.

"I don't like this," April said. "What if they charge mom's credit card?"

"They said credit cards weren't accepted."

"Oh, right."

They just sat there, staring at the screen for a couple of more minutes, before it went blank again as the computer returned to power-saving mode.

"I don't like this," said April.

"Yeah, it does seem weird," her brother replied. "Maybe it's just some stupid online game. Whatever it is, there's nothing we can do about it now. Let's just get out of here. We didn't really touch anything in the room. Benicia and Jonathan will never even know we've been in here."

"I suppose." April followed him out of the room, taking one last look back over her shoulder before they left.

"Alexa," Dylan said, "restore interior lock number 3."

Everything seemed to be normal when Aunt Serena picked the siblings up for school the next day.

She drove them to the campus and dropped them off ten

minutes early, the way she always did. The school grounds were decked out in black and orange bunting for the Halloween dance, although there weren't any witch or ghost decorations like there were on many of the neighborhood homes. A number of parents had made a stink about "demonic" imagery the previous year, and the school board had decided to avoid it—and the parents' wrath, which they feared more than any demon—this time out.

But something else was different, too: They arrived to find a group of students gathered around the front steps, talking excitedly about something. There were kids from all different grade levels there, which was unusual: They usually separated themselves into packs of all boys or all girls from different social cliques.

Something was obviously up.

"What's happening?" Dylan asked one of his friends as he approached, his sister close behind.

"Hey man," said Travis Litman, a tall, gangly kid of fourteen wearing a Slipknot T-shirt. "It's so fucked up. Haven't you heard?"

"Heard what?"

"About Sherri Luzinski, man."

April pushed her way forward. "What happened to her?"

"Get this," Travis said, laughing almost too hard to continue. "She got some email that said it was from that dude Rumeal—you know, that guy she likes from her homeroom."

"Yeah," said April. "Everyone knows she likes him."

"But here's the thing," Travis continued, reveling in his role as tea-spiller. "It wasn't from him. And when she opened it, it downloaded a virus onto her dad's computer that was full of illegal shit. I'm not gonna say what it was, but it was *bad*, if you get what I'm saying. She tried to delete it, but every time she did, it triggered the virus, and it just downloaded even more crap."

"Shit," said Dylan, trying not to look worried.

"Oh, that's not the worst of it," Travis continued. "Not half an hour later, the cops show up at her home and ask to see the computer!"

"No way!" said Dylan. "Don't they need a warrant for that?"

"Sure, but her dad didn't know anything about it. She'd been to scared to tell him and still thought she could find a way to get rid of it. So the poor ol' guy was clueless. He figured he had nothin' to hide. Why not let 'em in to have a look around, ya know? What's the harm? Well, then they found all those files on his PC and arrested him on the spot. Everyone says he's goin' to prison, and even if he doesn't, he'll lose his job."

April swallowed hard. She'd wanted to teach Sherri a lesson, but she never thought anything would happen to her dad.

She stepped backward, away from the others and over toward a tree, trying to contain the contents of her stomach. Fortunately, before anyone noticed, the warning bell rang and the kids started dispersing for classes.

Dylan walked over to her and hugged her. "Don't worry about it. Like I said, they can't trace anything to us."

She just stood there, trembling and still trying not to retch.

"We can't go back in that room, Dylan."

They stood there together, staring at the door to the Thibaults' office.

"We have to," Dylan said. "You know what happened was our doing. It couldn't have been a coincidence."

"No... I know... but..."

"So now that the job has been done, the owner of that server will want to be paid. We don't have the money. We have to find a way to..."

"To do what? You heard about what happened to Sherri when she tried to fix things. What if they've put the same kind of virus on this computer? The same thing could happen to us."

Dylan frowned, thinking for a moment. She had a point. "But we can't just do nothing," he said finally. "We'll just bring the computer out of sleep mode and see if there's anything new on the screen. Like a payment prompt or something. Then if there is, we'll... I don't know... I'll figure out something."

April looked doubtful, but she didn't have any ideas of her own, and she was used to trusting her older brother. They'd gotten through their entire life depending on each other, and now didn't seem like a good time to stop.

When they entered, the room looked the same as it had the previous day, and the monitor was still asleep, the way they'd left it.

Dylan walked quickly over to it, tapped the space bar, and let out a sigh of relief when he saw the Doxx and Swat homepage looked almost the same as the way he'd left it. No prompt had appeared demanding payment, and there was nothing to indicate that any new message had been received.

"What does that mean?" April asked, pointing to some small print in the lower right-hand corner. "I didn't see that before."

Dylan followed her gaze. "Yeah," he said, "I'm pretty sure that was there, but I didn't bother to read it. It says... "administrative console."

"Administrative console?" April repeated. "Doesn't that

mean...?"

Dylan frowned. "Uh-huh. It means whoever set up this website is operating it from this terminal."

"Benicia?"

"And Jonathan. Fuck! Maybe this is how they make all their money!"

"So that's why it didn't charge us. They're operating it, so they get to use it for free," said April.

"Right," said Dylan. "From the looks of it, they have a bunch of new targets today, too. Who knows how much they charge for this shit? Probably thousands of dollars." He started scanning the new names and addresses that had appeared since the previous day in the right-hand sidebar.

"Recognize any of them?"

"Not yet," said Dylan. Then, a second later, he pulled back, his face suddenly white. "Look at this one," he said, pointing.

April's eyes widened. "Wait," she said. "That's *our* address!"

"Holy fuck, what are we going to do?"

"We have to tell Jonathan and Benicia. We have to have Serena message them. Oh, god. What if Sherri's mom or someone got onto the site? What if she made Mom and Dad a target?"

"Mom and Dad? Since when did you start calling them that?"

"I don't know. But what if the same thing happens to them that happened to Sherri's dad? They've always been good to us, Dylan. What happens if they get arrested or something? We'll be out on the street. Or worse!" She was getting more upset by the second, wrapping her arms around herself and starting to sob.

"Hold on, Sis. Remember, the Thibaults run this system.

They wouldn't allow themselves to become targets."

"But they already have!" April wailed. "It's up there on the screen! Don't you see? It's already out there!"

Dylan didn't know what to say. She was right. There it was, right in front of them, and there was nothing they could do to erase it—even if they'd known how. The system was designed to be non-discriminating, but maybe the Thibaults never imagined it would be turned against them. Still, it didn't make sense to Dylan that they didn't demand payment up front. Creating their own targets free of charge was one thing, but allowing others to do so... that seemed like bad business.

As he was standing there, staring at the screen, there came a knock at the door.

Dylan nearly jumped out of his skin.

"Oh my God!" April whimpered. "Someone's here."

"You stay here," her brother said. "Let me go see who it is."

"No, don't leave me here!"

"All right, then," he snapped. "Come with me then." His own nerves were getting the better of him.

They crept slowly and silently toward the front door, like burglars in their own home, as though somehow this would protect them from whatever danger awaited beyond the front door. They could see through the half-circle window at the top of the door that the day's light was fading, but there wasn't an eyepiece for them to see who was on the other side.

"Should we open it?" April whispered.

"I don't know."

The knocking came again, more insistent now, and Dylan jumped again.

"Go away," he shouted. "We don't want any."

The response was not what he had expected. "Trick or

treat!"

"Shit!" said Dylan. He'd forgotten all about the fact that it was Halloween.

He opened the door to see a Little Mermaid, a young kid who couldn't have been more than six dressed like Yoda, and a taller teenager dressed like a Sasquatch. Dylan relaxed noticeably as he recognized Travis from school behind the mask. "Stuck babysitting Tessa and Gavin again?" he said.

"Hey, I'm Yoda!" the boy protested.

"And I'm Ariel!"

Sasquatch/Travis just shook his head.

"Sorry," said Dylan. "We don't have any candy. Benicia and Jonathan forgot to leave us any."

Travis shrugged. "Tell them," he said. "They're the ones who'll be fucking up your house for not anteing up."

"That's a bad word," the Little Mermaid said.

"So whatcha gonna do about it?" Travis said, raising a fist in mock anger.

The girl just laughed.

"OK," Travis said finally. "Catch ya later."

"See ya," said Dylan, closing the door.

"See?" he said, turning to April. "Nothing to worry about." But his tone betrayed the fact that he was trying to convince himself as much as he was talking to her.

"Dylan," she said. "I thought no one knew where we lived?"

Her brother took a deep breath. "Until our address went up on that site. Fuck, Sis, we're screwed. Travis and them had to get through the front gate and come all the way up here. That means all the electric fence is down and the gate is open. Whoever put our address up online must have found a way to..."

He hadn't finished his sentence before another knock came.

"Trick or treat."

"Don't open it, Dylan! Please don't open it."

But he had neglected to lock the door behind Travis and the others, and whoever was on the other side turned the knob and pushed it toward them.

Before him stood two older kids: One wore a Ghostface mask and held a gleaming kitchen knife, while the other one looked like Leatherface from *The Texas Chainsaw Massacre* and was carrying what looked like a very real Black & Decker chainsaw.

"Hey, killer costumes," said Dylan nervously, "but aren't you guys a little old for this shit?"

There was no response.

"OK, I'm sorry... like... we don't have any candy. So props for the costumes, but we gotta go."

Then he saw them, behind the two older kids on the lawn: the bodies of Travis and his little brother and sister, just lying there, blood staining the green grass around them a sickly shade of crimson.

He threw all his weight against the door in an attempt to close it, but as he did, the trick-or-treater in the Leatherface mask pulled the ripcord on his chainsaw and brought it down full force on the door. Chunks of wood flew everywhere, April screamed and ran, and Dylan again tried slamming the door hard in their faces... which knocked Ghostface off balance for a moment but didn't stop either of the masked intruders from forcing their way inside.

Dylan ran after his sister, but he was too slow. First, he heard the chainsaw rev, then he felt it come down on the back of his leg, slicing through his left calf muscle, all but severing his Achilles tendon, and turning his foot into a bloody stew of ground-up muscle and disconnected bone fragments. He screamed in agony and fell to the floor, trying to drag himself farther. But the chainsaw fell on him again, then pressed down on his right knee inexorably until his lower leg was separated from his thigh.

Without speaking, the chainsaw-wielding attacker gestured to his accomplice, who pounced on Dylan like a panther and sent an eight-inch-long steel knife blade plunging into his abdomen. He screamed a ragged scream of desperation laced with utter agony as the blade was raised and lowered again, with vicious force, "Ghostface" burying it deep in his shoulder and twisting it back and forth, slowly, grinding his muscles to a pulp.

In a state of shock, he passed out, never noticing that the chainsaw had been raised again. "Ghostface" pulled back his head roughly by the hair, and the motorized saw descended on his neck, the chain whirring and sputtering as "Leatherface" pressed down firmly and mercilessly, severing skin, tendons, vocal cords, and finally the teenage spine until Dylan's head was no longer a part of his body.

Bits of flesh and muscle clung to the chain, and blood covered the walls in splashes and swatches of bright red that made them look like the hide of a red zebra as depicted by some demented abstract painter.

When he was satisfied Dylan was completely and utterly dead, he and his companion turned their attention to Alice. Rather than flee out the back door, she had hidden in her secret hiding place: a section of half caved-in cellar beneath a trap door in the floor under a rug in her bedroom. She didn't make a sound. She tried not to even breathe as she heard the footsteps on the floorboards overhead, coming closer... closer... She shut her eyes tight and balled up her fists. She made herself as small as she could be. *No one can find me here*, she told herself. *No one knows about this place.*

But somehow, they did know.

Alice screamed as they threw back the trapdoor and the chainsaw revved to life. The monster wielding it came for her, waving it wildly through the air in an almost hypnotic pattern that made her stop and watch its deadly dance. Like a cobra surveying its target, it twisted and turned, rising up and lingering there for an eternal moment, teeth bared, before descending in a lightning strike upon its prey.

Alice's left eye was ground to dust as the chainsaw bore into its socket, then thrust deeper still into her skull. Bone fragments sprayed everywhere. Bits of brain matter came loose and hung like maggots from her broken face.

Like her brother, April lost consciousness before the fatal blow: The long blade plunged directly into her heart, sending blood streaming out of her chest as she convulsed and her muscles twitched again and again in frantic inevitability... until at last they—and she—lay motionless there on the dusty basement floor.

"Leatherface" removed his mask. "It's too bad," he said, as "Ghostface" followed suit. "We did everything for those kids. All they had to do was follow three simple rules. Was that too much to ask?"

The woman shrugged in response. "Kids have to have consequences," Benicia said. "Otherwise, they'll never learn."

"I guess they learned their lesson, right?" Jonathan said, chuckling.

His wife laughed with him. "I guess so."

"Ah well," he said. "I suppose you were right."

"Oh?"

"You never wanted kids anyway."

Sharon Marie Provost

Tiny Terrors

That little shit! Of course, he had to run home to papa and whine about the unfairness of "Mister" Vukovich's punishment. I shouldn't be surprised that the impudent little asshat can't even bother to get my title correct. It is DOCTOR after all... I worked long and hard to earn that distinction. Never mind the pompous bastard's abusive treatment of a fellow student for being the recipient of a hardship scholarship to this supposedly prestigious private academy for privileged little brats. We should ignore Sterling's infraction because that is the way the world works, right? Blessed are the rich, for they shall rule the earth... that is how that old phrase from the Bible goes, right? Fuck that shit!

Dr. Vukovich threw down the note from the headmaster that had just been delivered to his classroom. Sterling's self-satisfied smirk betrayed the fact that he knew exactly what that note had been about. Dr. Vukovich refused to give that kid anything more to gloat about, so he placed it in his satchel and resumed grading papers. The single sentence on that page kept running through his mind: "We need to discuss your recent questionable treatment of one of our diamond class students." As if the diamond class—insert insanely rich donor's child—mattered more than all the rest.

The students finished their math exams over the next 30 minutes. Dr. Vukovich had directed them to read the next chapter in their history books while they waited for the others to finish. His mind was entirely focused on his meeting later that afternoon, so he gave up trying to read their essays. Instead, he moved on to their multiple-choice science tests.

As expected, Sterling and several of the other diamond class students had done poorly on their exams. Yet they always passed each semester because of the extra-credit projects the staff was required to offer. Not that they completed those projects on their own... those were done by their bullied scholarship classmates, private tutors or nannies.

After what seemed like hours, but in truth was only 45 minutes, Dr. Vukovich's history lesson was interrupted by the final bell. All the students, including Sterling (who should have been held over for detention) jumped up, grabbed their knapsacks and rushed for the door. There was no sense trying to stop Sterling until this whole situation was resolved with the headmaster.

As Dr. Vukovich walked around to each desk and collected the maps his students had been filling in, he questioned his decision to become an elementary school teacher and part-time school psychologist after he'd moved here to the States. He missed his career and behavioral studies research at the Academy of Sciences in eastern Europe. All those years he'd spent in school obtaining a doctorate in behavioral neuroscience and then becoming a licensed psychiatrist seemed like such a waste.

His research had been showing great progress when the government shut down the program. That kind of research was no longer in vogue, and military strategies had changed over the past 20 years. At the time, he'd thought he would never get over the loss. The U.S. government would never allow that kind of research, so a career change made sense... or so he thought. But dealing with these children and the private school bureaucracy had made him seriously question his sanity.

Dr. Vukovich finished tidying up the classroom, placed the worksheets in his satchel and looked at his watch.

Well, it's now or never. Let's see what the blowhard headmaster has to say.

Dr. Vukovich locked up the classroom and headed down to the administration office. Nora, the school secretary, looked up from her desk in the reception area and motioned for Dr. Vukovich to enter the headmaster's office. When he entered, he found Sterling sitting with his father, Quincy Masterson, on the luxurious leather couch next to the stained-glass window.

Quincy rose with a sneer and reached out to shake Dr. Vukovich's hand, with that testosterone-fueled viselike grip common amongst his type. "Pleasure to meet you, Mr.

Vukovich," he growled.

"That's Dr. Vukovich, and yes, it is nice to meet you as well," he said as he matched Quincy's grip strength, giving the man's hand one final bone-crushing squeeze just before letting go. Headmaster Bertrand Peters waved Dr. Vukovich to the chair in front of his ostentatious, ornately carved walnut desk. It didn't escape Dr. Vukovich's notice that the donor recognition plaque with Quincy's name right at the top was displayed prominently on the corner of that desk.

"We are assembled today to discuss the incident and resulting punishment that occurred on Wednesday, September 4th between Sterling Masterson and one... Kent Anderson," Headmaster Peters said as he shuffled through papers on his desk.

"That Anderson boy is a troublemaker. He doesn't belong in this school," Quincy interjected.

Headmaster Peters raised his hand to pause the verbal onslaught before turning to Dr. Vukovich. "Can you explain what happened that day?"

"It was during art class. The boys had been seated together with several others because they all wanted to use watercolors. Sterling had brought his own extensive art supply set to class that day, and he began making fun of Kent because he had to use the art supplies provided by the school. Kent began to sniffle, so I was about to separate them when Christine needed help with a bloody nose.

"While I was busy getting her a tissue, the argument continued until Kent finally told Sterling to shut up. Sterling then began a very loud, inappropriate, and embarrassing tirade about how Kent was too poor to attend school. He began chanting an extremely rude nickname, and unfortunately the other kids picked up on it with him."

"And what was that nickname, Dr. Vukovich?" the headmaster asked.

"Indigent Kent. Now when is the last time you heard an 8-year-old use the word indigent? That is clearly something he picked up at home."

"That is neither here nor there. It is not for us to question what words his parents choose to use around him. After all, he did use the word properly. demonstrating his understanding of it. We should applaud our students expanding their vocabulary."

"Are you serious?" Dr. Vukovich scoffed.

Headmaster Peters maintained his unflinching stare as he nodded.

"I am all for our students expanding their vocabulary. But it is an entirely different matter for them to then use it to verbally assault a classmate. Further, it is a tragedy that his test scores in English and essays in class do not reflect that level of sophistication."

"Now wait one goddamn minute there, Mr. Vukovich. Now *you* are the one insulting *my* son," Quincy bellowed as he stood up, poking a finger into Dr. Vukovich's chest.

"That was not an insult... simply a statement of fact. Furthermore, it was not said in a public forum in order to embarrass him. This is a private conversation between his parent, his teacher and the headmaster." Dr. Vukovich placed his open palm on Quincy's finger and pushed it away."

"Gentlemen, this conversation is getting heated. I think we need to calm down and just deal with the facts. Now Dr. Vukovich, how did you handle the situation at that point?"

"I quieted the class down and tasked them with reading a

chapter from their books they had chosen for a book report. Then I put Sterling into the timeout corner while I dealt with Kent's emotional reaction to the situation. I ended up sending Kent to the nurse so she could call his parents to pick him up. There was only an hour left of school, and it seemed prudent to give him time to calm down at home. I sent him home with a note to his parents letting them know I would be calling them that evening to explain the situation.

"When class ended, I held Sterling over to discuss his inappropriate behavior and to serve detention. I had Ms. Clements supervise him while I went out to speak to his nanny, who was waiting to pick him up. I followed that up by stopping by the office to place a call to Mr. Masterson here to let him know about Sterling's behavior, and that I would be sending a reprimand letter home with him to be signed and returned to me."

"Is that true, Mr. Masterson?"

"Parts of it, yes. He did call me and tell me what Sterling had done. However, he did not tell me, nor you, the full story of what prompted Sterling to get upset and lash out at Kent. I didn't find that out until Sterling got home that night and told me. Sterling, will you please tell the full story to Headmaster Peters?"

"Yes, father. Headmaster Peters, I was working on my art project as Mr. Vukovich had asked us to do. Kent took my art supplies and started using them without my permission. I asked him to return them because they are very expensive, and my father had entrusted me to properly care for them. Kent called me a spoiled brat, and then he stole some of my colored pencils. He started saying bad things about my father... words that I am not allowed to say. I know I shouldn't have said what I did, but

I was very upset. I love my father. I didn't want to disappoint him by losing my art supplies."

"This is ridiculous, Headmaster. This story is utterly fabricated. None of what he just described happened. Besides, can't you hear that he was coached to say this? No 8-year-old speaks that way, yet alone young Sterling here. One look at his academic records will confirm that."

"Mr. Vukovich, that is slander. Neither I nor my son is a liar. As for those academic records, my son has a straight-A average. Am I wrong, Headmaster Peters?"

"Dr. Vukovich! He has earned those A's strictly by completing the extra credit work that Headmaster Peters requires that I offer. Looking solely at his scores on assignments and exams, he would have a C, at best, in all of his subjects—except for art and physical education, where he would legitimately earn A's."

"Excuse me! I think I have heard enough about this matter. I must tell you, young Mr. Masterson, that your behavior was unacceptable. I can see you were provoked, but we must learn to control our emotions and act responsibly. That being said, I think Dr. Vukovich's choice of discipline was excessive in this circumstance. I believe the detention you served yesterday is sufficient punishment for this infraction, especially given your remorse and acknowledgment of your wrongdoing. I will be requiring both you and young Mr. Anderson to apologize to each other. I apologize, Mr. Masterson, for wasting your precious time. We will be reviewing our policy regarding the handling of on-campus disagreements and punishments."

"Thank you, Headmaster Peters. I appreciate your prompt attention to this matter, as well as your fair adjudication."

Both men and Sterling rose to leave.

"Excuse me, Dr. Vukovich, if you could stay behind. We

need to attend to some matters."

"Good day, Mr. Vukovich," Quincy said as he turned away with a mocking smile.

Dr. Vukovich returned to his seat and folded his hands in his lap.

Now to get my ass handed to me because I hurt the little prince's feelings. This is bullshit! He smiled at Headmaster Peters as the door closed behind him. "So... what is it we need to discuss, Bertrand?"

"Dr. Vukovich, we cannot be handling difficult matters in this manner when it comes to our diamond class students."

"Seriously, do you hear yourself? Diamond class! Do you know the uproar that would ensue if the general public knew that we rate the importance of our students based on their parents' wealth? All students should be treated equally, regardless of social status, gender, sexual orientation, religious beliefs, and race.

"I fairly punished my student for his behavior: I treated him no differently than I would have any of the others. The three days of 15-minute afterschool detention I assigned to him was consistent with national guidelines, as well as our school guidelines, given the nature of the infraction and his grade level. If anything, it could be argued that I was lenient, given our society's current intolerance for bullying. There are schools in this nation that would have expelled him. Kent's family may even have grounds for a lawsuit alleging a hostile school environment for their child. Have you even considered that?"

"In light of the story presented by Sterling and his father, we had to... adjust... our position. I am sure it hasn't escaped you that his father is our largest benefactor."

"You let that man portray Kent Anderson as a

troublemaker. That child has never even had his name on the board once. I can't say that about most of the other students. He has a straight-A average as well, but his was earned honestly, by working hard on all his assignments and studying for his exams. That young man helps his sickly mother around the house when his father is out on long-haul trucking runs. He is the only minor allowed to visit his grandmother at the nursing home without a parent accompanying him because he is well-behaved and respectful. What you just allowed to happen is a travesty! The only slander that occurred today was against that young boy's reputation."

"You can choose to view this situation however you like, Dr. Vukovich. Simply stated, the only opinion that matters is mine. In the future, if you have any behavioral issues with any of the students, but especially with our diamond class students, I expect you to inform me about them. Do not single them out in class! Do not hold them over after school! Do not contact their parents! Come to me after school ends and inform me of the situation. Then I will do the required investigation and determine the proper method for handling it. Is that clear, Dr. Vukovich?"

"Crystal! Am I excused now? I have hours of grading ahead of me for this sham of an educational system we provide here for those above being required to actually learn."

"You are on a mighty thin ice here, Stefan. I would watch what you say if I were you. Otherwise, you might find yourself looking for teaching job at an institution that is far less prestigious than this one. You rode in here on your high horse, but I don't see you working at a public school in the inner city. You imply that I'm a slave to the system, only concerned about my own wealth and welfare. I don't see you passing up the money you make here in order to make a real difference. Maybe just a few too many questionable debts...?" Headmaster Peters trailed off, raising his eyebrows.

Dr. Vukovich's scowl faded amid a rush of shame: There was at least some truth in the headmaster's words. But then his anger returned. He *was* trying to make a true valuable difference. The rich shouldn't be able to rule the world singlehandedly, doling out reward and punishment at they saw fit, with money as the only determining factor.

Dr. Vukovich turned on his heel and walked out, shutting the door a little too hard behind him.

Nora looked up, startled by the vibration.

"Good evening, Nora," Dr. Vukovich mumbled as he stalked past her desk.

That egotistical asshole! He thinks he can make me feel guilty just because I receive a decent wage. Change has to happen at all levels. Even if I did work miracles with kids in the inner city, it still wouldn't make a difference: They never even have a chance because the wealthy are never held accountable for their actions. These parents think their little monsters are precious because they don't have to take care of them. Half the day, they are my problem, and the other half is spent being cared for by their staff. What would they do if those tiny terrors were unleashed on them?

Dr. Vukovich stopped by Aloha Liquors to pick up a bottle of Cemetery Gin. The distillery's motto was fitting for his stress level: "Guaranteed to embalm you... while you're still breathing." He might be stuck following the academy's rules for now, but he was determined to find a way to make them all pay. He spent the evening grading papers while sipping his drink.

Dr. Vukovich awoke with an epiphany in the middle of the night. Apparently, he still did some of his best thinking while sleeping. It was an old habit of his, which he had developed back in his research days, to keep a notebook and pen by the bed so he could jot down those ideas and not risk losing them.

Now he knew just how to get back at all of them.

An evil smile spread across his face as he imagined their horror on Halloween night.

The plan might be a longshot, but he had to try. The only problem was he didn't have much time to set it in motion—just under eight weeks, in fact. With that thought in mind, he jumped out of bed to email his old psychopharmacology colleague from the Academy of Sciences, hoping to schedule a call with him over the weekend, accounting for the nine-hour time difference between the two of them. All his scheming would be for naught if he couldn't get a hold of Serum MC14.

Dr. Vukovich tried to slow his racing mind so he could return to sleep. He knew tomorrow was likely to be a long day, between the headmaster watching him like a hawk and Sterling holding his victory over him. Besides, in class tomorrow he needed to implement Phase 1 of Project Tiny Terrors.

Headmaster Peters was surprised to see Dr. Vukovich walk onto The Wingfield Academy campus with a spring in his step and a smile on his face, whistling "Oh, What a Beautiful Mornin'." As he turned to enter his classroom, he couldn't suppress singing the last line of the chorus, "Everything's goin' my way." The children looked up, surprised, most of them laughing at him.

"What are you so happy about, Mr. Vukovich?" Sterling asked in a sarcastic tone."

Dr. Vukovich answered with a twinkle in his eye. "Why thank you for asking, Sterling. That was very kind of you. As for the answer, life is great. What is there not to appreciate? Besides, my favorite season and, therefore, my favorite holiday is approaching. Raise your hand if you want to guess the answers."

Twelve of the fifteen students' arms shots up in unison.

"Okay, Prudence. I think your hand was up first."

Prudence, ever the know-it-all, replied in a superior tone, "You like fall and Halloween."

"That is correct. And I have decided to do something special this year. I know how much you all love extra credit. If you complete a special writing project, you have the opportunity to earn 50 points of extra credit. How does that sound?"

The room resounded with a chorus of approving cheers.

"There are so many fun aspects to the Halloween season... from the costumes to the candy, to the decorations and fall festivals, corn mazes, candy apples and haunted houses... the list goes on and on. Plus, let's not forget the opportunities to scare each other. Myself, I have always been a fan of scary movies and books and telling ghost stories. I always chose to dress up as something scary like a vampire or a werewolf. Have you all decided what you are going to wear this year?"

The children's excitement bubbled over, just as he had hoped. All thoughts of raising their hands to answer went straight out of their minds. Instead, voices rang out with everything from vampire to ghost; Michael Myers to a Viking, a Grim Reaper, Jack the Ripper, Chucky, *The Purge* mask, a zombie, Freddy Krueger, Ghostface, Candyman and even Leatherface. Dr. Vukovich found it scary to think that these 8-year-olds, knew about monstrous characters from movies that came out before they were born. The few normal children's costume ideas came from his three scholarship students, who piped up with a cat, Mickey Mouse and a princess.

"Those are all wonderful ideas. I am glad you are all so creative. Do you want to hear about the extra credit now?"

"Yes!" was the enthusiastic answer.

"Do you remember when we went to the library a few weeks ago and learned how to look up books?"

"Yes."

"Once you make your final decision about your costume, I want you to write me a two-page paper about your choice. If you want to be a Viking, tell me about where the Vikings lived and what kind of life they led. Someone else mentioned Leatherface. I want you to tell me where this character came from, what he looks like, and any other information you find interesting. Then, I want you to tell me why you chose that particular costume and how you went about creating it: whether it is homemade or store-bought.

"Since some of you will be portraying scary characters from movies, you will need to get a parent's permission to wear that costume and do the research required for the assignment.. I will be sending you home this evening with a permission slip that you must return in order to participate.

"The project will be due on Halloween night. We will have a party in the afternoon on Halloween with cupcakes and juice. As part of your assignment, I will give you a prop at the end of class on Halloween, which you must hold while having your picture taken just before you go out trick-or-treating. Your parents will attach that picture to an email with your paper and send it to me that night. Does that sound like fun?"

"Yes, Dr. Vukovich!" Timothy exclaimed.

The children were more animated and attentive in class than usual that day. In fact, class went far better than Dr. Vukovich had expected, as even Sterling was on his best behavior. The headmaster only poked his head in once and left without a word when he saw the unusually industrious children and noticed Dr. Vukovich's continued cheerful mood.

Dr. Vukovich cleaned up his classroom quickly and headed home to check his email. He was delighted to see that his colleague Dr. Matthew Smirnov had messaged him back, and even more pleased to find that he was still employed at the Academy of Sciences. Dr. Smirnov had included his cell number and said he was available to consult by phone between noon and 7 p.m. Central European Summer Time on Saturday. Dr. Vukovich was relieved that he didn't have to get up nearly as early as he had feared.

Dr. Vukovich rose at 6 a.m., downed a cup of coffee, and then dialed Dr. Smirnov's number. The second ring had just started when Matthew's jovial voice greeted him, "Hey there, Stefan! Long time, no speak. How are you doing, my friend?"

"Great, Matthew. Thank you for taking my call. How are things going for you at the Academy?"

"Surprisingly well, actually. I am researching a treatment for Alzheimer's that involves the use of Klotho proteins as a neuroprotective agent. It is absolutely fascinating and may lead to a truly groundbreaking treatment."

"Wow! That is fantastic news. I am so happy to hear that you have found another rewarding field of research. That must have been quite the transition, though, from the behavioral modification research we had been pursuing."

"True. It was a bit of an adjustment. Speaking of transitions though, how is it working as an elementary school teacher and school psychologist?"

"That has been a bit more of a challenge—and frequently less fulfilling—than what you describe. It's not the job itself, but the bureaucracy and the particular circumstances of the children I teach: spoiled rich kids who have no work ethic. A few of my students attend the school on scholarship, and I have had some very rewarding experiences with them. I have helped others through counseling sessions at times, but most of these kids see highly paid private practice child psychologists."

"I can see your frustration there. That is definitely not the job for me. I admire your spirit though. So besides catching up, what did you want to speak to me about?"

"I was wondering if you still have any samples of Serum MC14 lying around the lab. I know when they suspended our research that they had destroyed most, if not all, of the supply we had on hand."

"Hmm... I do. Why do you ask?"

"I might have an opportunity to do some further research in the private sector. They aren't interested in the military super-soldier angle we had been pursuing. They're interested in... uh... adapting it to achieve behavioral modification treating mental illness."

"How did they hear about our serum? Our research was classified from the start, and we had to sign non-disclosure agreements when they shut us down."

"True. I took a closer look at that NDA though. It forbids us from talking about our exact research, but the document acknowledges the serum as our intellectual property, meaning we own it. We cannot talk about how we created it or what it was originally intended to be used for, but we have the rights to it."

"Well goddamn! You could push me over with a feather."

"If you can get me your copies of our research, the formulation and any samples you may have left, I can pursue it further if this deal goes through. No promises, but it is worth a try, right? After all the blood, sweat and tears—yet alone hours—we spent over those 10 years. If it works, we could be rich… maybe even win a Nobel Prize. While I pursue this, we can keep your name out of it if you want to protect your current research."

"Yes, please do. I trust you to share in the profits, should they ever develop, and the credit, should I choose to accept it, if this becomes a success. Over the past 10 years since our research ended, I have worked hard to distance myself from the disappointment of the project ending just as we were seeing positive results. As I said, my new research is also showing great promise. It's very rewarding to think we might be on the cusp of finding a way to treat one of the most tragic diseases known to man. My greatest fear is losing the essence of me and the knowledge I possess. I couldn't handle the loss of this research."

"Thank you, Matthew. You don't know how much this means to me. It may be some time before I know anything, if ever, but cross your fingers. I wish you the best with your research."

"I wish the same for you. I will express this to you on Monday. Take care, Stefan."

Damn! I truly hate lying to him, but I don't know what else to do. Besides, I have to keep his name far away from what I am about to do. In time, I can just get back to him and say that the deal fell through. Now it's time to implement Phase 2 of Project Tiny Terror.

Dr. Vukovich entered his classroom early Monday morning, arms full of child-size yoga mats. As the children filed in, he passed one out to each of them to store in their cubbies. He asked if they had brought back their permission forms and was pleased to find that every child had obtained a parent's signature. Just before the lunch bell rang, he made the announcement: "After lunch, we are going to try something new for the fall quarter for our PE class. We will be doing some yoga, Pilates and a brief meditation session before we enter our heavy brain power math and science lessons. How does that sound?"

The children smiled and seemed excited; several even piped up about their mothers taking yoga classes. The bell rang, and the children bounded out the door to the cafeteria, lunch bags in hand. He moved aside some of the desks in the back, so the children could lay out their mats when they returned. He would get them used to the yoga/meditation routine this week before introducing the serum slowly over the next six and a half weeks. He planned to dose them by mixing the serum in some Pedialyte to "bolster their hydration" before exercise.

The first week of the new routine went better than he could have hoped. The children enjoyed it. The headmaster came in during PE on Tuesday, gave Dr. Vukovich a thumbs up on his way out, and did not return to "oversee" the rest of the week. In fact, Dr. Vukovich received a note from the headmaster again on Friday, but this time it was all positive. It went so far as to praise him for being a team player and for expanding the Academy's diverse educational opportunities.

The package from Dr. Smirnov arrived on Wednesday. Dr. Vukovich spent his evenings reviewing their research to refresh his memory about safety, contraindications and side effects. It wouldn't do for one of the children to become seriously ill before he was ready to implement his plan.

Project Tiny Terrors was an exercise in behavior modification through the use of the drug known as Serum MC14 and hypnosis. A trigger object would be introduced during hypnotism to act as a green light, activating the modified behavior. During the same session, the subject would also be given detailed instructions as to *how* their behavior would be modified. To ensure success, the indoctrination procedure would be repeated many times over the course of several weeks with increasing doses of the serum.

The project he'd been working on for the serum's military application had been entirely successful in inducing the desired behavior changes. The last step had been to find the correct dose to cause the change for a 24-hour period as well as the proper dose to trigger it long-term until a counter agent could be administered. The first goal had been easy to achieve—the second was more difficult. A few of the test subjects experienced long-term effects, even after the counter agent was given. A few continued to experience the effects only for 24 hours. The study had been shut down just as they were in the final stages of determining a dose range that would slowly titrate an individual. They'd been on the verge of finding the sweet spot that allowed them to achieve their goal without administering too much of the serum and triggering side effects.

As the school psychologist, Dr. Vukovich had access to all of his students' medical records, including any health conditions the school needed to be informed of, as well as any long-term medications the child had been prescribed. Besides conducting the research and examining each child's medical records, he had spent the week going over the permission forms to create a spreadsheet listing each child's costume and pertinent information regarding that character.

His last task in preparation had been the most arduous: He needed to calculate a safe but effective dose for the children. When Sunday night rolled around, Dr. Vukovich was confident that. the next day. he would be able to begin the behavioral modification process— what the uneducated might refer to as brainwashing.

He placed a box near the front door that contained art supplies for each of the children to make their own trigger object. He had cut out 15 matching white posterboard 6-inch circles. Popsicle sticks were attached to the bottom, so each child could make a sign they could hold in front of them. The box also contained glitter, pipe cleaners, felt, and rhinestones they could glue in place to decorate the objects. Then they could use whatever writing implement they desired to write the words "Costumes tell a story" on it.

He would keep these in the classroom for their hypnosis sessions to attach the meaning to the trigger object, and they would take them home on Halloween after the party. The specific triggering event would be the flash from the camera when their picture was taken while holding that item and wearing their costume. A very specific set of circumstances was needed because it just wouldn't do for them to be activated inadvertently at the wrong time by some generic trigger.

The children were delighted on Monday when Dr. Vukovich brought in the special art project for them. Headmaster Peters stopped by and complimented him on the clever prop for the children to use with this writing project that both told the story of their Halloween experience as well as the story of their costume's inspiration. Dr. Vukovich humbly accepted the praise, a wide smile on his face as he imagined the chaos that would soon ensue.

The next six weeks were smooth sailing. The children enjoyed their PE class, and excitement built as Halloween approached. No one had experienced any ill effects from the serum. Each child could accurately recite their individual behavioral modification plan when asked under hypnosis. As the day drew near, Tabitha, the shyest child in class, asked if they could present their projects to each other in class on the day after Halloween, and Dr. Vukovich agreed at once. He even offered an additional five points of extra credit to each student who volunteered to practice their public speaking skills.

On the morning of Halloween, Dr. Vukovich rose early to load his car with the classroom decorations, cupcakes, apple juice, and the final dose of the serum to be administered during the afternoon party. He met the headmaster at the entrance as they both arrived at the same time. The headmaster accompanied him to the classroom, notifying him on the way that he had formally removed the writeup in his file given the drastic change in his attitude and treatment of the children over the past two months. He then helped him decorate the classroom before the children arrived, and gave him the key to the utility cabinet in the back of the room so he could stow the treats.

Dr. Vukovich could barely contain his excitement now that the day had finally arrived. He had prepared an easy day of lessons because he knew no one would be at peak concentration level—including himself. After they returned from lunch, they had a brief session of mediation and yoga to reinforce the trigger object. Then, he introduced a science lab lesson session about dry ice to give the classroom a spooky atmosphere before the party started.

He passed out the cupcakes and the serum-infused cups of apple juice he had prepared during the lunch period. This would be their last and largest dose of the serum: the one that would stimulate the behavior change for approximately 24 hours once the trigger mechanism was used.

Dr. Vukovich reminded the students to take a picture

before they went trick-or-treating in the evening, and to have their parents email their paper and photo before midnight.

As they left the classroom that afternoon, he passed out each child's trigger object and gave them a high five. Sterling was the last in line. Dr. Vukovich lifted his arm and shook it mightily, growling "Skol," before high-fiving Sterling. Sterling, ever the braggart, couldn't help but boast to his teacher, "My father is going to let me hold his Dane axe from his collection for my picture tonight. He is even going to let Alfred hold a scythe for his picture." Dr. Vukovich smiled broadly, "That's wonderful, Sterling. Have a great time tonight."

Dr. Vukovich spent the next hour cleaning up the disaster area his classroom had become after the party. He wanted to make sure his actions looked as normal as possible before the chaos ensued that night, so he spent a further hour grading papers. Then, he made his way down to the headmaster's office to return the key to the utility cabinet. He made some small talk with the headmaster regarding his eagerness to review the children's projects over the weekend before bidding him goodnight.

Then Dr. Vukovich walked to his car, singing "Don't Stop Me Now" by Queen under his breath. He stopped at the store to pick up an easy dinner to reheat, so he could be ready to watch the madness on television tonight. His backyard looked out toward the affluent Rawlings Ranch neighborhood, wondering what mayhem he might see over the course of the night.

Chrissy left the veterinary office where she worked and stopped by Cal Ranch to pick up a new weeding tool she had seen advertised online. The Garden Weasel Claw had four sharp, twisted steel tines perfect for ripping up the tenacious desert vegetation, foxtails and goat heads that had taken over the unused corner of her backyard during the summer. It would be dark when she got home, but she was determined to work for at least half an hour to clear the area where she planned to build a new pen for her goat Sprocket. Her husband had set posts set in the ground to mark the pen's boundaries earlier in the week. With any luck, it would all be ready by the end of the weekend.

As Chrissy approached her house, she saw Sterling running around in the front yard with his friend Alfred, dressed as a Viking and a Grim Reaper. It was obvious they were excited to go trick-or-treating soon. She waved to them as she pulled into her driveway, then entered her backyard through the gate. Her affluent neighbors were not fans of her four-legged menagerie, but the children all liked her.

Chrissy had been working hard for about twenty minutes when a clot of weeds became ensnared in the tines. She turned the claw upside down and leaned it against one of the posts as she began extricating the strong roots tangled around it. She gasped when she heard terrifying screams emanating from across the street. She turned toward the gate and began running to see if she could help. One last scream was cut off just as she realized it was coming from Sterling's house.

Chrissy ran up to the door and began banging on it, calling out, "Does anyone need help?" The door lurched open as Quincy Masterson leaned against it for support, a large antique axe protruding from his chest. He was gasping for breath. "What happened? Does anyone else need help?" Chrissy asked as she pulled off her jacket and pressed it against his chest to stanch the flow of blood.

Quincy breathlessly croaked, "Don't know. We took picture... Sterling. He... mad... came at me... axe."

Chrissy pulled out her phone, her fingers flashing across the keys as she dialed 911. She looked up as she heard Sterling's battle cry, "Skol!" as he ran a sword through his father's abdomen. Quincy Masterson collapsed, blood pouring from his lips and dripping onto his white polo shirt. Down the hallway, she saw a tiny Grim Reaper swinging a razor-sharp scythe he could barely lift, as he spun his body around, cleanly slicing off Claire Masterson's head.

"Oh fuck!" Chrissy screamed as she fumbled and dropped her phone, garnering the attention of both murderous children. She turned and began to run back across the street to her house. She grabbed the door handle, but it wouldn't turn, and she bounced off the front door.

Fuck fuck fuck! I didn't unlock the door, and my purse with my keys is still in the car. Why did I go straight into the backyard?

She looked back to see both boys approaching at an alarming speed. She turned and burst through the gate and into the backyard.

As she ran toward the back corner of the yard to hide in her shed, she tripped over the hose that had been dragged across the yard to fill the watering trough. She reeled for a few steps, trying to regain her balance, before she came to an abrupt halt against a fencepost. Blood trickled from the corner of her mouth as her gaze drifted down to the Garden Weasel protruding from her chest. Her knees grew weak as her blood pressure dropped.

Chrissy could hear the boys approaching from behind her, giggling as they saw she had impaled herself. She tried to turn her head to see them but lost her footing as her head spun. In her mad grab for the fencepost to stabilize herself, she fell forward plunging the claw through her body. Sterling reached out to catch the drops of blood dripping from the tines sticking out of her back and drew runes on his face to protect himself during the coming battle.

When the innocent victim in front of them was no longer of interest, Sterling and Alfred turned their rage on each other. Sterling ducked in the nick of time as the scythe skimmed over his head. He tucked and somersaulted toward Alfred, swinging his axe as he returned to a crouch. The axe sank into Alfred's thigh, blood geysering as he ripped it out and rose to his feet. As he spun around in a circle, he swung his axe up into Alfred's right armpit, and it came out through his left shoulder blade, severing his upper torso. Alfred slumped to the ground as Sterling let out a guttural scream of victory.

Across town, Tabitha and Bobby had just arrived at Kent's house to celebrate Halloween by watching the old black-and-white versions of *Dracula* and *The Wolf Man*. Kent was wearing a black shirt and red shorts with two large white buttons sewn on the front, along with white gloves and a pair of Mickey Mouse ears from Disneyland. Tabitha wore her favorite long pink dress, which was none the worse for wear despite how often she'd worn it to school. A silver plastic tiara with pink rhinestones crowned her head, and she held a silver plastic scepter with a star on the end. Meanwhile, Bobby arrived dressed entirely in black with a long black felt tail, presumably sewn by his mother, pinned to the back of his pants and sporting a headband with cat ears. His nose has been painted pink and black whiskers had been drawn on his cheek.

The two mothers dropping off their children had jumped out of their cars to join Kent's mom to take a picture of the children together with their signs. As the camera flashed, their behaviors changed in an instant. Bobby began to lick his hands as if they were paws and nuzzled his head against Tabitha's shoulder. Tabitha beamed as she began to pet the kitten before her. Surveying the scene, Kent declared in a high-pitched voice, "Oh boy! All you need is a little magic," as he touched the star atop Tabitha's scepter.

The three mothers were perplexed by the rapid change in the children's behavior but chalked it up to their vivid imaginations. They talked briefly, agreeing to be back at 9:30 for pickup, as the children filed into the house. The princess settled on the purple velvet chaise lounge in the corner of the living room. The kitten curled up at her feet, purring as he rubbed his hands across his eyes. Mickey entered the room singing, "Who's the leader of the club that's made for you and me?" before giggling nervously.

"Mickey Mouse!" the princess chanted dutifully, and the kitten meowed as it crawled across the floor to him and began to rub the length of his body across Mickey's shin. Kent's mother stood at the entrance to the living room watching the children's odd behavior, trying to decide whether she should be concerned. When they were still acting the same way 20 minutes later, she texted the other mothers to suggest that she drive them over to the Rawlings Ranch area to trick-or-treat at their classmates' homes. Both mothers readily agreed.

It wasn't easy, but she managed to wrangle the three children out to the car and get them seat belted safely. The fifteen-minute drive was quiet but uneventful, and she pulled up in an empty spot at the first house—the home of Chase, aka Freddy Krueger, from Dr. Vukovich's class. The princess rapped daintily on the door, holding out her pink satin bag when directed to do so by Kent's mother. Just as they were about to give up and leave, the door opened with a crash. Freddy Krueger appeared, brandishing a leather glove with steak knives taped to the fingers.

The kitten pawed at him and was rewarded with a devastating slash to the jugular. Dark red blood rippled down his torn neck as he turned with a gurgle to face Kent's mother. She screamed as her face was sprayed with bright red blood when another slash ripped through the princess' carotid artery. She grabbed Kent's hand and dragged him to the car, screaming for help, as Michael Myers appeared out of the hedges before her with a large kitchen knife. She dodged to the right, startled by a sudden rumbling directly behind her.

The mother fell to the ground, dragging Kent with her, as the chainsaw blade passed through her sternum and was drawn down, disemboweling her. She only saw a brief glimpse of Leatherface standing over her before she passed into unconsciousness and, shortly afterward, ceased to breathe.

Kent rose and waved with a cheerful, "Hello!" as two new figures appeared before him: Ghostface, brandishing a Buck Hunting knife, and a child wearing all black and a mask from *The Purge*, carrying a baseball bat. He dropped like a stone as the baseball bat him squarely on the side of his head before Ghostface pounced on him and stabbed him repeatedly.

When the new visitors had been dealt with, the killers began to attack one another. The brutal free-for-all that ensued left a killing field soaked with blood and only one costumed child still standing. Candyman, who had arrived late on the scene, was the sole survivor—albeit unsteady on his feet from the numerous serious wounds inflicted by the others.

Dr. Vukovich was surprised when the sirens began so quickly… a mere ten minutes after 6 p.m. Just as one siren died down, another started up as police and paramedics began the trek up into the foothills toward Rawlings Ranch. As darkness reigned, the neighborhood looked like a veritable Christmas tree with all the flashing first responder lights. The news vans made record time arriving on the scene, reporting the mystifying stories of the eyewitnesses on the scene.

The death toll kept rising, but early reports started at 31. One of the anchors in the studio questioned the on-scene correspondent about the startling reports that costumed children had been the perpetrators. As the correspondent began to answer, a child in black pants, a white dress shirt, red bowtie, and a long black cape lined in red satin appeared behind her. She bent down to ask him if he was okay, and he lunged at her neck. As a spurt of blood shot onto the camera lens, the report broke away to the stunned anchors stumbling over an apology for the graphic scene that had just occurred.

The news report continued through the night as more information came in. At dawn, the chief of police held a press conference. He explained that many children of the Rawlings Ranch neighborhood had inexplicably begun a killing spree that started with their parents and siblings, eventually extending to each other and innocent neighbors. The official death toll, barring any unforeseen circumstances, stood at 51. One child had been captured as he was thrusting a spear into the eye of his neighbor.

Dr. Vukovich marveled at the irony that the one child caught could be none other than Sterling Masterson. He received a call just after 5 a.m. from the school superintendent, letting him know that the Wingfield Academy would be closed for at least the next week. The superintendent explained that he had received a call from the chief of police regarding the incident. Besides his entire class being murdered, Headmaster Peters had been cut down in the fray. The superintendent offered Dr. Vukovich counseling, which he accepted on the spot.

Dr. Vukovich was called into the police precinct over the ensuing weeks as the tragic incident was investigated. Sterling Masterson's erratic, violent behavior had ceased soon after dinner the day after Halloween. At that time, he expressed no knowledge of the events of the previous 24 hours. He was transferred to the custody of a leading pediatric residential psychiatric treatment facility for assessment on the recommendation of social services and the court system. No one questioned the fact that Sterling's grandfather was a leading member of the state Supreme Court.

Dr. Vukovich took a leave of absence from the school, citing emotional distress, before moving away after the start of the year. In February, he called Dr. Smirnov to report that he had been unsuccessful in his effort to relaunch their research. He offered to send the material back, but Dr. Smirnov declined.

Dr. Vukovich returned to teaching at an inner city school in Chicago, where he felt he might have more of a chance of making a difference. When he found a new set of roadblocks, his thoughts returned to Serum MC14.

Stephen H. Provost

Trunk or Treat

Cannibals aren't typically party animals or social influencers. Mostly, they keep to themselves. Killing and eating people isn't exactly the most socially acceptable activity—even at Halloween. Most cannibals are kind of awkward. They don't make friends easily, and since there aren't that many of them, they tend to be loners. Those who do befriend them don't hang around long... either because they decide it's not good for their health or... well, cannibals *do* get hungry, after all, and their particular taste in food isn't exactly conducive to developing long-term relationships.

Earline Eakins wasn't a cannibal, but she wanted to be one. She had spent the past few years preparing herself to partake of her first meal of *homo sapiens sapiens* and had already decided what she wanted to try first. She had always preferred veal to mature cuts of beef. Why not apply the same principle to human dishes? Young and fresh would be best, she was sure, so she set out to find the perfect introduction to her new "lifestyle."

She didn't have to wait long. Earline worked at the corner drugstore across from Beechwood Grammar School, which happened to have an ice cream counter near the front. Beechwood kids would come in all the time to buy a banana split or cookie dough cone, but they usually showed up in groups at lunch or right after school left out. That didn't give a loner like Earline much opportunity to befriend any of them. Besides, most of them just made fun of her spindly arms and the way she kept her hair wound tightly in a bun on the back of her head.

Earline hated how mean they were to her and to each other, which made her feel less guilty about her desire to eat one of them. She just hoped their ugly attitudes wouldn't make them taste tough or "gamey" once she'd chosen a suitable subject—if she could even manage to procure one of them. They never stayed at the counter long, because they didn't like her, and they were always together, which meant it was hard to cull the most vulnerable kiddo from the herd.

Candace Watters was different. The 10-year-old girl with a face full of freckles and frizzy red hair came in on Saturdays by herself, when school wasn't in session. She always purchased a comic book, then came to the counter for a Neapolitan sundae in a bowl with hot fudge topping. She smiled at Earline when she saw her and never made fun of her. Instead, she just politely placed her order and said "thank you" when she picked it up. Then she went over to one of the round tables with the checkerboard tops and ate it while she quietly read the latest issue of *Wonder Woman* or *The Amazing Spider-Man*.

She was about to take her sundae over to her usual spot one Saturday, but before she turned away from the counter, Earline asked her a question. "Do you ever eat anything but ice cream?" she said with a nervous laugh.

Candy (as she preferred to be called) had said she did, but that she only had enough money to get herself one thing, and that ice cream was her favorite. Her foster parents gave her money for lunch at school, but instead, she saved it up all week to come in on Saturdays for her sundae and comic book.

"Don't you get hungry, though?" Earline had asked.

"Of course I do. But I wouldn't trade one of your sundaes for a whole week of spaghetti and ketchup at that stupid school."

"Tell you what," said Earline, leaning over the counter. "How about I take you to my house after you're done with your ice cream and make you up a real nice home-cooked meal. How does that sound to you, hmm?"

Earline had expected her to say no—she was very used to the other children all shying away from her and making fun of her—or telling her she needed her foster parents' permission. But she didn't. Instead, she answered with her usual politeness: "That sounds really good, Miss Earline. I would like that very much."

When Earline took her home, her mouth was watering at the thought of making little Candy her first meal. She wouldn't do it tonight, of course. She would need to butter her up a little (she laughed inwardly at her own choice of words) before that. Besides, since the girl had actually been nice to her, she at least deserved the home-cooked meal she'd been promised.

Earline went all out, buying groceries on their way to her mobile home so she could cook up a meal of filet mignon, asparagus, and baked potato. It cost her most of that week's paycheck, but it would be worth it. She knew she was a good cook and the meal would be delicious, and she also knew it would be the perfect appetizer for the next supper she planned with the girl.

"Do you live here all by yourself?" the girl asked her, gravy dripping down her chin.

"Yes," said Earline, smiling. "Do you like my home?"

Candy nodded eagerly. Earline hadn't been expecting this; she never let anyone else know she lived at Twin Oaks Park, because didn't like being called trailer trash. Besides, she valued her privacy.

What the girl said next surprised her even more. "I wish I could live here with you," she said. "My foster parents are always mean to me, and you seem like such a nice lady."

Earline's smile widened. "Then you can come over anytime you like. You can even come here trick-or-treating on Halloween. Just don't bring any of those other kids from your school. They don't like me."

Candy bowed her head. "Oh, I wouldn't do that," she said. "They don't like *me*, either. But my foster parents won't let me go trick or treating. They're very religious, and they say that it's a sin to go out pretending to be a ghost or a witch. So, they take me to their church instead for something they call trunk-or-treat. It's boring."

"They don't sound very nice at all," Earline said. "They would probably call *me* a witch!"

"I bet they would!" Candy agreed, and they both laughed.

"I tell you what," Earline said. "Halloween is next Saturday, so why don't you come over again after ice cream, and I'll have a costume ready for you, and we can take the trick-or-treat to them. We'll make them treat you the way you deserve to be treated, or we'll have a very funny trick to play on them. Do you like that idea?"

Candy nodded as she sliced off a piece of filet mignon with her steak knife and shoveled it eagerly into her mouth. "I think I do," she said. "This is so good. Can we have it again before trick-or-treating next week?"

Earline smiled but shook her head. "I have something even better planned for next week's dinner."

"Ooh, what's that?" Candy asked, her mouth full of potato slathered with butter and sour cream.

"You'll see, my dear," Earline said, her eyes narrowing and dancing mirthfully. "You'll see."

On Halloween, Candy came over to Earline's house right after ice cream, just as they had planned. She disappeared inside the woman's tan double-wide, but no one saw her after that. The neighbors didn't hear anything either, but they did smell the aroma of sizzling meat, covered in onions and mild peppers, carried on smoke through the window she left open a crack behind her drawn curtains.

When the meat was cooked and oh so tender, Earline put it on a plate and sliced it into little squares. Finally, the moment she'd been waiting for: She put it to her lips for a taste, and her eyes opened wide in amazement.

"It's even better than I expected!" she whispered. "This is too good to keep to myself. I must share it with my friends. Except, oh, that's right, I don't have any friends. Well, I'm not going to let that stop me!"

Earline took each of the tender bits of meat and tied them up in colored cellophane squares. Then she loaded them all into a sack and put them in her trunk before driving down the road to the Holy Lamb Baptist Temple—the church Candy's parents had wanted to take her.

They'll never take her there again.

When she arrived, she found the parking lot full of cars, each with its trunk wide open. The lot was decorated with hay bales and uncarved pumpkins, but no jack-o-lanterns or witches, and certainly no demons. Young children were going from one car to the next, where adults would take something from a bag in their trunk and pass it out to them. Earline noticed it was usually a small bag of gumballs or miniature chocolate bar, but some of the adults were giving out pocket Bibles instead. Many of the kids weren't dressed up at all, and those who were wore things like Mickey Mouse, princess, or kittycat costumes (no black cats, though).

Parking next to one, a black Chevy Colorado, she opened the door and got out. Her late-model Subaru looked decidedly out of place next in the line of high-end SUVs and luxury cars, and the man standing beside the Colorado studiously avoided looking at her as she walked around behind the car and popped her trunk.

Most of the kids avoided her, too (although one young girl came by for a sample of her "goodies"). This was nothing new. She recognized some of them from the ice cream counter at work, and she knew they'd be jeering at her and calling her names if they hadn't been at church where their parents could hear. She understood the truth of it, though: Their parents were thinking the same things in their heads; they just didn't have the courage to say anything out loud.

She'd only been there a few minutes when two adults approached her.

"Have you seen a 10-year-old girl with red hair and freckles?" the woman asked. "She sounded more inconvenienced than worried. "She was supposed to meet us here."

"I'm sorry, I haven't," Earline said.

"Aren't you the woman from the ice cream counter?" the woman said.

Earline nodded.

"She told us about you," she said in an even, offhanded way.

"I haven't seen her," Earline repeated nervously, hoping the couple didn't notice her tone.

If they did, they didn't seem to care.

"Well, thanks anyway," the man said distractedly. "I told you she wouldn't obey us. 'Folly is bound up in the heart of a child.' Proverbs 22:15." He paused for a moment and looked in Earline's trunk. "Oh, I see you brought something. Can I try it?" he asked.

Earline reached in and produced a wrapped piece of meat. "I'm sorry if it's a little cold," she said.

The man cocked his head to one side, unwrapped the morsel, and without paying much attention, popped it in his mouth. "That's... interesting," he said. "I think I like it. What do you call it?"

"Cooked Candy," she said simply.

The woman turned her head, her attention caught by the sound of the word. "Did you say Candy?" she asked. "That's our daughter's name."

"I know. She helped me make it. You might say she threw herself into the recipe." Earline shot them a mischievous gleam and winked.

The man looked as though he might be sick.

Earline returned home that night, having been kicked out of the parking lot at Holy Lamb Baptist Church.

There was, of course, no evidence that she had actually cooked little Candy Watters' and chopped up her body before serving it to those self-righteous bastards. She had been careful to cover her tracks.

Besides, she hadn't done anything wrong.

Candy got a good laugh out of it when she got back, and the two of them had another scrumptious meal together, finishing off the filet she had cut into pieces and handed out at the trunk-or-treat.

As for Earline, she decided to put her cannibalistic inclinations on the back burner, so to speak, at least for the present. In the end, she just couldn't bring herself to actually making "Cooked Candy." The girl was, after all, the first person who'd ever treated her with kindness. There would be others more deserving of the fate she had envisioned for the little redhead, but for now she was content with her new job as sous-chef at Maison Capri downtown.

It seemed her Cooked Candy had impressed that one girl who had tried it... and who recognized her from the ice cream counter. She just happened to be the daughter of the restaurant owner, who brought her in for a tryout... and hired her on the spot.

"Do you have any other recipes you'd suggest for our menu?" he asked her.

"Oh, I have one or two," she said. "But they're my own special secrets. Maybe I'll cook them up for you... when the time is right."

Sharon Marie Provost

The Lurker

There's that noise again! What the hell is that?

Elaine had heard that creaking noise in the roof again, like the house was settling in a heavy wind.

But there wasn't even a whisper of a breeze outside.

Lately, Elaine had been hearing all sorts of weird noises within her house that she hadn't noticed before. But when she looked around the house, she could never find their source. Maybe she was just noticing them because she was spending so much more time here lately—now that she had started working from home three weeks ago, just after the July 4th holiday. To be honest, she had never spent much time here before now. She had only moved in two months ago, and she had worked long hours previously. She got home with enough time to eat a late take-out dinner, take a long bath, and then head to bed.

Normally, a stupid creak or squeak wouldn't bother Elaine. But it was more than that. And it wasn't just because she had been under a lot of stress lately, either. The past few months, she *had* been under tremendous pressure from her job as she worked her way up the ladder... and then there was the loss of her mother. That's why she had decided to decrease her hours and start working at home. It had taken the unexpected loss of several family members over the past year, some of them heartbreakingly young, to teach her that life was precious and all too short. Maybe making partner wasn't as important as it had seemed in her own head.

But it wasn't just noises that she was experiencing. That's what was concerning. Items in her home would seemingly disappear; only to reappear later as soon as she didn't need them— and in a location that defied her meticulous, organized nature. In fact, they would reappear only after she had left the house, which wasn't often, since she was such a workaholic.

Weirder still: Items had appeared in her home that she staunchly couldn't remember buying. Yes, they were items that she had researched online and wanted to buy... eventually... but she was sure she had not pulled the trigger on those purchases.

Or had she?

It was this confounding mystery and the fuzzy-headedness she felt from nights of fitful sleep that kept her wondering if she was losing it.

Elaine realized she was obsessing again over all these issues instead of working, and she had an urgent deadline to meet.

What she needed was a soothing cup of chamomile tea before resuming her work. She filled the kettle and turned on the stove, wiping the sweat from her brow as she turned away. She was so engrossed in her thoughts, she hadn't noticed how warm it had gotten in the front of the house, where the sunlight streamed in each afternoon. She walked back to her room to change into her shorts. She stopped short at the door, a perplexed look on her face, when she saw her shorts lying on the bed. For the life of her, she could not remember having laid them out this morning.

Damn it! What is wrong with me? What is with my memory these days?

She shook her head as she began to change her clothes. After removing her sweats, she made a point to remember putting them in the laundry basket in the corner of the room.

The kettle began to whistle, so she returned to the kitchen to prepare her tea. The rest of the afternoon passed quietly as she dove into her work, finishing the project just as the last rays of daylight passed behind the mountains. To her thinking, she had earned a treat after the long day of work, so she ordered takeout from Olive Garden.

Forty minutes later, she returned from picking up her food and headed out to eat her dinner on the patio in the cool evening air. To her surprise, she found the back door unlocked. She chastised herself for forgetting and vowed to be more responsible.

Elaine's frustration at her own negligence lately knew no bounds. If asked for one word to describe her, surely most people you asked would say "responsible." If not that, then "trustworthy," "reliable," "steadfast," or "stable." None of those words seemed to apply, though, in the past few weeks.

She finished her dinner quickly and decided to go to bed early. She had finished her last project that would require overtime. From now on, it would be normal business hours for her: Monday through Friday from 8 a.m. to 5 p.m. If she started getting enough sleep and developed some work-life balance, surely her head would be clearer, and her problems would resolve themselves.

Elaine walked down the hall to her room and found the door shut. For the life of her, she could not remember having shut the door when she rushed out earlier to get the kettle. No matter—she was making changes to her life. She would be done with this issue soon. She climbed into bed wearily and fell asleep almost instantly.

She awoke a few hours later to the sound of a door shutting... and then another... and then another. She peered desperately into the darkness in the hall, but she couldn't see anything—not even a shadow. A moment later, she stifled a scream when her bedroom door closed as well. She quietly jumped out of bed and ran to lock the door. Her hand shook as she dialed 911 to summon the police.

The operator kept her on the line and tried to calm her as the police headed over. When they arrived, she told the operator where they could find her hide-a-key on the porch. She was much too afraid to go out into the hall and let them in, even if she hadn't heard any more noises since her door shut.

A short while later, they knocked on her bedroom door and identified themselves. The operator on the line verified that they were the officers who had been dispatched to the scene. She opened the door quickly and, in a breathless rush, began to tell them what had happened:

"Last night, I went out to get dinner. and when I came

home my back door was unlocked. I thought I had forgotten to lock it, but when I went back to bed later, my bedroom door was shut. I never shut it... not even at night. I have been under a lot of stress lately. I thought I was losing it. Anyhow, I went to bed early and fell asleep right away. I woke up 15 minutes ago when I heard a door down the hall shut and then the other two and then my own. I didn't see anybody, but it was dark. Did you see anybody? Was my home broken into?"

"Ma'am, please calm down and take a breath. Let's start at the beginning. When you found your back door unlocked, was there any sign of it having been broken into? Was anything missing in your home?"

"No, I don't think so. I'm not an expert, though. Can you look? And no, I think all my belongings are here."

"And do you know what doors were shut, besides your own that is?"

"You just walked down the hall. I am sure you saw there are only three doors in the hallway besides my own... the bathroom, the spare room and my office. They are the only doors in the house besides the front and back doors and my en suite bathroom," she replied haughtily, frustration clearly in her voice.

"Ma'am, I am not trying to be obtuse. It's just that there are no doors shut besides your own. The front door was locked and showed no signs of forced entry. The back door was shut and locked. As you mentioned, we did not see any signs of forced entry there either. When we just came down the hall, all the other doors you described were open. Nothing looks disturbed. Could you have been dreaming?"

"No, sir... er, I mean Officer. My door was shut when you arrived because SOMEONE SHUT IT. I *never* shut my bedroom door. Can you dust the doorknobs for fingerprints? Will you check all the rooms to make sure no one is hiding? I am not crazy. I am not a child suffering from nightmares."

The officers looked at each other and nodded as they let out nearly inaudible sighs. They spent the next hour searching the house, each and every room. No intruder was found. Next, they dusted the knobs for fingerprints. They took pictures of each print found before lifting them with tape. Neither of them was a fingerprint expert, but all the prints appeared to be from the same three or four fingers. They promised to deliver the prints to their crime lab and asked Elaine to come down to the station the next day to give her prints for exclusionary purposes. They then wished her a good night before taking their leave.

Elaine locked up the front door, and then proceeded to double check that the back door and every window was locked as well. She left her porch light on as well as a light in the kitchen and living room. The curtains or blinds were all shut, so no one could see in, but they would see the glow of the lights on and maybe leave her alone. Finally, she climbed back into bed, and eventually she fell into a restless slumber.

The next morning, she rose early and headed down to the local precinct. The officer at the front desk greeted her politely and then looked up the report number she provided. He quickly and efficiently obtained her prints and promised to have someone call her with the results as soon as possible. Later that afternoon, she received a call from a technician in the crime lab.

All the prints that had been obtained were hers.

She thanked him and hung up quickly before letting loose a scream of frustration. She knew what she had heard last night. Her door had shut right in front of her eyes. Yet, the officers had found no unidentified fingerprints, and all the hall doors had been open.

Elaine spent the afternoon investigating all the possibilities she could imagine that might possibly explain her situation: a brain tumor, sleepwalking, stress, the paranormal, stalkers, and even mental illness. But nothing seemed to explain the specifics of her situation.

She called her employer, telling them she was ill and needed a week of personal leave. She then made an appointment with her doctor, who prescribed her a sleeping pill and told her to relax for the next week... maybe even go on vacation. He even provided her with a note for her employer.

Elaine returned home and promptly logged onto her computer, not to work, but to reserve a room at a hotel. She closed out the Amazon page she'd been using to research a book and some household items she wanted to buy soon.

She had promised herself that one day she would go out into the desert to explore some of the many local ghost towns. Now seemed like the perfect time. She booked three nights down in Tonopah at the Mizpah Hotel so she would have time to visit Goldfield, Beatty and Rhyolite. Then she booked two nights in Yermo, so she could go see Calico, and then make the relatively short drive for a day trip to Oatman, Arizona. She would start the drive home Saturday and spend one final night in Mammoth Lakes before returning home on Sunday to prepare for work the next day.

Elaine quickly packed only the bare necessities, opting to leave her laptop at home to unplug from the world at large. She once again checked all the doors and windows to make sure everything was locked up tight. Then she did a quick inventory of the house, so she would notice if any changes occurred while she was gone. She would either prove that an intruder had been visiting her home, or she would be able to relax, knowing this had all been just a terrible mix-up caused by stress and a lack of sleep.

The week of vacation was just what Elaine needed. She couldn't remember having slept that many hours each night since she was a child. The tension headaches disappeared. She did not experience any unusual activity—not that she had expected to—so her stress level dropped each day. She was even able to spread her mother's ashes in the wilderness near Mammoth, as she had promised to do. She finally felt a peace she had not known in years. As much as she loved to work, it was clearly not the key to her happiness.

With great reluctance but a clear mind, she began her drive home on Sunday.

She entered the house to find everything just as she had left it. No items were moved. Nothing added. Nothing removed. The house was locked tighter than a drum. She released an audible sigh of relief as she began to unpack, then went to the kitchen to make dinner. The evening passed peacefully with no worries, and Elaine slept soundly as she had on her trip.

The next day, she began work bright and early. The hours passed quickly as she worked to catch up on projects from the previous week. Her concentration was broken by a sharp knock at the door. Elaine considered ignoring it, since she wasn't expecting anyone, but she heard a noise by the door. When she opened it, she was surprised to see it had been an Amazon delivery. She couldn't remember having ordered anything lately. And it wasn't like she really had any friends or any family left who might have sent her something.

Trepidation rose within her as she struggled to break through the tape on the package.

She soon found that the contents were no cause for concern: It was simply a book she had saved in her Amazon cart for a future purchase. But she remembered closing the Amazon tab the week before. She *knew* she hadn't actually placed her order... at least not deliberately. Maybe she had accidentally clicked on the "place order" button in her haste to book her vacation. Yet... she didn't see how she could have done that. Her mind battled with itself, trying to resist the temptation to worry.

She placed the book on her side table and decided to return to work. However, her mind kept drifting to the book. Finally, she decided to resolve the mystery by looking up her Amazon account. To her shock, there it was: The purchase *did* appear on her account on that very day. She checked her email, and there was the message confirming the purchase.

Her eyes darted to the time and date the email was received. The purchase had occurred on the day she left, but hours *after* she had departed. She *couldn't have* accidentally placed the order. It was impossible. She hadn't even been home and hadn't taken her computer with her.

She returned to her Amazon order page and looked up the details of the purchase. It had been made using an Amazon gift card.

She had never been given an Amazon gift card, yet alone purchased one herself.

She called customer service right away to see who the gift card belonged to; however, to her dismay, she learned that it had been purchased at a third-party retailer.

With cash.

There was no way to track the owner..

She resolved to put the book out of her mind. Yet it spun

with all the possibilities.

Could she have left her old work computer at headquarters logged into her Amazon account? Perhaps a co-worker had seen it and bought her that book as a kind gesture.

Could there have been a computer glitch at Amazon?

A stalker? But What kind of stalker buys you gifts?

None of these answers made sense. Yet there had to be some kind of reasonable explanation, even if she couldn't come up with it right away.

Elaine set the book aside and returned to her work.

The rest of the afternoon passed without disturbance, so her nerves began to quiet as well. She quit working at 5 p.m. and went to the kitchen, determined to stay on a 9 to 5 work schedule.

She began making dinner and nearly jumped out of her skin when she heard the creak in the roof once again... followed shortly by the click of a door in the hall shutting. She grabbed her largest knife out of the woodblock and quietly crept through the kitchen. She checked the living room mirror on the opposite wall and couldn't see anyone in the hallway, so she began to make her way quietly down the hall.

She hadn't imagined the sound of the door clicking: The door to her office was closed. She searched every corner of the spare bedroom, pulled back the shower curtain in the bathroom, then checked her own bedroom—peering into the bathroom and walk-in closet—before approaching the office.

She slowly turned the knob, then jumped into the room with the knife raised above her head.

The room was empty.

She searched all the other rooms again but couldn't find a single item out of place.

All the doors and windows were locked.

How could someone have been in here but left no trace? How could the door have closed on its own? The HVAC isn't on. The windows aren't open, so there isn't a draft in the house...

Elaine couldn't keep from trembling as she walked back down the hall to the kitchen, where she resumed her dinner prep and tried to put it all out of her mind.

It's an old house. Old houses are drafty, even when doors and windows are not open. You are being paranoid. This is ridiculous. Get your shit together!

After dinner, she retreated to her room to snuggle in bed and read the book she had received. She was trying to convince herself that all was well, as if she had received it under perfectly normal circumstances. Still, she had left the lights on in several rooms because their warm glow made her feel safer.

She was just starting to relax when she heard a shuffle in her closet.

Elaine jumped out of bed like a shot and bolted across the hall to her office, slamming the door and locking it behind her. Something tripped her as she backed up toward the desk, and she fell to the floor. Her eyes swung toward the object: It was the vacuum she had saved in her Amazon cart along with the book she hadn't ordered. And she MOST DEFINITELY hadn't ordered the vacuum cleaner, either.

Elaine stifled a scream as she heard footsteps in the hallway coming toward her. She scrambled to her feet and grabbed the phone, frantically dialing 911... but there was no dial tone. She screamed when the doorknob started turning and the door bounced on its hinges, as something, or someone, bounced off of it.

Elaine rushed to the window, quietly unlocked it, and

snuck out.

She ran to her neighbor's house, the closest person to a friend she had, across the street and banged on the door, pleading for help. When the door opened, she rushed inside and asked to use the phone to call the police. Once again, the 911 operator stayed on the phone with her as units were dispatched.

The sirens came shortly.

Then the police arrived in two squad cars...

But they found the front door still locked.

The officers from one squad car set a watch at the front and back entrances, while the other officers approached Elaine and asked for the key. She gave them a spare key, which she kept at the neighbor's house, and they rushed in to begin their search.

Once again, they found no intruder, nor any evidence that anyone had been there. The house was locked up, her bedroom closet looked undisturbed, the office door appeared undamaged, and they found no vacuum in her office.

This time, the officers were not as polite when they told her their findings. Clearly, they no longer believed her. The second car left the scene as soon as it was apparent that nothing had been found. Then the remaining officers began to question her about her life and health. They even went so far as to ask if she had a therapist, then issued a stern warning about filing false reports.

Elaine pleaded with them to believe her, but soon realized it was useless. She couldn't explain in her own mind where the vacuum or the intruder had gone, so there was no sense trying to convince them.

After they left, Elaine returned to her room and locked herself in. She spent the night crying, wracking her brain to find *some* explanation for the weird occurrences in her home.

It was fruitless.

The next day she rose, exhausted, and emailed her boss rather than calling in, then fell into a blur of alcohol-induced haze and depression. She no longer reacted when she heard noises in the house. The vacuum reappeared, this time in the hall closet, but she didn't even acknowledge it. When she went out to the liquor store to buy more gin, she was nonplussed when she found flowers on her kitchen table. When she found her lingerie was missing from her dresser, she took it in stride. Elaine wallowed in her belief of being a helpless victim of some paranormal entity or a stalker who always evaded detection.

Meanwhile, the strange noises in the back of her house were becoming more frequent. The more she ignored them, the more often they occurred.

Finally, on Halloween night, she was so tightly wound that she screamed down the hall, "What do you want from me? You win. I give up." The noises stopped instantly, and the rest of the evening passed silently. She had turned off her porch light, so she hadn't been bothered by all the children she had heard streaming up and down the street trick-or-treating. Elaine was too tired to care one way or the other, so she retired early.

Sometime in the middle of the night, she was startled awake by a scraping noise inside her closet. Then it dawned on her: The intruder must have been using the access panel to the crawlspace. That's how he'd been getting in.

But even as she realized this, the closet door was already opening. Her fear overwhelmed her. She didn't dare run past it or look over to confront what—or who—was coming at her. She squeezed her eyes shut, hoping it would leave her alone.

Minutes passed without a sound, but she could feel someone watching her. Goose bumps and chills ran up and down her body. Her flesh tingled as she waited to feel its touch. When she could no longer stand the suspense, her eyes popped open to confront the sight... of a man smiling down at her.

"Well, hello there, sunshine. It took you long enough."

Elaine opened her mouth to let out a shriek, but he was faster. His finger was upon her lips instantly as he began to shush her.

"That is not very nice of you. Your lover has come to greet you after you finally gave yourself to me earlier. That is no way to treat me after all the presents I have given you."

Elaine's pupils dilated as she listened to his words, her fight-or-flight instinct finally kicking in. She opened her mouth and lunged forward, slamming it shut around his finger, severing it.

Blood squirted all over her face.

"Never! I will never be yours," she screamed as she turned to leap out of bed. She never saw the fist coming at her head, once and then again. She felt the blood run down her temple as the pain shot through her head like a lightning bolt. The room was spinning, but she fought the dizziness as she tried to run. The second blow came in a flash, and her vision faded to black as her body slumped over the edge of the bed.

"Hey, did they finally find her? Is she the one selling the house?" the mailman asked as he stopped his truck in front of the house.

The real estate agent was pushing the for-sale sign stakes into the lawn. She paused to answer him. "No. It has been seven years since her disappearance. She was declared legally dead by the courts. The probate court found she didn't have any family left, so the state is liquidating her assets." Elizabeth resumed her efforts with the sign.

"That was one strange case, I tell ya. No sign of foul play. None of her belongings were missing, including her purse and money. She was expected at work the next day for a meeting with the board. I heard she had made partner. No one could explain her disappearance, and no one has seen her since. How could she disappear like that?" The mailman pointed to the house across the street and one over from Elaine's house. "That woman over there is a regular Mrs. Kravitz," he snorted as he laughed at his own joke and used his thumb to wiggle his nose, pantomiming Samantha from *Bewitched*. "She is up all hours of the day staring out her front window. She keeps track of all the goings-on in this neighborhood. I heard she didn't see anything strange in the days leading up to her disappearance. She saw that lady come home that day with groceries—and then she was mysteriously never seen again. Whooo-ooooo-ooooo!" he trilled as he wiggled his fingers in the air laughing again.

Ass!

Elizabeth nodded her head distractedly as she straightened the sign in the holder. "It was all very strange, but truly none of my concern." With one final stomp, she jammed the stakes deep into the ground and turned her back on him before heading into the house.

She was truly perfect for my collection. *I never get tired of rewatching her reactions on the videos.*

He removed the thumb drive from his computer, walked over to the leather case and flipped up the latches to open it. He reverently placed the drive back in the slot labeled *My Sweet*

Elaine July 2-October 31, 2023. It joined 23 matching drives, each labeled with a different woman's name and time periods varying from three weeks to three months. His thumb softly stroked the top of the drive, then he closed the case with a sigh. He returned it to the wall safe hidden behind his favorite signed piece of art by Luis Royo.

The art depicted a mostly naked woman in the clutches of a monster, possessing her body and soul. It depicted exactly how he felt about those women in his collection. He watched them... he lurked on the fringes of their lives... taking in every moment of their private existence at home alone. Then, slowly but surely, he insinuated himself into their lives, taking control of their thoughts and emotions. They were obsessed with the thought of him, even if they didn't even know of his existence.

Then when he finally had complete control over them, he removed them from the world... from the influence of others who may try to steal them from him. Each time, he would find just the perfect time to surprise them and introduce them to the object of their obsession. They always tried to pretend they didn't know him, and that they didn't belong to him. But he knew they were just lying bitches, like all women. The bitches of the world unite—girl power and all that shit. Down with the patriarchy! Fuck that shit! He would not accept that kind of behavior from these bitches or any others.

Eventually, when he came to make them him his... officially, they always made him mad. They were his belongings... one way... or the other. Unfortunately, their damn feminazi nature always got in the way of the happy ending. They made him hurt them—kill them. Then there was just the matter of where to keep them. At home, he only dared to keep the videos he made of them in their home when they thought they were alone, then when they began to question if they were... and, finally, when they accepted that they were not.

Their bodies were an entirely different matter.

On one of his many long hikes, he had found an abandoned mine deep in the desert, surrounded by a tall fence and covered in warning signs. It was obvious no one had been there in many, many years. It was the perfect location.

He would drive out there in the dark of night and, when the early rays of dawn shone, he would carry their bodies to the mine's entrance and drop them down hundreds of feet to their new home. He couldn't see the women in his collection, but he knew they were there, safe and undisturbed. Besides, he had his movies to watch whenever he wanted to visit them.

He had acquired several girls before Elaine and many in the seven years since. But she still held a special place in his heart. She had been his longest courtship and become his favorite gal. That bitch had been a fighter though. The evidence was clear when one looked at his left hand; the index finger crudely amputated near the junction with his palm. He had finally broken her on the perfect day, Halloween. No one thought anything about seeing people dressed in all manner of costumes and carrying a variety of props. Even when things did not go as planned, and he left seemingly (or, in this case, actually) carrying a body wrapped in a sheet.

No one in the neighborhood ever reported seeing anything suspicious that night.

Of course, he had to take a trip down memory lane and watch her video today after he saw the story on the news about the court's official death declaration and the dissolution of her estate. But now it was time to get going. He had a new gal, after all, and she would be home soon. It was time to sneak back into her home and work on breaking her down. This new one was a little different, more subservient. He just knew it would work this time.

If not, there was still plenty of room in his collection.

Stephen H. Provost

Once Upon a Star

The clouds looked darker than they had that morning, which was strange: The weather report had called for clearing skies.

Erron stepped out of his Ford Focus and shut the door, staring up at the sky—or what he could see of it. Except for a faint golden glow on the western horizon, his view was obscured by those clouds.

They weren't the kind of clouds that chased one another across the sky, hurling bolts of lightning and bleeding buckets of rain. They were the sort that hung down from the sky like a drenched towel that clung to Erron's skin tenaciously, defying its own purpose: Towels were supposed to keep you dry.

The dimming light of late afternoon made the wet mist feel all the more oppressive.

Erron glanced around him, unsure of where he was. He hadn't been paying attention when he headed north from Fresno, his mind consumed with more pressing thoughts—at least to him—than where he was going.

"Anywhere but here," he'd said to himself.

This "anywhere" was in the middle of nowhere.

And he was stuck here now, having neglected to fill his gas tank before setting out and having been too preoccupied to notice the needle edging closer to empty. His cellphone was dead, too: He hadn't thought to charge it. Not a good look for someone who'd just finished his junior year in college with a 3.88 grade-point average.

He had a good excuse, he told himself, for neglecting things he would normally remember. The curves on this two-lane road north of Mariposa had taken every last shred of concentration… apart from that which he devoted to the events of earlier that day.

That's when he'd seen them together: Curtiss and Maricia. He'd been with Maricia for six months—not a particularly long time, but long enough to fall in love. After seeing her hang all over Curtiss, though, it was clear to Erron that his feelings were not shared.

Curtiss, he felt sure, couldn't love anyone. But he had that greasy-haired, unwashed Daryl Dixon kind of look. Women loved that shit. They said they cared about love and devotion and all that medieval chivalry crap, but they'd drop you in a hot minute if they got a whiff of that bad boy vibe.

He'd thought Maricia was different, but he'd thought

wrong. Her whole "shy girl" persona was just an act. She was just like all the rest.

Maybe what he needed was a medieval girl, or at least a woman from a time when Daryl Dixon didn't exist and love still meant something more than hooking up with the hottest guy. Not that his buddies were any better. They saw big tits or a tight ass, and they were all about that.

Romance was dead.

Erron knew he didn't belong in the 21st century, but he wasn't sure where he belonged.

Just "anywhere but here."

A high, shrill cry jarred him loose from his bitter musings, startling him so much that he jumped in place. It sounded like a woman being attacked, but though he looked frantically around him, he could see no one.

Then it came again, joined by a second, overlapping shriek.

What was happening?

Erron had to do something. He ran, desperate, in the direction of the cries, but when the next one came, it sounded more distant. He stopped, listening in hopes of getting a fix on it. But there was only silence, amplified as it echoed off the low-lying clouds that reached down as if to embrace the lonesome buildings on either side of the road. Abandoned and forlorn, they looked more than a century old, constricted by vines and shrub-trees. Growing amok, the ailanthus burrowed into the earth with tenacious roots and wrapped their gnarled limbs around brick and wood and plaster in a mad embrace.

Cracked windows and weathered boards teased the promise of shelter—however dank and drafty—from the wet chill of twilight. But "no trespassing" signs, slapped on corroded green iron doors held fast by padlocks, reneged decisively on that promise.

Erron wondered if they were meant to keep the curious from entering for the sake of the owners or for the wellbeing of intruders. Or perhaps to protect the ghosts who dwelt within.

Erron didn't believe in ghosts, even now, so close to Halloween. Maricia had been all into that. She'd gone on and on about the "veil" between the spirit realm and our world being thinnest around All Hallows'. She'd even encouraged Erron to hire a medium so she could contact her dead sister.

"What a waste of money," he'd told her. The dead were dead.

Maybe he should have gone along with it, though. Maybe if he had, she wouldn't have hooked up with Curtiss, and he wouldn't be alone in this desolate town on the first week of summer vacation.

He shoved these thoughts from his mind and walked back toward his car, pulling his arms close to his body against the chill. There were no motels in sight, and he had to find a place to sleep.

Resigned to being stuck where he was, he clicked his electronic key to release the trunk. Thank God he'd left the sleeping bag in there from that camping trip he'd taken with Maricia to Dinkey Creek a couple of weeks back.

They hadn't taken a tent because they'd wanted to see the meteor shower.

"We could wish upon a star," Maricia had said.

He'd made his wish, but it hadn't come true.

"Superstitious bullshit," he grumbled to himself. "Just like ghosts and that thin veil crap."

Erron thought he heard a woman's voice beside him: "You're too young to be so jaded." But it was less than a whisper, and Erron dismissed it as his own mind filling in the silence that surrounded him.

He looked up at a large two-story building. Vacant and soundless like the rest, it loomed over him, dark and menacing against the fading light. The front porch, strewn with broken patio furniture and lawn tools left to rust by some former occupant, sat shielded from the street by broken latticework, its white paint chipped and faded.

Another of those "no trespassing" signs had been affixed to the front door frame, which bore the address 10001 Main Street. Erron laughed to himself, unsure which was funnier: that this abandoned one-lane strip of cracked asphalt should be called Main Street, or that an address of 10001 should be needed on a street that appeared just a block or two long.

He passed the building and came to an open field beside it, overgrown with weeds and grasses but as good a place as any to bed down for the night... as long as it didn't rain.

Erron cast an apprehensive glance overhead, but the clouds still didn't seem like storm clouds, and he reassured himself that it was safer to risk a little rain than to ignore the "no trespassing" signs. Maybe squatters had already claimed these places, or maybe they were being used by druggies who'd set up pot grows or meth labs inside. This place was far enough away from everything that either was entirely possible.

He unrolled his mummy bag and climbed inside, staring up for a moment at the darkening near-night sky. He didn't exactly feel safe, but he was too tired to care. And maybe a little adventure in a ghost town was just what he needed to distract him. He would go back to the highway in the morning and try to flag down some help.

He was just about asleep when he heard the distant sound of a woman's terrified scream.

When he awoke, everything had changed.

Erron sat up abruptly in bed and rubbed his eyes.

In bed.

Where was his sleeping bag, and how had he gotten here?

He was in a hotel room with high ceilings and a window that admitted sunlight through lacy spider-web curtains. The bed was comfortable enough, indeed almost luxurious, with fluffy down pillows and crisp, clean white sheets. No wonder he'd slept through till morning.

But it was lacking in amenities. No TV or even a radio; no evidence of heating or central air; not even a fan or overhead light. At his bedside, an oil lamp sat on an ornately carved cherry wood table whose clawed legs curved gracefully down to the floor.

"No phone either," he observed aloud, checking his pocket reflexively for his cell and remembering it wasn't charged... a split second before noticing it wasn't there. "Shit. Must've dropped it."

His luck was only getting worse.

Erron moved to the window and drew back the curtain to take a look at his surroundings. Below him, he saw what appeared to be the same road he'd come in on—Main Street—but while many of the buildings looked familiar, they were no longer abandoned. Fresh coats of paint and open doors greeted pedestrians who, while not numerous, were certainly not absent, as they had been when he arrived.

Two Asian man passed by, wearing long braids that emerged from underneath wide, almost umbrella-shaped bamboo hats. They wore loose-fitting, billowy clothing, and shoes with amply cushioned soles. No one dressed like that anymore. Erron had seen old black-and-white movies with white actors made up to look Asian dressed like this. But these men looked authentic and anything but self-conscious as they walked down the street. They acted like they belonged here. They *seemed* like they belonged here.

But where was "here"?

More to the point, *when* was here?

A woman passed below him (he was clearly on the second floor of wherever he now found himself), attired in a frilly summer dress and carrying an equally frilly parasol. A young man pedaled a bicycle, its front wheel bigger than the rear, down the street, somehow keeping it upright even on an unpaved road, full of ruts and stones.

Main Street hadn't been in good shape before, but it had been asphalt, Erron was sure of it.

The hum of conversation drifted up to him as Erron craned his neck to peer up the road in the direction where he remembered parking his car.

He couldn't see it. He hoped he'd simply lost his sense of direction or that it was just out of view, but a feeling nagged at his suddenly queasy stomach that it just wasn't where it was supposed to be. Or maybe *he* wasn't where he was supposed to be.

Not only could he find no sign of his car; he couldn't see a single automobile either parked or being driven down the street. He hadn't seen any cars last night, either, but then everything had been closed up and there hadn't been a soul in sight. Today, the street only seemed to be getting busier as the minutes passed. More pedestrians were venturing out and, more remarkably, there *was* traffic on the street—it just wasn't automobile traffic. Men on horseback and wagons drawn by horses (or in one case, by oxen) moved up and down the road.

A light knock came at the door, and Erron opened it to discover a young woman holding a covered silver platter engraved with the words "Garrett House." That must be the name of the hotel.

"Your breakfast, sir," the woman said softly, averting her eyes and extending her arms to offer him the platter.

He couldn't determine her exact age—close to his own perhaps, but with a timeless beauty that defied speculation. Soft black curls cascaded down to her shoulders on either side of a face so smooth it could have passed for porcelain. She wore a demure and frilly petticoat dotted with red roses, but there was a hint of sadness behind her polite smile.

"Where am I?" Erron asked.

She seemed unfazed by the question. "You're at the Garrett House, sir, on the Sonora Road. But I'm afraid you didn't sign the register. If you would be so kind, after breaking your fast, to visit the front desk..."

"Sure," he said. "But I..." He was about to say he didn't know how he'd gotten there but realized that would make him look either crazy or drunk.

"I need to know where the nearest gas station is. I ran out of gas, and..."

She frowned.

"I'm sorry. If you don't know, maybe I should ask Mr. Garrett."

She put a hand to her mouth to obscure a laughing smile.

It was Erron's turn to look puzzled. "What?"

"The Garretts haven't owned the hotel for years. My father, the Count, is the proprietor here, and has been for many a year now."

"The Count?" Was he in Transylvania?

"Count Christian William Hugo Solinsky." Each of the names rolled off her tongue with pride. "I am his daughter, Maggie."

She did a shallow curtsy, the best she could manage while still holding the tray.

"Sorry," Erron said. Realizing his thoughtlessness, he hastily took it from her and set it on the bed.

He suddenly felt self-conscious and awkward.

Maggie blushed. "I should go. The noon stage will be coming in before long, and we need to get the dining room ready to receive our guests." She paused a moment, looking at Erron closely.

He liked the feeling of her eyes on him.

"What is it?" he said finally.

"Forgive me, sir." She lowered her eyes, and her blush, which had never fully faded, deepened. "I have just never seen anyone dressed the way you are. But I suppose I shouldn't be surprised. You are quite an exceptional man." She paused a moment, then said, "I am sorry for my rudeness in staring. You should break your fast, sir. You rose late, and it will be getting cold."

Did she wink at him? He must have imagined it, but shuffled his feet awkwardly, nonetheless.

"Please remember to check in at the desk, Mr. Collins."

Erron started. How had she known his name? He was sure he hadn't mentioned it, and if he hadn't signed the register—which he hadn't—she couldn't have seen it there.

"Yes. Collins. Erron Collins. My parents spelled it E-R-R-O-N, not like the guy in the Bible. They weren't religious."

She paused. "Are you, sir?"

"I don't believe in superstitions."

She smiled, and that hint of sadness returned. "You should

wish upon a star sometime," she said, very seriously. "That will change your mind."

"I doubt it," he muttered, looking away from her.

She reached forward and put a hand on his arm. "Just be patient, sir... Erron..." she said. "It took a long time for me, but my wish came true just today."

When she spoke these words, it seemed like she opened a floodgate of thoughts and feelings that had been locked inside her for a very long time. "We must speak again," she gushed. "I have waited so long for you. I have so much I need to tell you about the future. About life. About everything." Her voice was still soft and quiet, but almost conspiratorial, and there was an eagerness about her tone that spoke of excitement... or was it desperation. Perhaps both.

Erron nodded and smiled. "I can't wait," he said, then cursed inwardly for sounding too eager himself. There was something about this girl he couldn't put his finger on. The word "soulmate" slipped through his defenses and into his mind, and he fought to dismiss it. Still, it lingered there, and he realized that, whether he'd revealed too much or not, he really couldn't wait to see her again.

A loud bell rang just as Erron was leaving his room to head downstairs, and the clamor of horses' hooves outside was followed by the rush of perhaps a dozen men and women through the hotel entrance.

They didn't stop at the front desk, but scurried down steps that must have led to the basement.

"May I help you, sir?"

Erron turned from the disappearing crowd toward the sound of the voice and found himself facing the front desk. He had hoped to see Maggie there, but the voice was a man's, speaking in measured syllables and dignified tones, and the figure was even more obviously masculine.

Standing nearly six-and-a-half feet tall, the man who could have been no one but the Count gazed at him through a pair of glasses over a slightly lifted nose, not in condescension but in practiced pride. His silver hair had largely receded, and he wore an immaculately groomed handlebar mustache. His coat, dark brown with tails, appeared formal but slightly worn. He nodded slightly with a studied hospitality.

"How may we be of service?"

Erron cleared his throat. "Maggie... your daughter... asked me to come down and check in."

"Very good, sir." The man sounded like a butler from a 1940s film. "The register is here. How long will you be staying with us?"

"Just last night... I think." Erron found himself hesitating. He wanted to see Maggie again. Maybe ask her for her number... He looked around on an impulse, but there were no phones down here either. And this was the front lobby. How on Earth did a hotel take reservations without a phone?

Just as he was wondering this, a man wearing a wide-brimmed hat and dusty brown coat and vest burst through the front door, a large bag slung over his shoulder. He looked comically like a cross between Santa Claus and a poor man's Clint Eastwood in *High Plains Drifter*. He sauntered up to the Count and dropped the sack onto the front desk with a thud.

The Count glared at him. "The post office is across the street, Mr. Jackson."

The newcomer just waved him off. "And Maggie's here. Seen her?"

The Count pursed his lips.

"SEEN HER?" the man called Jackson demanded again, stepping closer to Solinsky and half-snarling.

"Who says she wants to see you?" The words were out of Erron's mouth almost before he realized he'd opened it.

Jackson whirled around. "Her FIANCY, that's who. And just who the hell are you?"

Erron took a step backward. "Just a friend."

"Maggie ain't got no friends without my say-so. Your name wouldn't be Erron Collins, would it?"

Erron was struck dumb for a second. Did everyone here know his name? And why did this Jackson fellow spit it out with such contempt. The man had moved a step closer to him and looked angrier than a nest of hornets. What had he done to make this guy so mad? He'd never even met him.

"Don't deny it," Jackson was saying. "I've heard her talk about you when she doesn't think anyone's listening. Erron Collins. I caught her practicing writing her name—her name: Maggie *Collins*—on an envelope once. She thought she'd crumpled it up and thrown it away before I saw it. But see it, I did! Normally, I'm a congenial man. But no one, not NO ONE makes a fool of me by consorting with my Maggie!"

The Count had, smoothly and silently, stepped out from behind the desk, and now interposed himself between the two men. Jackson didn't seem at all like a "congenial man." He appeared to all the world like one hot-headed sonofabitch, and most people would have just stayed out of his way. But the Count stood nearly a foot taller than he did. Despite his age, Christian Solinsky was not a man to be trifled with.

"And Maggie will not marry you without MY say-so. I would advise you to put a sock in it, Mr. Jackson. This gentleman is a guest at Garrett House, and as such is entitled to the privilege of a peaceful and quiet repose here. Or need I remind you of the importance that *reputation* confers upon this fine outpost—which Maggie will inherit upon my departure from God's green Earth?"

Jackson ground his teeth together. "A PAYING guest, I hope. Or is business so bad that you're givin' rooms away again?"

The Count stood up straighter, and Erron looked awkwardly to one side. He had NOT paid, and his wallet was nowhere to be found in his empty pocket. It seemed to have walked off with his cell phone.

But before either of them could answer, Maggie strode into the lobby from a side door. Placing herself directly in front of Jackson, she put her hands on her hips and declared, "Yes, he has paid, Thomas." (That must have been the man's given name.) "And if you would like to continue being my 'fiancy,' you had better use proper manners toward my father and our guests. If you do not, you will no longer be welcome here. Do I make myself plain?"

Erron mouthed a "wow," his eyebrows raised. Was this the same modest, soft-spoken girl who had brought him his breakfast—and who, if he was not mistaken, had flirted with him? If anything, he found himself even more attracted to her now.

Jackson was still seething, though. He reached down beside him and pulled a six-shooter from his holster, quick as a flash.

"What is he to you?" he demanded, staring down Maggie but waving the gun toward Erron.

She didn't back down. "A guest in Father's hotel. He speaks to me with a lot more kindness than you're showing me in this moment. What's gotten into you, Thomas? This isn't like you at all. You've never behaved like this before."

"Well, I ain't never come face to face with a man who wants to steal my woman!" he shouted. "And as for him being a guest here, I can solve that problem for ya right quick. If he's got a bullet in his skull, he'll be a guest at Doc Stratton's place, convalescin' instead," Jackson said. "Or inside one of Louie's fine coffins." He chuckled.

For the first time, Maggie's resolve appeared to falter. Her shoulders tensed, and her voice cracked when she said, "He's *just* a guest."

The smile that crossed Jackson's face was both self-satisfied and deadly. "Your protestin' tells me he's a whole lot more'n that ta you, Megs. I knew you were carryin' on behind my back with this Erron Collins lowlife. Thank you for clearing it all up for me."

"No!" she said. "It is nothing like that. I brought him here. It was my fault, not his!"

Erron didn't know what to think about any of this. Maggie hadn't brought him here. He'd run out of gas. There hadn't been any mirrors above the bed in his room, and Maggie hadn't served him pink champagne, over ice or otherwise. But now all he was seeing were stagecoaches and wannabe cowboys waving six-shooters. Where the hell was he? Westworld?

"Oh, you admit it! You harlot! Bringing *him* here when I'm out runnin' the line up ta Big Oak Flat. How often has he been here, Megs? Has he deflowered ya ta boot?"

He was waving that revolver around so wildly, Erron was sure it was bound to go off.

"Now see here!" the Count interjected. "I will not have my daughter's honor impugned!"

But Jackson didn't seem to hear him.

He fired the gun.

Maggie screamed, and it sounded for all the world like the scream Erron had heard when he'd arrived the night before. Plaster fell from the ceiling where the bullet hit.

Erron ducked to avoid it, which was a good thing because it was the only reason he avoided a second bullet that whizzed right past his left ear.

"What the...!?"

"Please, Thomas." Maggie was crying and pleading now. "This isn't like you. And it's not his fault. He doesn't belong here."

"Damn right he don't belong," Jackson shouted. "That's why I'm sendin' him back to his maker."

He aimed again, directly at Erron.

"Erron, run!" Maggie cried. But he was way ahead of her. He'd already taken three steps toward the front door when he saw a giant figure dive at Jackson from seemingly out of nowhere.

Solinsky.

Erron stepped out onto the front porch at the same time he heard another gunshot. Far in the distance behind him... farther than it should have been. Almost an echo. Then, even farther away, a scream. A scream of terror. It was Maggie.

He had to go back.

Erron turned on his heels and took a step back toward the hotel.

Except it wasn't there.

Erron stared through glassy eyes at the vacant lot. It was, he knew, the same lot where he'd laid out his sleeping bag the night before. But the sleeping bag wasn't there, and neither were the weeds that had been growing all across the place when he'd arrived. The lot neatly kept, with a well-manicured lawn, a vegetable garden to one side, and a flower garden up near the wall of a building across the way.

He recognized that building as the two-story house, or fraternal hall, or something that he'd seen looming over him when he got there: 10001 Main Street. But it, like the yard, was well-kept... and apparently occupied. He could see a light in one of the windows upstairs.

The post office building across the street was still there too, but not locked up tight behind iron doors as it had been on his arrival. A sign hung out front on two chains, swaying softly in the wind. "Morris Store," it read. And a sign jutting out from one corner of the building declared it to be the "Auto Stage Office," offering "free baggage room" to anyone using the service. Nearby, an arrow pointed the way to Yosemite Road.

Has to be Highway 49.

Auto Stage was an odd term. But it must have meant the business offered some kind of a car rental service, maybe something like Uber. Or maybe it was a tour bus business with service to Yosemite.

Cars would be an improvement on the horse-drawn wagons and odd-shaped bicycles he'd seen before, and indeed, he did see a car across the way, in front of the Auto Stage Office. It was obviously an antique, no doubt owned by one of those classic car collectors who spent their money buying and restoring Model T's, Model A's, and Model whatever else they had back in the early 20th century.

Still, the street was much quieter than it had been before: not as quiet as when he arrived, but not nearly as busy as it had been that morning. Most of the businesses were closed, and some buildings seemed vacant, as they had when he arrived. He didn't see any pedestrians on the street, and the only place that seemed open was the Morris Store.

Erron rubbed his eyes. Everything was off. His vision seemed blurry, and as the shock of everything that had happened began to wear off, he was acutely aware of another feeling: a sharp stinging pain in his shoulder that radiated out across his entire torso.

Doing his best to ignore it, he stumbled forward. He needed answers, and he hoped that whoever was behind the counter at the Morris Store would be able to provide them.

The door creaked slightly as Erron entered, closing it behind him.

Half-empty shelves ringed the store, holding everything from tins of tobacco to yeast, from baking soda to boxes of cold cereal—one bearing a familiar logo and the name Kellogg's Toasted Corn Flakes. He saw bottles of liquor and jars of pickles, some covered in a fine layer of dust. A hat rack showed off a few bowler hats for sale, and a large upside-down barrel at the center of the store served as a display table for cans of tomatoes.

On the counter, a bucket of candy for the kids sat alongside a scale for weighing sugar and flour. The cash register, which Erron could see from its side along a counter to his right, looked as much like an antique as the vintage car out front. Multiple keys arranged in rows covered the surface of a curved copper-colored quarter-cylinder, above which was a window that displayed the price.

A balding man with a gaunt face and a humorless

expression glanced up at him from behind the counter, where he had been tending to his ledger.

"How can I help you?" he said reflexively, then his eyes widened as they came into focus. "You've been shot."

Erron's own eyes widened as he realized the man was right. He brought his hand up to the source of the stinging pain in his shoulder and drew it back, his fingers now covered in blood.

He winced, the pain all the more acute at the realization of its cause.

The man moved quickly toward him from behind the counter and caught Erron as his knees give way. He felt lightheaded, and suddenly, he had no idea how he'd been able to make it across the street without passing out.

"I'd call for Doc Stratton, but he's out on a house call down near the Crimea House."

Stratton. That was the same name he'd heard used for the town doctor before. At least something was still the same here. But if they kept referring to the same guy, that probably meant the town had only had one doctor. Otherwise, the merchant would have summoned a different physician—one who wasn't away making house calls.

What doctor still makes house calls?

What's an auto stage?

Why is this store open now when it was shuttered and abandoned when I arrived?

Finally, Erron thought to ask the one question that mattered most: "What year is it?"

The merchant frowned. "That's a bad wound, son. You're losing your faculties. It's 1918. What other year would it be?"

Erron shook his head, but that only made it hurt more.

"Here," the merchant said. "I've got a cot in the back you

can use for now. We'll get you bandaged up, and I'll fetch some whiskey. I've got an elixir here somewhere. China Sam swears by it. It's supposed to cure everything from rheumatism to whooping cough. That should tide you over till Doc gets here."

He pulled Erron cautiously to his feet and draped the wounded man's good arm around his neck. The wound in his other shoulder was throbbing, and Erron wondered whether the bullet had gone straight through or was still lodged somewhere inside.

The merchant, who looked like he was in his late sixties, wasn't a big man but was still strong enough to help Erron to the cot in the back. He left for a moment, then returned with a glass of whiskey. And he hadn't skimped: Erron guessed he must have poured out five or six shots. Erron clenched his teeth as the merchant dabbed a wet cloth gently on the site of the wound, then wrapped it in a cloth bandage.

Then he pulled a stoppered bottle from his apron.

"Tilt your head back."

Erron complied, and the man removed the stopper, pouring the contents into his open mouth.

He nearly retched. It tasted rancid.

"China Sam's elixir," he explained. "If the old man's to be believed, it'll cure anything."

Erron's head felt like it was swimming in a vat of hot syrup or molasses. He must have been running a fever. *If the old man's to be believed*? Hadn't the merchant ever tried this shit out on anyone else, or was he, Erron, an unwitting guinea pig? It sounded like more superstition, in the form of snake oil, to him, but he was in no shape to protest, let alone refuse the so-called medicine.

"You haven't told me your name," he rasped.

The merchant smiled. "I'm Saul Morris. I've lived in these parts all my life, but I'm getting ready to finally move on. I was planning to close up shop early next month."

"Why?" Erron managed to ask.

Saul grimaced. "Some power lines hit my telephone line and caused a fire." He pointed to a blackened spot on one of the walls. "We tried to rebuild, but we'd need more money than what we've got. We sued the power company, and we'll win... eventually. But you know how the courts are: slower than a turtle going uphill. We can't afford to wait, and we still don't even have phone service here. It was time to call it a day.

"It's a good thing you didn't get shot a couple of weeks from now," he added, chuckling as the edges of his mouth curled up just slightly. "Those iron doors out front would be closed, and most of the other places in these parts already shut down a while back. We're the last one standing, so to speak. You rest now. You'll be right as rain in the morning."

In the morning? How was that possible? Maybe he'd misheard the man. Maybe that was when the doctor would be returning. He didn't have the energy to try to reason it out. That vat of syrup encasing his mind was getting hotter. And thicker. The fever was getting worse, not better. He had to sleep. He closed his eyes and saw stars swirling against the back of his eyelids. He picked out one and focused on it.

And he made a wish.

The last thought he had before he passed out was of Maggie.

When Erron woke, the fever had broken and the pain was gone. It hadn't just subsided; it was gone. He raised his hand to the wound and pressed on it gingerly, closing his eyes tight to brace himself against the burst of pain he knew was to come.

But he felt nothing.

The blurred vision and the feeling of being stuck in molasses were gone, too. He felt, as the merchant had predicted, "right as rain."

Cautiously, Erron raised his fingers to his face, anticipating the sight of blood, but there was none.

"Saul?" he called out. "Mr. Morris?"

The merchant entered the room a moment later, brushing aside a curtain that separated the back office from the store proper.

"How do you feel?" he asked.

"I don't feel anything. Not a stab or even a twinge of pain. Did the doctor remove the bullet while I was sleeping?"

"Doc hasn't been here," Saul replied. "Must be the tincture."

Erron scowled at him. He didn't know that word.

Saul elaborated: "The Chinese medicine."

"What's in that stuff?"

"Search me. Herbs. Ground-up poppy seeds. Vinegar. Vodka—'cept they call it Baijiu, and it tastes a lot different, I'm told. Never tried it myself."

"You're not missing anything," Erron quipped.

He threw his legs over the side of the cot and sat up. Still no pain. No fever. Whatever that "tincture" was, it was nothing short of a miracle cure. If the bullet was still inside him, it must have dissolved that sonofabitch. If that was even possible. Erron was sure it wasn't, but he had no other explanation.

"Mr. Morris," he said, "do you know a girl named Maggie?"

Morris chuckled. "A lot of people've come through here. Not as many these days as there were a time ago: They didn't call it the Crossroads of the Southern Mines for nothing. Black Bart used to buy candy here in this very shop, and Joaquin

Murrieta stole a horse just up the road a bit. Stopped at the local Smithy and had Louie shoe it for him."

"Louie?" Erron had heard that name before.

"Egling. The wagon-builder. He built the bridge in Knights Ferry, too. Longest covered bridge west of the Mississippi, and that's a fact. He was the undertaker, too. Built coffins. Lived right here in town for most of his life before he moved north to Angels Camp. Most everyone has moved now—north or west or east or somewhere. It's quiet here. Too quiet. That's why I've decided to move on."

Erron scowled. This fellow was a storyteller, and he was easily sidetracked. Erron didn't care about some blacksmith or what bridge he'd built.

"But Maggie doesn't sound familiar?"

"Do you know the girl's family name."

Of course. Erron should have known the man would need more information. "Sol-something. I can't quite remember..."

But the merchant's face brightened. "Solinsky? Would you be referring to Maggie Solinsky?"

"Yes, that's it."

"And why would you be asking after her?"

"I think I'm in love with her." The words were out of Erron's mouth before he could think twice about uttering them. He'd just broken up with Maricia, but since he'd met Maggie, he hadn't thought of his ex. Not once. Maggie just felt right to him, and he hadn't even kissed her. He couldn't explain it, but he knew.

Saul's face darkened again. "Maggie hasn't been in these parts for twenty or thirty years. Moved to San Francisco with her husband, Thomas, then from there to Modesto. As far as I know, that's where she lives now."

Erron's first thought was one of relief: She wasn't dead. Jackson hadn't shot her.

But then came the second, agonizing thought: He *had* married her.

He swallowed hard. "Are you sure they got married?"

Saul went over to a rolltop desk in the corner and pulled out a large scrapbook stuffed with newspaper clippings. "I keep everything of note in here," he said, rummaging through it. "I hope to write a history of the town one day... Ah, here it is."

He pointed to a short clipping that read: "We have received an elegant card bearing the following: 'Miss Maggie F. Solinsky and Mr. Thomas W. Jackson married March 28, 1892.'"

It couldn't be! If he hadn't run out that front door at the Garrett House, he might have prevented it all from happening. But he'd been shot, so what good would it have done? The bastard would probably have shot him again, and then no Chinese remedy would have been enough to save him.

But there was more. Next to the clipping was another from ten years later that read:

"News was received here last week of the death of Thomas W. Jackson in San Francisco, caused from inanition. The deceased was the only son of G.W. and Emily Jackson of this city and was born in this valley February 22, 1866, and up to about 12 years ago was a resident of this city. He left here and for some years was a stage driver at Sonora and to Yosemite Valley. He married Maggie Solinsky, by whom he had three children. Mrs. Jackson and two of the children survive him. Mr. Jackson was a very congenial man and made friends wherever he went. He was thoroughly honest and upright and more considerate for the welfare of others than for himself."

There was that phrase again: a "congenial man." Jackson

had used it to describe himself, and others apparently thought the same. Or maybe they just didn't want to speak ill of the dead.

But Jackson was dead, and had been for some time. Erron had seen the term "inanition" once before, in a college textbook on anatomy and biomedicine. It was an old-fashioned word for... malnutrition. The man had died of hunger.

"You knew her?" he asked after a moment.

Saul smiled again, almost wistfully, "Oh, everyone knew Maggie. The Belle of Main Street they called her. Never an unkind word for anyone. Her father was full of Old World courtesy—the kind you just don't find anymore. Ran the Garrett House the way I run my store: Put the customer first and the ledger last. You can always make up for lost profits, but you can't make up for an angry customer.

"But Maggie, she was the soul of that place. It was the last hotel still open in town, the way we're the last general store. It outlasted the Eagle, the Granite House, and the El Dorado—Jim Peacock's old place. She treated it like the jewel that it was, with all her father's dignity plus the biggest heart in the world. Too big in some ways. Rumor has it she loved a man who deserted her, and pined for him, waiting in vain for him to return. Wait here..."

Saul hopped up from the stool he'd been sitting on beside Erron's cot and stepped back over to the rolltop desk, where he began rooting through some papers.

"Ah, here it is," he finally said, holding up a small booklet.

He leafed through what he called an autograph book before his hand settled on a certain page that bore a short message in immaculate handwriting:

Friend Saul:

May your virtues ever shine
Like peaches on a pumpkin vine

Your Friend
Maggie Solinsky

The message was dated January 14, 1884.

"See what I mean about her havin' a big heart?" he said.

Erron nodded. "You don't need to convince me of that."

Saul tried to suppress a frown—which Erron noticed but decided to ignore. He was suddenly full of hope again: Maggie was alive, but Thomas Jackson was long dead. Maybe he still had a chance with her... even if she would have to be in her fifties now, and he still looked his proper age of twenty-three. It didn't matter. Love was eternal.

"Why did she leave town?" he asked.

"The Count—that was her father; a real Polish count he was—died, and Jackson insisted that she sell the place. She would have inherited it, too: Her brother went off and became a big-shot attorney, so she could have stayed there to run the old House. But Jackson wanted to move to back to San Francisco, where he was born, and she didn't have much choice in the matter. Like I said, though, she was the soul of the place. With her gone, it got rundown, and no one stopped there anymore. Finally got burned up in a fire, and by that time, nobody cared. They didn't even try to put it out. A real shame."

Erron swallowed hard.

That's why the hotel wasn't there anymore. But he hadn't seen any flames: It had disappeared the minute he stepped out the front door. It just suddenly *wasn't there* anymore. It didn't make any sense. And then there was the way the streets seemed to change: Boarded-up buildings one minute; a thriving commercial center with stagecoaches and cowboys the next; and now something in between—vintage cars and a town in decline. It felt as though he was hopping around in time.

This was, he knew, impossible. He didn't own a DeLorean, and he didn't know Doc Brown. There had to be some other explanation, and he didn't want to sound crazy, but this Saul Morris seemed to know everything there was to know about the town and about Maggie.

So, he had to ask.

"What is it about this place?" he asked. "I feel like I'm lost somewhere in time, but that 'somewhere' keeps changing."

He expected the man to look at him like he'd lost it, but a knowing expression crossed his face, and he nodded sagely. "Do you believe in ghosts?" he asked.

"Not particularly."

"Well, let me tell you a story that might convince you otherwise. Way back when, there were thousands of Chinese people here. They came to work the mines. But now, there's only two of them left: China Mary and China Sam. Those aren't their real names, but none of us stupid white folk could pronounce them, so we just called 'em that. They said they didn't mind, but when Washington passes a law against any more folks like you comin' into the country, you tend to *act* like you don't mind.

"Anyway, like I said, they're the last two. And there's a Chinese cemetery just up the road where a lot of 'em were buried, but most of 'em ain't there anymore. Know why?"

Erron shook his head.

"They dug 'em up and sent 'em back to China."

"How come?"

"I'm not rightly sure. But I have a theory: This place... isn't quite right. I told you it was the Crossroads of the Southern Mines, but it's been at the center of something for a lot longer than that. China Mary came into the shop one day and said something, out of nowhere, that stuck with me. She asked if I'd ever been to what she called a nexus, where the laws of nature don't apply. Like a gravity hill, where a car might seem like you're rolling uphill against gravity."

Erron nodded. He'd heard of a place like that, up the coast in Santa Cruz, called the Mystery Spot. Tall people looked shorter than short folks there, too. He'd always thought it was just an optical illusion some guy rigged up to make a few bucks off passing motorists.

"Now, some people say the Chinese dug up their dead because they thought they'd be at peace in their homeland. That's probably true, but I think there's something more to it: My theory is they *don't* think they'll be at peace *here*. This place doesn't just mess with gravity; it messes with time. But only around All Hallows' Eve every year. That's when they say the veil is the thinnest."

Erron bit his tongue and resisted the urge to spit out some rude comment about the thinning of the veil. It reminded him of Maricia, who had been so convinced that such things occurred.

They couldn't.

Or could they? Was he in the middle of some Halloween haunting right now?

Saul was ready with an answer to this unasked question: "I've heard reports of people coming in here who say they've seen ghosts, but what they describe—some of them, anyway—isn't just seeing a *ghost*. It's seeing the *whole town* the way it used to be, back during the Gold Rush. Or even how it's going to be:

all boarded up and abandoned."

Erron sat up straighter. "Yes!" he said. "That's exactly what I've been seeing."

Saul nodded knowingly and pressed the tip of an index finger to his nose. "And how can anyone be at peace if they're constantly hopping twenty years forward or a hundred years backward?"

It all seemed absurd and impossible to accept, but Erron couldn't help wondering about the implications of what old Saul was saying—if, by some impossible stretch of the imagination, it might be true.

"So, if I was hit with a bullet in, say, 1890, and I arrived here thirty years later, the wound would have had that much time to heal."

Saul frowned. "Theoretically..." he began. "But you were bleeding when you got here. So the bullet must have hit at the precise moment you jumped from that time to this one."

"Then why did it heal so quickly?"

Saul shrugged. "That Chinese remedy is supposed to be damn good."

Erron wasn't convinced, but he was less concerned about the abstract ideas behind this nexus Saul had mentioned than he was about its practical application. Suddenly he remembered something odd Maggie had said when she was pleading with Jackson. "I brought him here," she'd said. "It's my fault." What could that have meant?"

He wasn't sure Saul would know, but it didn't hurt to ask.

"Ah," he said, but he stopped there. Then, when it was clear Erron was intent on hearing more, he said, "I'm not sure, and I'd rather not guess—though I'm probably right. I think that's something she would prefer to tell you herself."

This gave Erron renewed hope. Maggie was still alive—at least in this "now," 1918. And if she was living in Modesto, that wasn't too far away.

"Now all I need to do is find a way to get to her," he said. "Modesto is how far from here? Thirty miles?"

"More like 45. But you're not up to it."

"Bullshit. I feel fine," he started to stand up, but then the dizziness returned, and he found himself careening downward toward the cot again. It made no sense. He'd felt perfect just a moment ago.

But he wasn't ready to give up just yet: "OK, so I'll take it easy. I don't have to drive. My car is actually... well... out of gas or something, but you have an auto stage company, right? It says so right there on your sign. You can just drive me to Modesto. I'll find a way to pay you, I promise."

"I don't even know she's there. Or where she lives in Modesto if she's there. It's not a small city."

"You can find out."

"It's not that simple."

"Fine. I don't need your help. I'll walk to Modesto if I have to."

Saul was shaking his head, though. "I'm afraid you'll have to wait for her to come to you. You're in no condition to travel. Tell you what I'll do: I'll send a cable to Modesto and ask if she's there. I'll say her old friend Saul needs to talk to her. If she's there, she'll get in touch with me. Just do me a favor, will you? Watch the store for me while I go and fetch a few things to close 'er up for good tomorrow..."

"Tomorrow?" Erron interrupted. "I thought you weren't closing for a couple of weeks."

Saul laughed. "That was two weeks ago," he said. "That's how long you've been out of it!"

Two weeks?! Had he been in a coma? Or maybe it was just another case of time playing tricks on him in this godforsaken place.

Saul was talking again: "If a customer comes in and doesn't have the right change for somethin', don't let it worry you. Just offer 'em a discount or let 'em have the thing free, for all I care. It'll be one less thing for me to bother with when I hightail it outta here."

He laughed again. "Think you can do that?"

Erron nodded and rose, more slowly this time to fend off any dizziness, and followed Saul into the main store area, setting himself down on a stool behind the counter.

"I'll see you in a little while," the merchant said on his way out. "Don't worry. You won't have any customers."

He didn't. Not a single person came through that door, and Erron passed the time playing solitaire with an old deck of cards the man had left lying on the counter. The joker smiled back at him when he came to it, and he flung it into a corner. He'd never liked clowns. Besides, he was starting to feel like he'd been played for a fool by Saul, who seemed to be taking forever on his errand.

He didn't know how many hours had passed before he nodded off to sleep, but he awoke with a start to find himself sitting in near darkness. The iron doors had been closed, and a musty smell wafted its way into his nostrils.

"What the hell...?"

Had Saul locked him in?

He had said he couldn't leave. Had the man asked him to look after the store as some excuse to keep him here? But if so, why?

"Saul?"

There was no answer.

"Mr. Morris?" he called louder, but was met with silence.

Then he heard it: That sound of a woman screaming in the distance.

"Maggie?"

He stood too quickly and, although the dizziness was gone, he stumbled over a box of letters behind the counter.

That wasn't there before.

The scream came again, but it was farther away this time, and Erron decided to stay where he was. He didn't want to trip over anything else, and his eyes would only need a moment or two to adjust.

When they did, he realized that the entire layout of the store had changed. In fact, it wasn't even a store now. Gone were the half-stocked shelves of merchandise, the scale, the cans of tomatoes on that upside-down barrel, and even the cash register. In their place he found an old postage stamp machine, empty mailbags, and a carousel of dusty old greeting cards.

He suddenly remembered the place had been a post office, but it couldn't have been *just* a post office until after Morris closed his store.

The aging merchant said Erron had been asleep for two whole weeks before; how long had he been out *this time*?

Stepping past the box of letters he'd stumbled across before—which he now saw had been stamped "Undeliverable"—he made his way to the back room. Maybe Morris had left some last news clipping in his scrapbook that provided a clue to what had happened. The rolltop desk was gone, and there was no sign of the scrapbook, but he did find several stacks of old newspapers in a corner labeled "Rural Free

Delivery." They'd been bundled together with twine, but the threads had become frayed and worn in the dampness that must have caused that musty smell.

The newspapers were all copies of the *Sonora Union Democrat*, bearing various dates: 1971, 1958, 1954, 1947, 1937... all long after Saul had closed the store and a whole lot more than two weeks. Erron realized he must have jumped through time again. It always seemed to happen in his sleep for some reason, and he had no control at all over where he ended up.

He spent the next couple of hours searching through the stacks for something that might help him make sense of it all, but there was less and less news from this lonesome town the further forward he went in time. After paging through a couple of issues from 1971 and 1958, he decided to go back to the earliest bundle he'd found there, from 1937. He had looked through several copies from different dates by the time he came upon the news he'd been dreading:

"Margaret F. Jackson died yesterday at the age of 76. The mother of three children by her late husband, Thomas Wilburn Jackson, she was the daughter of the former Polish count, Christian Solinsky, who owned the Garrett House hotel for many years, and Mary Amelia Solinsky. Mrs. Jackson was married to her husband in 1892, and he preceded her in death in 1902, passing away in his native San Francisco. Following his death, Mrs. Jackson moved to Modesto and never remarried. She is to be interred at Memorial Lawn Cemetery in Sebastopol. Services will be private."

Casting the newspaper aside, Erron sat on a stool beside the stacks and put his head in his hands. He was too late. This cursed time warp had deposited him back here, probably in his own time or close to it, decades after Maggie's death.

He could still hear her excited voice in his ears: "I have so much I need to tell you about the future. About life. About everything."

Now the future had passed them both by, and she was gone. That conversation would never happen... unless he could somehow find a way to get back to her. But what was it Saul had said? "I'm afraid you'll have to wait for her to come to you."

Yet that was impossible. It had become impossible on September 27, 1937, the day she died.

Erron buried his face deeper in his hands and began sobbing, tears flowing through the spaces between his fingers and down onto the floor, where they seemed to simply disappear, overpowered by the thick coat of dust there that had consumed everything else. Why not his tears as well? What did they matter? He wept for a love that should never have been and, in the end, could never be.

All that was left was to get out of this place, locate his car, and find some gas to get back on the road again.

He wouldn't go back to Fresno.

He wasn't sure where he'd go.

But anywhere was better than here, and anytime was better than now.

He heard the call again, the sound of a woman screaming, but it sounded more now to him like a cry of mourning. And in the train of its echo, he heard the whisper of a voice he recognized, but knew beyond all certainty he would never hear again.

"Erron."

Despite that certainty, he turned slowly around, and there, standing before him, stood Maggie, not a day older than when he'd first seen her, wearing those same dark curls and that same petticoat dotted with red roses she'd worn the day they met.

His eyes widened, old tears still lingering there and new ones forming.

"How?"

"I've waited so long for you, Erron. You have no idea. But I was selfish. I knew we could never be together, but I called you to me anyway. It ruined everything. I'm so, so very sorry." She flung herself into his arms and in the same moment began sobbing every bit as much as he was.

"It's OK. It's OK." He ran his fingers across her hair, pushing it back gently off her forehead and allowing them to run through her locks down the back of her neck. He had wanted to do that the moment he first saw her, but he hadn't dared. Now, it felt every bit as wonderful and natural as he'd dreamed it would.

"Can you ever forgive me?" she pleaded, looking up at him.

"For what?"

"For loving you when I shouldn't have. For bringing you into all this. I loved Thomas; I really did. He was a good man. What you saw... it was the worst part of him, and you only saw it because I betrayed him."

"For me?"

"Yes. If I hadn't brought you to me, he would have never been like that."

"Then why, if you loved him...?"

She started sobbing, even harder now. "Because I loved you more. This place, this..."

"Nexus?"

"Yes, this nexus. It gives some of us the ability to jump ahead in life. For most people, it just happens. They have no control over it. But I was always different: I could control it, at least some of the time. I was in love with Thomas, and I wanted to see what our future together would be like. He told me not to look, but I couldn't resist. I wanted to see us growing old together, with grandchildren, but when I pulled back the veil, I saw him lying in bed, unable to eat and deathly ill, just ten years after we were to be married.

"I couldn't bear the thought of living without my one true love, so I told myself he wasn't the one. He couldn't be. I began searching through time for the person I was *really* meant to be with—the one person who could spare me the life of loneliness I knew I would live if I married Thomas."

"And you found me."

"Yes. And I brought you to me. I didn't know I could do it until I tried, but then there you were that morning in the upstairs room, which had been vacant the night before. I knew it was you from the first, and I knew I was the reason you had come. Oh, Erron, please. I didn't mean to... But you were everything I dreamed you'd be and more. You made me feel things Thomas never did, just in the short time we were together. And I couldn't let you go then, I just couldn't. But I had no idea he would be so jealous. That he would find out and draw that cursed gun of his. He'd never been like that before. I swear. I had no idea. You believe me, don't you?"

"Shhh," said Erron softly. "Of course I do. But it's OK. Saul Morris gave me some Chinese home remedy he had in his store, and it fixed me right up. See? I'm good as new." He pulled back and smiled down at her. "Nothing to worry about."

"Oh, dear, dear Saul," she said softly. "Always the most virtuous man..." But she hadn't stopped weeping. If anything, she was crying harder now.

Erron was confused. "What is it? I said I'm OK."

But she was shaking her head. "Come with me."

Maggie took Erron's hand and let him out through the back of the building. The door had been boarded up, but the wood was weathered and cracked, allowing them enough room to make their way outside.

The sun shone brightly down on them from a crystal blue sky, so different from the overcast pall that had hung over the place when Erron had arrived, seemingly a lifetime ago. Squinting and shielding his eyes, he saw his car, just where he'd left it.

That must be a good sign. We can get some help and get out of this place.

Maggie led him past the car and up the road, past a convenience store and bar with an "OPEN" neon sign flashing in the window. On seeing it, he realized he had been just *that close* to help when he'd broken down. If he'd walked in a different direction, he could have saved himself this entire ordeal. But if he'd seen it then, he would never have met Maggie, and they wouldn't be together now.

"C'mon," he said. "The place is open. Let's go in and get some help."

But Maggie didn't seem to hear him. She kept a firm grip on his hand as she led him away from the store and across the road, to a large cattle gate, which she opened before grabbing his hand again and pushing him through.

A dirt and gravel road led from there eastward up a hill, and as they climbed the gentle grade, an arched sign came into view: "CITY CEMETERY" it read.

"What are we doing here?" Erron asked, slightly out of breath. "Is this where Thomas is buried? Or your father?"

Maggie nodded. "Yes, Father's grave is here, but not

Thomas'."

She opened the gate beneath the arch and led him across the grassy knoll to a simple gravesite with an old, weathered headstone. The lettering was so faint and worn, Erron had to get down on his hands and knees to make it out, but when he was finally able to read it, he fell backward in shock:

Erron Collins
Born: ?
Died: 1918
Rest in Peace

"This is impossible," he said when he finally caught his breath.

"I wanted to be buried here, with you," Maggie sobbed. "But my family would never have understood. All those years, I never told them who you were to me. I had children. Thomas' children. They would never have forgiven me."

"But I can't be dead," Erron stammered. "I'm right here in front of you."

"And I'm right here in front of you, not a day older than when you first met me."

"Of course you're not," said Erron. "You jumped through time to meet me here. To find me. Oh, Maggie, I'm so happy you did!"

But she was shaking her head slowly. "I didn't," she said. "I didn't jump through time. I appear as you first saw me because I can appear to be any age I want now... now that I'm..."

Erron's mind flashed back to the newspaper clipping.

Her obituary.

"No!" he shouted.

But she was nodding sadly. She took his hand, and they sat

on the grass together, staring into each other's eyes. Erron couldn't even cry now. There was nothing more to say.

Finally, after a few moments, she broke the silence. "The time is short for us," she said. "The thinning of the veil is near an end. Tomorrow is the vernal equinox, and the times and worlds that overlap here will be lost to one another for another year. "Just hold me until the stars come out, and stay with me until it happens."

Erron nodded and kissed her deeply. At least he would get to do that this once.

He wrapped his arms around her and they lay back on the soft grass, staring up at the sky as darkness fell and stars began to peek out from the firmament one by one. After a time, the sky appeared as a brilliant skein of diamonds, and the pair of them lay there, their bodies entwined, as the first shooting start of the evening flashed in an arc across the California sky.

"Did you make a wish?" she whispered.

"I did."

"But I thought you didn't believe in superstitions," she chided him playfully.

"I don't believe in superstitions, but I do believe in love. I always have."

She smiled at him.

"That's why I brought you to me."

They lay there, silent for a moment, and then she said, "I don't need to ask you about the wish you made."

He smiled. "I'm sure it was the same as yours."

"And it's come true now, hasn't it?" she said. "Didn't I tell you? Sometimes you just have to be patient."

No women cry out in the town today, but peacocks live

there, and their voices sound very much like a scream or sad lament. Some people say that's all they are. But those who have read this story know better.

Just don't tell too many people. Not everyone believes in love.

Postscript: This story is a work of historical fiction. Virtually all the people depicted here really lived in a town called Chinese Camp, which is today a virtual ghost town on California's Highway 49. The dates and places are depicted accurately, as well. Count Solinsky, his daughter Maggie, Saul Morris, Doc Stratton, Louis Egling, and Thomas Jackson really lived there.

China Sam and China Mary really were the last two people of Chinese ancestry in town (they left in the early 1920s). The Count really ran the Garrett House; Louis Egling really built wagons and acted as the town undertaker; Saul Morris really owned the Morris Store, which really did close in 1918; and Thomas Jackson really drove a stagecoach (and was a companionable, well-liked fellow). The marriage announcement for Maggie and Thomas, as well as Thomas' obituary, both quoted here really appeared in the Ukiah newspaper. Maggie's salutation to Saul was taken directly from his actual autograph book. Erron Collins is a purely fictional character who never played any role in the history of Chinese Camp.

Or did he?

Learn more about the history of Chinese Camp in the author's book, *Chinese Camp: The Haunting History of California's Forgotten Boomtown*, available on Dragon Crown Books.

Bonus story…

Stephen H. Provost

To Murder a Crow

The scarecrow seemed to cast a shadow against the sky. There was a full moon, but the rest of the cloudless veil was blacker than it should have been.

Halloween was almost over.

The scruffy old man in the rickety ticket booth called out, "Fifteen minutes till closing."

The boy with the tousled brown hair was the only one there to hear him.

His given name (the boy's, that is) was Alex, which was

short for Alexander, after the great conqueror, the long-ago king of Macedonia.

The boy was there by himself at the entrance to the corn maze on the outskirts of Moravia, Iowa, the entrance to which was guarded by the silent scarecrow. It didn't seem to bother the scruffy old man in the rickety ticket booth didn't that Alex was there by himself. An orphan, who had lived with half a dozen foster families, he was only in his current home because his guardians needed the government stipend that came with him. They didn't much care about where he spent his time, as long as they got their check. So he had come here, to the maze, alone.

But he had paid to be there, using most of his allowance, and that was what mattered to the man in the ticket booth.

The corn maze had been open for a month, and it wouldn't be open past tonight. Unfortunately, the old man—who owned the place—had yet earn back the money he'd put into it, because the weekend rain had kept too many customers away. He was on his hands and knees now, like a bloodhound with a saggy, weepy belly, hunting for spare coins that might have fallen through the booth's wooden slats onto the muddy-puddly ground underneath.

He muttered something: "Last time. No more."

Then he glanced at the boy again. He was not going to look for the child if he got lost. It was none of his concern. "Better get started," he called out. "Fourteen minutes."

The boy stared up at the nameless scarecrow, which seemed to stare back at him, though this was, of course, impossible. The paint that had been used to create its mouth ran down its chin, where the earlier rains had carried it. One of its eyes, which previously been potatoes, had sprouted roots that clawed blindly at the night. The other had gone missing altogether, as someone had removed it.

"I did it! Rrawk!

The voice caught the boy's attention, and he looked around to see where it had come from.

Its owner was dark as the night itself. But then, the boy saw movement: a glisteny, feathery head, pecking persistently at the potato-eye that remained.

"What is your name?" the boy asked.

"Rrawk!" came the reply.

"Pleased to meet you, Mr. Roark."

"Rrawk!"

"Mr. Rrawk, then. Beg your pardon."

He wondered how the crow could speak, but he didn't think much more about it, because it clearly *had* spoken, and there was no disputing that fact. There was, therefore, no use in worrying too much about it. Besides, the night was getting on, and the air was growing chill. The boy felt his goose-bumped skin give a fateful shiver beneath his winter jacket, whereupon an idea occurred to him. It was little more than a fancy, but a real idea nonetheless.

"Mr. Rrawk, since you can fly, might you be willing to guide me through this corn maze?"

The one who called himself Rrawk said "Rrawk!" again, as if to make sure the boy knew that was his name. Then, he said, "That would be cheating."

The shadow of a frown drifted across the boy's face against the dark night. No matter, then. It had been worth a try. Even so, the boy was lonely. He had been lonely for as long as he could remember *being* anything. And so, he opened his mouth again and ventured the admit: "I would be grateful, at the least, for your company."

The crow seemed not to hear him, intent as he was at pecking the potato eye.

Alex was not too disappointed. Rrawk was, in fact, only a crow.

The crow paused in his pecking. "Heard that!" he squawked.

Alex tilted his head to one side. "Heard what?"

"That thing you said. In your head."

"You couldn't have. I didn't say it."

"Ah, but you did. To yourself. And your self is the most important audiences." He bowed like an actor on stage at the end of a performance.

The brows over Alex's young eyes pressed down on them. "Then what did I say?"

"That would be telling!"

Alex did not believe the crow had heard anything, nor was he even sure, any longer, that he even wanted the creature's company. So, instead of pursuing the matter further, he set his eyes once again upon the corn maze and put his feet upon the path that conveyed him thence.

The crow finished his meal and followed.

So did the scarecrow.

The corn maze wound down and around and up and through, back in on itself and across again. It reminded Alex of learning to tie his shoe. He'd been stubborn about that. Instead of observing how others did it and copying them, he had insisted on figuring it out himself—and in consequence had created all manner of intricate knots that were nearly impossible to untangle.

"Rrawk! Where are you going?"

The boy turned around, surprised. "Are you still there? I thought you weren't coming."

"That's what you get for thinking."

"I suppose so," the boy said coolly. He was not about to admit that he was glad for the company, or that he was hopelessly lost. Already he had been inside the maze long enough that he imagined the proprietor had closed the rickety ticket booth and gone home.

"Lost?" asked the crow.

"No," said the boy.

"Lost," the crow declared.

The boy stopped and sat down on a hay bale, in exaggerated fashion, as though admitting defeat. He avoided looking at the crow, and instead focused his attention on pulling bits of hay from the bale, one by one.

"You won't find your way like that."

Alex raised his head and fixed the crow with a withering gaze. "*You* said you wouldn't help me."

"Rrawk! I did not!" The crow seemed wounded. "I only declined to guide you, not to help you!"

The boy was about to say something more, known only to him, but the crow did not wait for his answer and instead flew away in a scurry-flurry of night-black wings.

"Figures," Alex muttered, pulling more bits of hay from the bale as he sulked.

"Yes, it does."

The boy's head shot up at the sound of a voice that was not the crow's. It was higher-pitched and scratchy like an opera singer with straw stuffed down her throat. It belonged, as it happened, to the scarecrow.

"How did you find me?" asked the boy.

"It was not easy, let me tell you, since that evil crow plucked out my eyes!"

"He did not seem evil to me," said Alex. "Just annoying."

"You might feel differently if he'd plucked out *your* eyes," said the scarecrow.

Alex had to admit that this was true.

"Well, what do you want, then?"

"Revenge, of course!" said the scarecrow, as though it should have been self-evident. "If you help me get it, I will be your guide." She nodded her head, and it fell off. Fortunately, she caught it before it hit the ground and resituated it on the space between her shoulders. (Alex assumed it was a "she" from the sound of the scarecrow's voice, although there was honestly no other way to tell.)

Alex noticed for the first time that she was carrying something: a bow and a quiver full of arrows. He was sure he would have seen it if she'd had it outside the maze, and he had no idea where she might have gotten it. Of course, he had no idea how she managed to move at all, let alone converse with him, in the first place, so it wasn't as shocking as it might have been otherwise.

"For you," she said, handing him the bow and removing the quiver to offer it, as well.

The boy took it reluctantly, amid the nagging feeling that it wasn't exactly a gift. "What am I supposed to do with this?" he asked.

"Why shoot him, of course," said the scarecrow, as though it should have been as plain as day—even though it was night.

The boy shook his head. "I can't do that. That would be murder."

"Yes, a murder of crows!" the scarecrow threw back her head and laughed at her own joke. "Or in this case, one crow."

Alex didn't understand the joke, but he didn't care to.

The scarecrow suddenly stopped laughing, and her raspy voice turned quite serious. "You will need my help to reach the center of the maze," she warned. "And you must reach the center before you can get back out."

Alex scuffed his heel against the dirt path. That didn't make sense. "I can just go back the way I came," he said.

The scarecrow laughed again, but there was less mirth in her tone this time. "And which way would that be?"

She had a point. Alex doubted he could retrace his steps and find his way out quickly on his own. But how big could the maze be? He was bound to stumble upon the exit eventually, even if he had to push his way through spaces in the walls. Except there were no spaces in the walls. The corn grew so thick he could not even *see* through it, let alone *walk* through it. Even if he could, would he be closer or farther from the exit? There was no way of knowing.

"I don't know," he confessed.

"Then we have a deal," the scarecrow said firmly. "We will wait here until the crow returns, you will shoot him, and I will take you to the center of the maze."

Alex frowned. "Why don't you just shoot him yourself?"

"It's against the rules."

"What rules?"

"We're only supposed to scare the crows, not kill them. It's written down in triplicate, and all of us are required to sign in blood. Please don't make me fetch you a copy."

Alex shook his head, idly wondering whose blood was used, considering scarecrows did not seem to have any.

"Then it's settled," the scarecrow said.

Alex said nothing. He just sat there, trying to figure out what he would do if and when Mr. Rrawk returned.

The scarecrow hid behind a corn stalk as the crow flew into view. He was carrying something in his beak and wearing something on his head, but the boy couldn't tell what either was.

"There he is! There he is!" the scarecrow whispered excitedly. "Be ready with your bow."

Alex raised the bow tentatively and aimed it in Mr. Rrawk's general direction.

"Wait till he's in range! But don't let him see you!" The tone in the scarecrow's raspy voice was a cross between giddy and desperate.

"You promise to get me out of here?" the boy asked, seeking to reassure himself and assuage his already-guilty conscience. The crow was flying nearer now, and was close to being in range. Nervously, Alex fingered the bowstring, feeling the tension, a match for the tension within him. He reminded himself of how sorry he felt for the scarecrow, at having her eyes pecked out so cruelly. But then he thought of how mean it was, also, to scare the poor bird away from his meal. He had only been hungry, after all. And if the scarecrow had let him feast on the corn, he would never have been tempted to peck out her potato-eyes! Still, he hadn't needed to do it.

"Why does life have to be so complicated?" Alex said inside his head.

The truth was, he realized, that *he* was being tempted now. Of all the reasons and motives that tumbled around inside his skull for doing the scarecrow's bidding, the one that made him even consider such a thing was his own desire. Truly. He wanted to be free of the maze. The longer he remained inside it, the more he lamented that he might never find his way out again, and it was this fear that drove him to contemplate the madness of actually shooting Mr. Rrawk.

Suddenly horrified at himself, he loosed his hold on the bowstring and watched as the arrow fell harmlessly to the earth.

An odd sound reached his ears a moment later, like two straw brooms being slapped repeatedly together.

He turned to see the scarecrow.

She was... applauding.

"Bravo! Well done!" she announced in her creaky-croaky voice as the crow descended to alight on her shoulder.

Alex's eyes went wide.

"But...," he protested.

"Rrawk!" said the crow. It sounded oddly like a laugh. "Fooled you, did we not?" he said, seeming overly pleased with himself.

"You passed our little test," the scarecrow added. "I must confess I was worried for a moment there, but you came through with flying colors."

"Test?" said Alex. "Then you are ...?"

"The best of friends," the scarecrow announced. "But we had to make you think otherwise, to be sure you were worthy to reach the heart of the maze."

"We've become quite good at acting," Mr. Rrawk boasted. "She pretends she wants to scare me, so I can eat the farmer's corn."

"And he only eats the ears of corn that fall to earth, so I can keep my job!"

"But—your eyes!" exclaimed Alex.

The scarecrow chuckled. "Really, now, dear boy. Could *you* see with a potato?"

"Well, I suppose. ..."

"I don't need eyes to see, in any case—no more than I need a tongue to speak."

Alex looked again at what was left of the scarecrow's painted-on mouth: the bits that hadn't run down her straw chin in the rain. "Please don't stare," she said curtly. "It's impolite. I *know* I need to do my makeup!"

The boy averted his eyes quickly. He had no wish to be rude. Or cruel, for that matter. He had been the one and nearly the other in the space of just a few minutes.

Then it occurred to him that the crow and his accomplice had been very rude to *him*. They'd played a not-so-nice practical joke on him when he was facing a crisis that the scarecrow herself had told him was quite serious: If she was right, he couldn't get out of the maze unless he found the center first, and then he'd have to navigate his way out again. He was beginning to despair of doing it all by morning.

The sky was dark, the moon was dipping below the corn stalks—which seemed to be growing taller by the moment—and he was all alone. Except, that is, for two new companions who shouldn't have been able to talk, much less think rationally... yet had already outwitted him and might abandon him at any moment.

If things looked discouraging for Alexander, this was nothing compared to what lay ahead. He felt that time was of the essence, yet he was about to discover the essence of time.

"To Murder a Crow" is an excerpt *The Talismans of Time*, the first book in *The Labyrinth of the Lost Academy*. Originally published in 2019, it is available for sale on Amazon, along with its sequel, *Pathfinder of Destiny*.

Did you enjoy this book?

Recommend it to a friend. And please consider **rating it and/or leaving a brief review** at Amazon, Barnes & Noble, and Goodreads.

About the authors

Dragon Crown Books publisher Stephen H. Provost has written several books about life in 20th century America, including a dozen books on America's highways. During more than three decades in journalism, he has worked as a managing editor, copy desk chief, columnist, and reporter at five newspapers. Now a full-time author, he has written on such diverse topics as dragons, mutant superheroes, mythic archetypes, language, department stores, and his hometown. Visit him online and read his blogs at stephenhprovost.com.

Sharon Marie Provost, chief operating officer of Dragon Crown Books, is a longtime resident of Carson City. She is the author of *Shadow's Gate* and the co-author of *Christmas Nightmare's Eve.* Sharon also owns and has trained several champion dog-trial poodles. You can find her at "Sharon Marie Provost, Author" on Facebook.

The Nightmare's Eve Collection

Available from Dragon Crown Books and Amazon

Made in the USA
Columbia, SC
11 September 2024